Praise for
When We Fall

"Brimming with detail and emotion, [. . .] ture of the gilded lives of the hedge fund elite, as the arrival of a young widow sends shock waves across an affluent suburban enclave. Add in a crumbling marriage, a lethal frenemy, a love interest, and a dizzying cascade of wealth and entitlement, and Emily Liebert's latest will keep you turning pages long past bedtime."

—Beatriz Williams, *New York Times* bestselling author of
A Hundred Summers

"Emily Liebert is peerless in her ability to craft fabulously flawed, compelling characters you alternately root for, love to hate, and hate to relate to. *When We Fall* is the best sort of novel—the kind you can't wait to finish and that leaves you desperately wanting more when you do."

—Jenna McCarthy, author of *I've Still Got It, I Just Can't Remember Where I Put It: Awkwardly True Tales from the Far Side of Forty*

"Emily Liebert has written a wise, warm, and deeply compassionate novel about the complex bonds between women—mothers, daughters, sisters, and friends. Her characters will move right up off the page and into your heart—which is exactly where they will stay."

—Yona Zeldis McDonough, author of *Two of a Kind*

Praise for
You Knew Me When

"A wonderful book for anyone who has ever longed for an old friend or dreamed of returning home after what feels like forever."

—*New York Times* bestselling author Kerry Kennedy

"[Liebert] has a knack for crafting realistic, witty dialogue. An emotionally honest novel full of nostalgia for old friendships, the struggle of reconciliation, and the everlasting power of female friendship." —*Booklist*

ALSO BY EMILY LIEBERT

You Knew Me When

WHEN WE FALL

EMILY LIEBERT

 NEW AMERICAN LIBRARY

New American Library
Published by the Penguin Group
Penguin Group (USA) LLC, 375 Hudson Street,
New York, New York 10014

USA | Canada | UK | Ireland | Australia | New Zealand | India | South Africa | China
penguin.com
A Penguin Random House Company

First published by New American Library,
a division of Penguin Group (USA) LLC

First Printing, September 2014

 REGISTERED TRADEMARK—MARCA REGISTRADA

LIBRARY OF CONGRESS CATALOGING-IN-PUBLICATION DATA:

Liebert, Emily.
  When we fall/Emily Liebert.
    pages cm
  ISBN 978-0-451-41945-3
  1. Female friendship—Fiction.   I. Title.
  PS3612.I33525W64 2014
  813'.6—dc23   2014005367

Printed in the United States of America
10 9 8 7 6 5 4 3 2 1

Set in Palatino
Designed by Spring Hoteling

For my grandmother and best friend, Ailene Rickel,
who always picks me up when I fall

Acknowledgments

With this, my third book, under my belt and at least two more on the way, I feel like I'm living the dream. There are so many people to thank for setting me on the path to achieve this dream and for supporting me as I make a career of putting whatever comes to my mind to paper.

First and foremost, I wouldn't be writing if not for my agent, Alyssa Reuben. I call her my "literary goddess," which she seems to be cool with. Alyssa: You are my partner in crime, my dear friend, and so damn good at your job that you make it seem easy, which I know it's not. As always, I look forward to being your favorite author forever.

This novel would not have seen the light of day without my phenomenal editor, Kerry Donovan. Kerry, I'm not sure what I'd do without your extraordinary ability to take what I write and make it readable, good, actually. You have been both a devoted champion of my work and a trusted friend. Who else can I go to with questions on grammar and potty training?

Big thanks also go to Jason Yarn and Laura Nolan at Paradigm. And to everyone at NAL and Penguin Random House who contributed to the conception of this book, including Diana Franco, Rick Pascocello, and Craig Burke.

I could write the best books in the world and no one would

know about them without the tireless efforts of my publicists, Sarah Hall, Lisa Marie Gina, and the entire Sarah Hall Productions team. You're my extended family, and I am continually amazed by how hard you push and how much you make happen on my behalf. Thank you, Sheryl Press and Meredith Ford. Thank you a million times over!

It's been a true pleasure working with Canyon Ranch to spread the word about this book and about their fantastic resorts and spas. So many exciting things in the works!

And now a special thank-you to the people in my life—friends and colleagues alike—who've supported me throughout my career: Kerry Kennedy, Mariah Kennedy Cuomo, Cara Kennedy Cuomo, Michaela Kennedy Cuomo, Andrew Cuomo, Tom Yellin, Sara Haines, David Goffin, David Eilenberg, Alessandra Meskita, Devin Alexander, Jake Spitz, Jill Kargman, Jane Green, Beatriz Williams, Sarah Pekkanen, Karin Tanabe, Jenna McCarthy, Yona McDonough, Tamra Judge, Patti Stanger, Diane Neal, Zoe Schaeffer, Jayne Chase, Vanessa Wakeman, Jene Luciani, Gwen Wunderlich, Dara Kaplan, Monica Lynn, Ryan & Mindy Smith, Hyleri Katzenberg, J. D. Myers, Jennifer Heitler, Blake Harris, Robin Homonoff, Emily Homonoff, Jill Brooke, Amy Kallesten, Catherine MacDonald, Lisa Lineback, Julie Chudow, Danielle Dobin, Karen Sutton, and Jen Goldberg, who takes the most gorgeous photos of me, even when I'm not looking my best! Not to be forgotten, my new Westport family: Debbie, Scott, Taylor, and Dylan Mogelof. Thank you for becoming instant friends!

To my cherished friend and fellow author Shari Arnold. I depend on your sage wisdom more than you know. Cheers to all of your success to come!

ACKNOWLEDGMENTS

As always, a heartfelt thank-you to Jessica Regel, who took a chance on me in the very beginning.

To my best friend, Melody Drake. You keep me both grounded and on my toes, if that's possible! I love you, love you, love you!

Thank you to my in-laws, Mary Ann Liebert, Peter B. Liebert, and Peter S. Liebert, and to my sister-in-law and brother-in-law, Sara and Alex Liebert.

My family is everything to me. My parents, Tom and Kyle Einhorn, support me unconditionally, which is a gift. My brother, Zack Einhorn, is a lifelong friend and more talented than I'll ever be. My grandmother Ailene Rickel, to whom this book is dedicated, is one of my best friends and my best publicist! Thanks also to my grandmother Pat Einhorn. I love you all so much!

Last, but definitely not least—my boys. My tolerant and adoring husband, Lewis, deserves more thank-you's than the space allows. Jaxsyn and Hugo, my little chickens. You are my world. I love you to the moon and back.

Sometimes the pain was so visceral, she wanted to crawl out of her own skin. Sometimes it was there right in front of her, swinging back and forth like a pendulum, taunting her to reach out and grab it. To wring it until she'd squeezed it to a pulp. But, instead, she closed her eyes. And when she awoke, it was morning.

WHEN WE **FALL**

Chapter 1

"But I don't want fruit for breakfast, Mom!" Gia planted her chubby elbows on the granite countertop and scowled at Charlotte. "I want pancakes. With lots of syrup."

"Gia, we don't have time for pancakes today. Mommy has an appointment at ten thirty with Aunt Elizabeth. Maria will be here any minute. And I still have to shower. So please eat the fruit, sweetheart." Charlotte darted around the kitchen in her silk La Perla robe, tearing through her morning to-do list. Let dog out in backyard. Feed dog. Give dog fresh water. Make list for supermarket. Load dishwasher. Gather dry cleaning to be dropped off. "It's good for you, Gia. Fruit is good for you." The first day of school couldn't arrive soon enough.

Gia folded her arms across her chest and shook her head defiantly. "Fruit has a ton of carbs in it." She pushed the plate away from her as if to declare pancakes carb free.

"Who told you that?" Charlotte glanced at her nine-year-old daughter, the apparent nutrition expert, in her oversized Justin Bieber nightshirt.

"Olivia's mom. She knows everything about healthy stuff. She's really skinny."

"Is that so?" Olivia's mom, Avery—who was precisely the type of person to have a name like Avery before names like Avery were even trendy—*was* really skinny. Too skinny, actually.

"Yup. She said I have to eat only protein and vegetables if I want to look like her."

"Interesting." Charlotte didn't appreciate the unsolicited advice from skele-mommy. "Well, I think you look perfect just the way you are."

In Charlotte's opinion, prepubescent girls were not meant to be starving themselves or adhering to stringent dietary restrictions. There'd been none of that in her day. Charlotte had been pleasantly plump, as her maternal grandmother had affectionately referred to her, until she was at least fourteen, at which time she'd shed most of the baby fat. After that, her physique had been what one might call "sturdy" or "solid." *Fat* wasn't the right word. But *thin* wasn't either. And *skinny* was out of the question, given her genetic inheritance. Charlotte's own mother, while striking in many ways, had thighs so substantial she used to brag, "I could crush a can of creamed corn between these babies!" And her father's protruding paunch preceded his entrance into every room. The writing was on the wall.

Still, by the time Charlotte was a freshman at Cornell University, she'd found a way to tame her voluptuous figure with control-top stockings and other gut-sucking paraphernalia. And by the time vanity had really set in, she'd found a way to stick her finger down her throat following every meal. It wasn't ideal, but it was a means to an end: finding a rich, handsome husband to take care of her.

"Then why are you making me eat fruit?" Gia arched an eyebrow, a signature gesture that evoked her father. The same father who'd insisted that Gia was "unnecessarily overweight" and that if she didn't slim down she'd be tormented by the kids at school. He'd suggested that the sooner she learned to adjust her diet to reflect the crawling metabolism she'd been bestowed with—a dig at Charlotte's side of the family—her life and theirs (that part had been left unspoken) would be much easier.

Of course, Charlie had a point. Charlotte didn't want Gia to be persecuted by her classmates any more than he did. But she also didn't want Gia to grow up insecure about her body, desperate to conceal her ample rear end and padded midsection, as Charlotte had. It was easy for Charlie to set forth directives, especially when the onus was on Charlotte to follow them. He wasn't the one who had to put a plate of fruit in front of Gia every morning. Or make up excuses to leave the playground early, before the ice-cream truck arrived, so that she didn't have to deny her daughter the simple childhood pleasure of a snow cone. So what if she was a little overweight? She was only nine, for God's sake! Nine-year-olds deserved to eat snow cones!

"I'm not making you, Gia. Clearly you haven't taken one bite. Can you please just eat it, so I can get ready? You can have pancakes tomorrow. I promise." Charlotte sat down at the kitchen table—adjacent to the breakfast bar, where Gia was perched on a barstool—sinking her tired body into one of the six cushioned chairs upholstered in deluxe celadon linen. She surveyed her *Architectural Digest*–worthy kitchen with its stark white frameless cabinets, black granite worktops crafted from volcanically formed natural stone, top-of-the-line stainless-steel appliances, and the pièce de résistance—an Italian glass chandelier, a modern interpretation of vintage Murano, that she and Charlie had purchased on their honeymoon in Florence—to preside over it all. She knew she was blessed.

"I don't want pancakes tomorrow. I. Want. Them. Now!"

Charlotte sighed. She didn't have the energy to fight with Gia. Not today. Especially since it wasn't her battle; it was Charlie's. She still had to deal with her sister, and it wasn't even nine a.m. And that would extract every morsel of vitality from her being. It always did.

"Fine, sweetheart. Whatever you want." She stood again, defeated, walked toward the freezer, retrieved two Eggo buttermilk pancakes, slid them into the toaster oven, and swiped the bottle of syrup from the refrigerator, setting it on the counter in front of her triumphant offspring.

"Great." Gia revealed a complacent grin and dropped her arms to her sides. She'd won and she knew it. Granted, Charlotte hadn't put up much of a fight, but then, she rarely did. She was the pushover parent. The good cop, if you will. Something for which she knew Charlie resented her.

It was impossible to pinpoint when things had turned for her and Charlie. There wasn't a day or a month or even a year when their relationship had suddenly morphed from two people so madly in love it felt incomprehensible that they'd ever been able to breathe without each other to two people passing through the hallways of their house and their lives with little more than a quick conversation, a peripheral smile, and a chaste peck on the lips. What she wouldn't give to return to that dispassionate contentedness. Now things were different. Most days, it felt as if she were dangling from the roof of the tallest skyscraper, which had been erected with layer upon layer of resentment. One rancorous floor on top of another, the windows welded shut to constrain the dense fog of suffocating bitterness. After all, it was one thing to be miserable. But quite another for people to know about it.

It would have been easy enough to blame their troubles on parenthood, a common scapegoat and credible culprit in destroying marriages, transforming them from spicy to icy faster than you can say "breast pump." But that wasn't the entirety of it. Charlotte would have loved more children. Gia hadn't been an easy baby, but wasn't there some sort of memory-erasing serum that obliterated all the physical and emotional pain inherent in childbirth and child rearing in those first few years? The sleepless nights. The hundred-and-four-degree fevers. The projectile vomit. The lavalike poops that seemed to erupt at the most inopportune times, like when you'd been waiting in a long line at the supermarket and were just about to load your items onto the conveyer belt at checkout.

They'd tried for a second baby when Gia was four. Charlie had wanted a boy. But month after month, test after test, the words *not pregnant* had taunted her. Three characters fewer and she'd have been a mother of two. Maybe of a Charles Crane, Jr. Would that have made things better?

They'd gone through five rounds of IVF, which had only intensified the ubiquitous strain in their marriage. Charlotte had been hyped-up on hormones. Charlie had grown intolerant of her radically swinging moods. And Gia, just a toddler, had been forced to listen to her parents throw down over things as innocuous as a glass of spilled milk. Turns out it was something to cry over.

There were still good days, though they were few and far between. Occasionally a whole week would pass without a fight and, for a brief space in time, Charlotte would remember why she'd fallen in love with Charlie in the first place. She could tell he was feeling the same way. Something in the way he looked at her, even touched her. If she was really lucky, she'd wake up to him caressing her back, knowing that he'd been watching her sleep with a certain fondness she cherished and tried desperately to preserve. How was it possible, she'd often wondered, that one person could evoke such radically far-flung emotions in another? How could she feel such intense tenderness for Charlie on any given Monday and by Wednesday have to restrain herself from wringing his neck?

"Here you go." Charlotte placed Gia's second pass at breakfast in front of her. "Just don't tell your father."

"My lips are sealed." She pretended to zip her mouth shut with the tips of her thumb and index finger pressed together. "As soon as I eat these." She giggled.

"Thanks." Charlotte smiled as her daughter drenched her pancakes in a puddle of maple syrup. Sometimes it was easy to forget she was just a little girl.

Once Maria had arrived, a few minutes before nine, as she always did, rain or shine, Charlotte withdrew to her expansive white marble master bathroom to treat herself to a relaxing steam shower before meeting Elizabeth. It was remarkable, really, the way Gia's whole attitude shifted when she was in the presence of anyone but Charlotte or Charlie. Suddenly she became obedient—polite, even—dispensing *please*s and *thank you*s as if she had an excess to relinquish. But as soon as Charlotte so much as walked by the room where Gia and Maria were playing, invariably Gia's diva demeanor would rear its ugly head. And then some.

Charlotte cranked the faucet all the way to hot, slipped out of her robe, and let it fall to the floor, where Janna, her housekeeper, would find it later on and dutifully return it to its hook on the other side of the bathroom, which was the size of a studio apartment in New York City. This was Charlotte's favorite time of the day. The one hour of peace and quiet between Maria's arrival and commencing the myriad errands and appointments that typically confronted her. There was no one to tug on her arm or interrupt her train of thought with a question that, surely, they could answer on their own.

Sometimes she had to remind herself that she'd gone to an Ivy League school and graduated magna cum laude. That she'd then landed a coveted position, albeit entry-level, at one of Manhattan's most distinguished advertising firms and that, during her two-year tenure, she had been tapped as the company's rising star. Then she'd met Charlie and decided to marry him within months, had gotten pregnant shortly thereafter, and had taken a "leave of absence"; still, that did not mean she'd forfeited her brain cells in exchange for a sprawling lawn and designer shoes.

Charlotte examined herself in the mirror, as she did every morning, zeroing in on each imperfection. The crow's-feet radiating from the corners of her eyes and fanning down her cheeks. The sagging breasts. The way the undersides of her arms flapped like slabs of meat. The fact that her inner thighs kissed when she walked. And the saddest truth of all: her visibly bulging belly nine years post-baby. She needed a spray tan, a bikini wax, and either a diet plan that might actually work or liposuction.

Charlotte knew she wasn't fat, per se, but you didn't have to be fat to be considered fat when you lived in the Manhattan suburbs. If you were so much as average, you weren't thin enough. Ladies' lunches were salads only. Oil and vinegar on the side. Sugar-free iced tea or water with lemon, and no carbonation for fear of bloating. Regular exercise classes were a given—no less than six times per week, pick your poison, depending on how much you were willing to sweat. Personal trainers were another option, but not nearly as social. Because, ultimately, it wasn't just about how you burned off your salad. It was about who saw you burning it off and how good you looked doing it—clad in Lululemon with a fresh blowout and an artfully made-up face, just enough effort to make perfection appear effortless.

Charlotte grimaced and slathered a mud mask on her face, which she'd let set while she exfoliated the rest of her body. Short of plastic surgery, it was the best she could do. She opened the heavy glass door to the shower, releasing a gust of thick, warm steam, and stepped inside the one place where she could shut off from the rest of the world, even if only for ten delicious minutes of solitude.

But before she could close the door behind her, the phone rang, dislocating her serenity. She didn't have to answer it. What could be so important? *Who* could be so important? Gia was home with her. Charlie was at work. Her parents were definitely still asleep. And she was about to go meet Elizabeth. Most likely, it was a prerecorded message from some insurance company, informing her that—no matter what rates she currently had—they could do better. Still, she couldn't fully relax without knowing who was on the other end of the line.

She scampered across the bathroom and into her bedroom, her damp feet padding through the plush white wall-to-wall carpeting, which they had to have cleaned every two months thanks to their dog Lolly's eternally muddy paws. The phone chimed for a fifth time as she lunged for it.

"Hello?" she answered breathlessly and somewhat accusatorily. As in *What could be so important that you have to interrupt my steam shower?*

"The appointment was rescheduled," Elizabeth droned through the receiver.

"What do you mean it was rescheduled?" Charlotte propped herself against the side of her king-sized bed. Heaps of pillows in different shapes, sizes, and patterns dressed the ornate wrought-iron headboard. It was hopelessly romantic. *Hopelessly* being the operative word.

"I mean it's not happening today, so you're off the hook." Elizabeth delivered the news without so much as a hint of gratitude that Charlotte had rearranged her day to accompany her sister to her new shrink. The new shrink that, with any luck—more like a minor miracle, actually—would be the last in a long line of shrinks who Elizabeth had decided "didn't get her." Or "didn't understand all that she'd been through." Because no one could ever understand the depths of her sister's pain. No matter how hard they tried or how many degrees they had hanging on their office wall.

The thing was, Charlotte had actually been looking forward to this appointment. Sure, she'd sat alongside Elizabeth for more therapy sessions than she cared to remember, but this time she had a purpose. A goal. She'd planned to tell this counselor— psychologist, psychiatrist, whatever she was—that she needed her sister's help. That, while she understood—perhaps better than anyone else—the impact of the unthinkable tragedy Elizabeth had endured, there had to be a light at the end of the ten-year tunnel. And if there wasn't, Elizabeth had to find a way to function as a normal, or at least useful, member of society, which meant assisting Charlotte in taking care of their sick parents. She'd pilfered the last part from Charlie.

"I don't want to be off the hook. I was looking forward to meeting Dr. Lisa," Charlotte griped, though she'd been instantly skeptical of the informal designation. In her estimation, anyone who used their first name to follow their title came off sounding more like a late-night radio-show host than a steadfast medical practitioner.

"Well, sorry."

"So what happened?" Charlotte walked back into the bathroom to turn off the shower and to dab at the hardened mask on her face with a wet washcloth. "Did you make a new appointment?"

"Not yet. I have no way to get there," Elizabeth mumbled.

"I don't understand."

"What's not to understand? I. Have. No. Transportation."

"What's wrong with the Jeep?" Just three months earlier, Charlie had succumbed to Charlotte's unremitting pleas to buy her sister a new car. Elizabeth's twenty-year-old Volkswagen, which she never washed or had serviced, had smelled like a garbage dump and had been breaking down twice a week, and Charlotte, the ever-dutiful sister, had been driving all around town picking her up.

"Nick has it." Nick was Elizabeth's boyfriend. Her notoriously irresponsible boyfriend, whose penchant for gambling at Mohegan Sun and Foxwoods every few weeks had earned him his "winning" reputation.

"Okay, well, where's Nick's car?" Charlotte rolled her eyes in anticipation of the answer. Rather, the excuse. "Don't make me pull teeth here, Lizzy."

"I don't know." She was immediately defensive, as well she should be. They both knew, at this point, that it was more of an indictment than an innocuous query. "He said something about a friend borrowing it."

"A *friend*." Charlotte exhaled dramatically. "I see. So, what? He took your car for the foreseeable future, leaving you bound to your apartment indefinitely? That sounds like a good plan."

"Don't start."

"Start? You think this is the beginning? This has been going on for three years, Lizzy. It's not only your life that's inconvenienced by his crap." Charlotte flung her muddy washcloth into the laundry basket and instinctively ran the palm of her hand over her skin to make sure it was as supple and smooth as the bottle had promised.

"Oh, I'm sorry. Did I get in the way of your regular facial or massage? Which one was it today?"

Charlotte clenched her jaw and balled her free hand into a tight fist, coaching herself to breathe in and out. In and out. She wasn't going to allow herself to be sucked into Elizabeth's vortex of misery. Again. "Let's drop it, okay? Just try to give me a little advance notice when you reschedule."

"Fine."

"Do you want to use the Range Rover until Nick gets his car back?"

"That would be helpful."

"I'll pay for the cab over here."

"Can't you come get me?"

"Lizzy . . ." Charlotte stopped herself and took another deep breath. "I'll be there in twenty minutes."

Chapter 2

"I can't believe how great this place looks." Allison scooted around the kitchen's center island and knelt in front of a low cabinet so she could reorganize the piles of neatly pressed linen place mats and napkins her mother had picked up, along with "a few other necessary items," as she'd referred to the collection of brimming shopping bags littering the already congested foyer. "Can you hand me that orange tablecloth?"

"Just a minute, sweetheart." Her mom fluttered across the space, swooping from drawer to drawer, cupboard to cupboard, and in and out of the refrigerator so many times that Allison's ten-year-old son, Logan, had said that Grandma was making him dizzy—at which point Allison's father had suggested that "the men" take a trip to Dunkin' Donuts for a tête-à-tête. And even though Logan had no idea what that meant, anywhere Grandpa was going, he was more than happy to follow. Over the past four days, that had included three separate trips to the toy store—apparently one could never have enough sporting equipment in suburbia—a visit to Grandpa's office followed by a tour of the hospital where he did his rounds, and countless excursions to the Wincourt Library, where "the men" would get lost in the stacks for hours, while Allison and her mother whipped the house into tip-top shape.

Allison had no expectations that either Logan or her father would help unpack and organize things. When it came to complicated brain surgery, her dad was your man. But folding T-shirts and screwing in lightbulbs were not part of his repertoire. On the other hand, Allison's mom had been making preparations for their arrival since the house had been purchased in June. They'd arrived to working telephones, a cable package with more channels than any two people could hope to watch, and a refrigerator bursting with prepared meals—lasagna, chicken casserole, beef chili, you name it.

Allison had been anticipating their move out of Manhattan for months and had been promising herself for weeks that she wouldn't let Logan be the strong one. Resilience was deeply embedded in Logan's DNA, as it had been in his dad's; in Logan's case, it was coupled with the heartbreaking circumstance of growing up without a father. How many times over the course of the past decade had Logan been the one to remind her, even when he couldn't speak, that he needed to be fed, or dressed, or read a bedtime story? And he never cried, not even as a baby. Well, not never, but rarely. All the mommies in her mommy-and-me classes had been incredulous. Allison had chalked it up to God owing her one. A dead husband and a colicky baby; now, that would have been downright cruel.

It wasn't the norm for Logan to play parent. It certainly could have been if she'd let herself be pummeled by the forceful waves of anger, depression, and fear that had submerged her more often than she cared to admit. But she'd refused to do that to her baby. Logan—or at least the promise of him—had been the lone shaft of light illuminating the dark abyss that was her life. Her life *after*. Because that's how Allison defined it. Before Jack's death and *after*. She'd thought about terminating the pregnancy for a fleeting moment, when one of the few "bus tragedy" widows she knew had done it without so much as a hint of penitence. "It's not fair to bring a child into this world without one parent and with another who can barely get out of bed in the morning." She'd said it so matter-of-factly. As if she didn't have a choice. As if a piece of her husband hadn't been living inside her. At the time, it had seemed evocatively hollow to Allison, but her mother had been quick to point out that everyone had her own method of grieving. And that what was right for this woman didn't have to be right for her.

She barely remembered being pregnant. Nine months of doctor's appointments, an ever-expanding belly, and knowing smiles from strangers had elapsed faster than a good night's sleep, an experience that, for Allison, had perished along with Jack. She hadn't returned to their marital bed *after*. She'd slept only on the living room couch, waiting for him to walk through the front door. Until his body was recovered, there was a chance he could come home, she'd rationalized.

Eventually, Jack's body had been identified—or at least parts of it had. Allison's father had handled those details, keeping anything remotely grizzly well concealed, while Allison's mom had tended to things like grocery shopping and making sure her pregnant daughter was maintaining as healthful a lifestyle as could be expected for a woman who'd just lost her husband.

Her parents had also facilitated her move from the one-bedroom Upper West Side apartment she'd shared with Jack—their "love nest," he'd dubbed it upon first sight—to a bright, spacious-for-Manhattan two-bedroom on the corner of Eighty-fifth Street and Lexington Avenue. The quiet of their West Side neighborhood, which had once seemed beguilingly romantic, had suddenly become haunting. Not to mention that every inch of space had reminded her of him. She'd needed noise around her. Something to drown out the unceasing turbulence in her head.

Initially, her mom had suggested, in her gentle way, that Allison move back home, to their intimate suburban enclave forty-five minutes from the hustle and bustle of New York City. If only for a few months, a year at most. But Allison had been resolute in her decision to stay put. She'd maintained that she craved the familiarity but had deliberately left out the truth—that she was terrified to leave Jack behind.

Now, eleven years later, she was still terrified to leave him behind. But she knew she was doing it for the right reasons. To give Logan the upbringing he deserved. And to give both of them a fresh start—a long-overdue fresh start. Logan was ready. For him, their move wasn't the volatile cocktail of mixed emotions it was for her. He wasn't beset with guilt over leaving behind a father he never knew. Or tortured by a slideshow of reminiscences looping in his head. He wasn't even mildly bummed out about forsaking the only place he'd ever called home. Thankfully, these weren't the kinds of things ten-year-old boys dwelled on and, fortunately, Allison had enough perspective to realize this. Just because Logan acted grown-up didn't mean he was. And she'd be damned if she'd burden him with her own anxiety.

Perhaps Allison was the one who wasn't ready. Perhaps she never would be, not entirely. "You have to take a leap of faith," her mom had reminded her, although this was easier said than done, they both knew.

Still, when they'd arrived at their new home late Wednesday morning and Logan had dubbed it "the best place on earth," Allison had been markedly relieved. Apparently, to Logan, living in Wincourt near his grandparents and having a big backyard where he could play baseball and soccer on a whim was just about as magical as the kingdom itself. Maybe she *could* put off the long-overdue Disney World vacation she'd been considering for a bit longer!

Allison had been pleased to find that she too felt immediately comfortable in their new home—a recently renovated white colonial with polished black shutters situated on a quiet side street five minutes from town. She delighted in walking through the front door into the two-story entryway bathed in sunlight, which gave way to hardwood floors with intricate inlays leading to a gourmet kitchen complete with a suspended pot rack and a walk-in pantry. The kitchen rolled effortlessly into an airy and bright great room, which overlooked the backyard, complete with a fenced-in vegetable-and-herb garden, a mahogany deck, and a stone wall ideal for displaying vibrant flowering plants. Instantly, Allison could picture Logan playing a game of tag football with her father and their neighbors while her mother grilled burgers and dogs for the voracious crew, and she ran through the vegetable garden barefoot, plucking ingredients for a festive salad. She could also see herself lounging on a recliner, sipping her morning coffee, and enjoying a warm croissant al fresco while Logan was at school. But, above all, the most enticing feature of their outdoor spread, certainly as far as Logan was concerned, was the built-in fireplace ready for roasting marshmallows at a moment's notice.

As far as Allison was concerned, her brand-new art studio, nestled in a quiet corner on the first floor, with French doors that opened onto the patio, was reason enough to flee Manhattan. "If you love copious amounts of natural light when you paint, this is the home for you," was what her Realtor had said before showing her the house last April. And she'd been spot-on. The original owner had been a sculptor, she'd informed Allison, who'd considered this co-incidence a sort of divine providence.

Allison had also been lured by the peace and quiet, something she'd grown to covet, having been a single mom in New York City for a decade. That and the master bedroom outfitted with two custom walk-in closets and a sprawling marble master bath with double sink, extra-deep walk-in shower, and two-person Jacuzzi tub. It felt fit for royalty or, in this case, one lone queen, even though Allison knew that, compared to the other houses in Wincourt, hers was ordinary at best. It was hard to imagine that all this space was hers and Logan's, when they'd so contentedly occupied an apartment half the size for close to a decade.

She'd fallen in love with the property at first sight, before the couple living there—who'd just become pregnant with their fourth child in six years—had even put it on the market. The price tag had been heftier than expected, but thanks to the income from a few of her pricier paintings, which had sold for Valentine's Day and Mother's Day, along with the steady stream of money that Jack's parents, Nancy and Bill, funneled into her account, she could afford it. That was the thing about Nancy and Bill. Physical presence was practically impossible for them, but they were nothing if not prompt and generous when it came to providing for her and Logan. Jack had come from a notoriously wealthy—and controlling—New England family. They drank more than they ate, always with stiff upper lips. And they couldn't be counted on for more than an occasional call, reserved for major holidays and birthdays only, but when it came to assuaging their guilt via financial support, Nancy and Bill had yet to disappoint.

Logan had met them only three times, which was why—to this day—he still called them by their first names. Three times in ten years. Once when he was five months old, which arguably didn't count since he had no recollection of that encounter. Once when he was four. And then again when he was eight. Initially, Allison had felt apathetic toward their indifference when it came to Logan. Nancy and Bill had been unpleasant to deal with when Jack was alive, so not having to deal with them once he was gone had seemed like an unexpected gift. Until Allison had held her sweet son in her arms and promised to give him everything in the world, including a relationship with both sets of grandparents. Whether she liked it or not, life was no longer about her.

They'd been invited to Logan's bris but had declined, offering a friend's daughter's wedding as their excuse. They'd also been invited to every birthday party over the course of a decade, but there'd always been one reason or another—nothing of any real merit—why they simply couldn't make the arduous drive from Boston to New York to celebrate an important milestone with their one and only grandchild. "Maybe it's too hard for them to face him, since they lost Jack," Allison's mom had suggested, acknowledging the profound physical resemblance between father and son—slightly cleft chin, empathetic brown eyes, obnoxiously flawless olive complexion—while at the same time doing what she always did: trying to see the best in everyone. Even if there was no best to be seen. "If I died, would you stop seeing Logan?" Allison had countered, knowing full well it was not only a ridiculous thing to ask but an insensitive one. "Stop seeing him? I'd adopt him!" her mom had declared, immediately adding, "And don't say things like that," after which she'd deliberately turned the conversation to her friend Martha Horowitz's botched total hip replacement.

Allison had stopped coddling Logan a long time ago, if only when it came to Nancy and Bill, once she'd finally realized that promising they'd come visit soon was doing more damage than good, since they never showed up. If they didn't realize how sweet and special her son was and how lucky they all were to have a piece of Jack with them forever, then it was their loss.

Initially, Allison had been wary of accepting their money. She'd felt like a kept woman, hired to ease their grandson into the reality that they weren't going to show on Christmas, despite the dozen or so shipped boxes they sent of toys, cloth-ing, and tickets to whatever kiddie show was currently live at Madison Square Garden or Radio City Music Hall. But Allison's mother, relying on her predictable Pollyanna pos-ture, had insisted that Nancy and Bill were doing what they could do, the best way they knew how. She'd also told Allison not to look a gift horse in the mouth—some months her paintings sold and some months they didn't, so she should be thankful for Nancy and Bill's benevolent contributions.

"Mom, the tablecloth?" Allison looked up to find her mother balancing thick chunks of juicy red tomatoes on top of a precarious heap of shaved turkey, paper-thin Swiss cheese, and crisp Romaine lettuce. "Hungry much?" She stood and walked over to the counter.

"You need to eat something." Her mother didn't make eye contact.

"I told you I have no appetite, Mom." Allison sat down on a barstool.

"Voilà!" Her mother added a slather of mustard and a sec-ond hearty slice of sourdough bread to her masterpiece and reached for a knife to cut the sandwich in half. "Here you go." Allison's mother nudged the plate toward her. "You need sustenance."

"But I'm really not—"

"Eh-eh." Her mom wagged her index finger. "I don't want to hear it. You're already skin and bones. And I don't want what happened last time to happen again."

Last time. There were so many different ways her family and friends referred to it now. Besides actually saying it out-right. *Last time* was a common one. As in *We don't want you to get frail and dehydrated like last time.* Other euphemisms came in the form of *You know what? Let's not talk about* you know what *in front of Logan.* And her all-time favorite: *Since the accident. How's Allison doing* since the accident? Popular among her parents' acquaintances.

No one liked to think about the fathers who would never again throw a baseball in Central Park with their sons. Or walk their daughters down the aisle. The mothers who would never again hold their newborn babies or toddlers or teenagers so close to their hearts they could feel the rise and fall of their chests. The children, sisters, brothers, aunts, uncles, cousins, and friends who'd done nothing more than decide to go on an innocent company-wide ski trip only to have their futures, and the countless milestones inherent in those futures, annihilated. It was heavy stuff. Too heavy for someone who was just trying to be polite.

"I promise you I'll eat something when I'm hungry." Allison smiled, rubbing her mom's arm affectionately and pecking her on the cheek. "In the meantime, looks like you've got your work cut out for you." She motioned to the sandwich on steroids.

"One bite?"

Allison shook her head.

"Fine, I'll wrap it up for Logan." Her mom grimaced. "Now, where did I put the aluminum foil?"

"Second drawer to the right of the stove." Allison sat back down on the hardwood floor to continue folding napkins. "It feels good to be home."

"I'm so glad to hear you say that, sweetheart." Her mom walked into the pantry. "Cup of tea?"

"Sure." Allison got back on her feet and reached for two blue mugs so big they resembled soup bowls. She'd bought them because they were the exact same color as Logan's room in their New York City apartment. "It's amazing how much has remained unchanged in Wincourt."

"Like what?" Her mother dropped a tea bag into each mug and took one at a time from Allison, filling them from the instant-hot-water tap.

"All the stores in town. The school, at least from the outside." Over the last decade, Allison had barely been home. She'd seen her parents at least once a week, but typically they'd been the ones to come to her. Making things easier on Allison had become their life's mission, and that included not asking her to travel outside her comfort zone any more than was absolutely necessary.

"There are so many new things too. Wincourt has flourished in your absence, my dear." Her mom tasted her tea and sat down for what seemed like, at least to Allison, the first time in days.

It was hard to ignore the visible proof that Jack's death had aged her mother. But until recently, Allison had been unable to consider the fact that the ramifications of her unthinkable loss had set off a domino effect extending well beyond her and Logan. Not that anyone had dared to mention *their* pain. Certainly not to the grieving widow and newly minted single mom of a child with no father.

Allison's mother had been breathtakingly beautiful in her day, with a glossy mane of sumptuous blond hair cascading midway down her back, which in her mid-forties she'd cropped into a stylish shoulder-length bob. For as long as Allison could remember, her mother's skin had been implausibly luminescent, she swore from nothing more than bargain-brand soap and Oil of Olay. Much to Allison's delight, her mother's most striking feature—her pale gray eyes—had been passed down to her, along with her long blond hair. Though the one thing Allison had not inherited was her mother's straight and slender nose. Instead she'd been the hapless recipient of her dad's crooked honker, which—as luck would have it—actually suited her face.

Jack had adored her mom. They'd been like partners in crime. Sometimes Allison would come home late from the art gallery where she'd been working at the time and the two of them would be on a movie date without her. Her mother was easily lured by the prospect of swinging into the city for an "artistic flick," and her father always appreciated Jack's willingness to sit through subtitled French films with his wife, refusing to endure the "chore," as he referred to it. In fact, to this day, he still said the same thing whenever her mother asked him to see a foreign film: "If I wanted to read, I'd stay home with the paper."

"Is that so?" Allison couldn't help but laugh. Wincourt was barely as big as a Manhattan neighborhood. "It's a cultural mecca now, huh?"

"Very funny. You'll see." Her mom furrowed her brow. "Is Logan excited for tomorrow?"

"Are you kidding? He can't wait. All he can talk about, outside of being with you and Dad, is making new friends and meeting his teachers and what sports he can get involved with." Jack had been the athletic one. The type who, at twenty years old, having never skied before, had taken the chairlift directly to the top of an intermediate slope and found his way to the bottom as gracefully as someone who'd been at it for at least a few months. In turn, Allison—who'd been skiing upward of a dozen times—had found her way to the bottom on her rear end. Of the two of them, who would have guessed that a ski trip would have been the cause of *his* demise?

"It's remarkable." Allison's mom nodded definitively. "He is remarkable."

"I know." Allison swallowed a lump in her throat. "He's amazing. I can't believe how well he's handling all this."

"Thanks to you."

"Yeah, right."

"You should give yourself more credit, Ali."

"Maybe." She scrunched her nose.

"What is it?"

"Nothing."

"I know that look."

"It's stupid."

"Get on with it." Her mother waved her hand.

"What if I don't make any friends? You know? What if I don't fit in with the suburban mommies?"

"Like me?"

"They don't make 'em like you anymore, Mom."

"I can't see that happening, Ali. You were always very popular in school. And at summer camp. Weren't you team captain or something?"

"Red Team." Allison smiled wistfully. It was a big deal to be a team captain. Only four seniors got picked. And everyone

knew Red Team was the best. Jack had been one of her lieu-
tenants.

"Betty Miller's daughter still lives on Oak Drive. I could introduce you."

"Mom, I went to school with Sara Miller."

"Reintroduce you, whatever. She's a lovely girl."

"She's a nun."

"So? What do you have against nuns?"

"What could we possibly have in common?"

"You both like to wear black and white." She smirked.

"Very funny." Allison rolled her eyes. "I think I'll take my chances with the moms at Logan's school first."

"Up to you."

"I bet it's really cliquey."

"Isn't it always?"

"I guess." She groaned, thinking back to how it had been in the immediate days, months, and years following Jack's death. How so many of her friends—the ones she'd met since moving to the city after graduating from college—had made futile attempts at being supportive, showing up at her front door with bagel and cookie platters. But once it had become abundantly clear to them that gossiping over lunch at the corner café was no longer part of the fabric of Allison's be-ing, they'd dropped like flies, buzzing off together to exist in a world where breaking bread didn't include sobbing into your Cobb salad. It was almost as if they'd deemed her tragic existence contagious. *Don't touch the widow or you might catch dead-husband disease.*

Allison had also lost touch with some of her real friends, mainly because she'd been rendered incapable of maintaining relationships and at some point the physical and emotional distance had become too vast. All except her best friend, Melanie, whom she'd met the first day of freshman orientation at Brown. Melanie's dedication, unlike the others', had been stalwart. She'd made monthly visits from Chicago, shouldering the cost of expensive hotel rooms without so much as a mention. She'd flown back and forth, landing at LaGuardia late on Friday night and returning to O'Hare late on Sunday evening, so she could devote every minute of her spare time to extracting Allison from the depths of her despair. Ten years later, Melanie was still living in the Windy City and she was still a steadfast ally. Only now, there was a husband and a brood of four kids, with a fifth on the way. Even uninterrupted phone calls were challenging.

"Well, I'm not worried. As I said, you've never had a problem making friends before."

"I was never the woman whose husband died before."

"You're still the same person you always were." Her mother tipped her head downward.

"I hope you're right."

"Right or not, I'm proud of you." She looked back up, and Allison could see that her eyes were bloodshot. "I suspect moving up here is, in some small way, a second kind of loss for you." She cleared her throat. "You know, having to part with that physical connection to Jack you may have felt in the city."

"Maybe." Allison let her mother hug her, and, slowly, she could feel the weight of the last few days release from her body.

"It's going to be okay." Her mother squeezed her tight,

like she'd done so many times when Allison was a little girl and scared of the monsters living under her bed.

"I hope so." She straightened up while—out of the corner of her eye—admiring the sliver of a diamond wedding band still twinkling on her right hand.

"I know so." Her mother nodded decisively. "Just you wait and see."

Chapter 3

Charlotte identified an isolated booth, tucked into the hindmost corner of the Wincourt Diner, and was dutifully escorted there by the college-aged hostess, who was smacking her watermelon-flavored bubble gum and humming Carly Rae Jepsen's "Call Me Maybe." Under normal circumstances, seeing and being seen would have been paramount to Charlotte, but not when it came to dining with her sister.

She slid into the booth, shucked her dark brown quilted jacket, and watched the front door so she could wave Elizabeth over as soon as she arrived. Late. Always late. Even though they both knew she had perfectly suitable transportation in the form of Charlotte's navy Range Rover, with plush, cream-colored leather seats and coordinated navy piping.

"Can I get you a drink, ma'am?" The waifish teenage waitress, with an arm sheathed in vibrant *Twilight*-inspired tattoos, appeared with pen and paper poised to take her order. Charlotte frowned at the designation. When had she become a ma'am? Probably somewhere between baby and Botox.

"I'll take an iced tea, no sugar. Not Snapple."

The waitress nodded. "Is someone joining you?" She motioned to the empty seat opposite Charlotte with a ketchup-soaked straw she'd retrieved from the soiled diner floor.

"One would hope." Charlotte smiled politely and the waitress stared at her blankly. "Yes, someone is joining me. Any minute. I think." She exhaled, beleaguered by having to justify her sister's boundless incompetence yet again. Namely to someone whose main concerns were evidently ornate body art and extreme piercings—Charlotte had counted six gold hoops in each ear plus one of those ghastly silver barbell-like thingies impaling the tip of her tongue. Who knew how many more there were in regions that, gratefully, Charlotte would never lay eyes on.

"Okay, so do you know what this person wants to drink?" The waitress wound a section of stringy brown hair around her middle finger as her beady green eyes darted from table to table in pursuit of a diversion.

"She'll have the same." Charlotte scanned the restaurant, anxious to make sure there was no one she recognized or who might recognize her. To say that the Wincourt Diner was not her usual stomping grounds was the understatement of the century, except where Elizabeth was concerned. Charlotte far preferred Chez Louis' grilled shrimp and vegetable platter or the poached salmon at the Ivy Grill. But, predictably, Elizabeth wanted greasy griddle food. And what Elizabeth wanted, Elizabeth got, which was just fine by

Charlotte, since her sister's soggy stack of pancakes came with a welcome side order of anonymity.

"Okay." The waitress disappeared into the throng of indistinguishable servers, and Charlotte rifled through her monogrammed carryall to find her iPhone.

The Louis Vuitton had been a gift from Charlie for their tenth wedding anniversary, which meant he'd given her permission to buy something for herself. *Within reason.* He'd never bothered to ask what he'd gotten her. One bag was the same as the next to him—their definitions of *clutch* being, quite clearly, very different. In Charlie's world, a clutch was what Derek Jeter came through in with two outs in the bottom of the ninth. Charlotte scanned the e-mails in her inbox, which were mostly snippets of gossip from her best friends, Sabrina and Missy. There was also a slew of "immediate action required" notes from Gia's school principal, since fourth grade would officially commence the following day. It was hard to believe that almost a decade had elapsed since Gia's birth, an occasion that, for most new parents, would have been indisputably blissful. But not for Charlotte and Charlie. Any joy they'd articulated in the weeks leading up to, at, or immediately after Gia's birth had been swiftly squelched by Charlotte's mother, for fear that it would intensify the excruciating agony stemming from Elizabeth's catastrophic loss. And the agony wasn't confined to Elizabeth. There'd been a sinister cloak of despair encasing her entire family for at least a month.

"You would not believe the fucking traffic I just hit on the Post Road." Elizabeth's snarky voice called Charlotte to attention. Her sister appeared purposefully casual, as usual, wearing a crinkled white men's shirt tucked into faded and shredded blue jeans, the soles of her perfect size-seven feet flattening the back of an old pair of Vans sneakers and her auburn hair gathered into a messy chignon. Often, Charlotte wondered how Elizabeth managed to look so good with such little effort and even less money for shopping.

It was hard to remember a time when she hadn't been jealous of Elizabeth's naturally lean physique, her warm olive complexion, and the way her enviable blue eyes illuminated when she was passionate about something. Elizabeth was by far the more desirable sister, in Charlotte's opinion and—she felt quite certain—in the opinion of anyone who'd met them. She was also the more outgoing and possibly smarter sister, though Charlotte always made better grades in school thanks to her staunch work ethic.

"Shhh." Charlotte surveyed her surroundings again, perusing the thankfully unrecognizable faces.

"What? We're not at the ballet." Elizabeth dropped all one hundred and three pounds of herself into the plush booth with a thud.

"I know, but do we really need the f-bombs?" Charlotte sniffed and widened her eyes. "Are you smoking again?"

"What?" Elizabeth flailed her lean, tanned arms to summon the waitress, who promptly rolled her eyes.

"You heard me." Charlotte tucked her skillfully straightened, collar-bone-skimming brown hair, highlighted with streaks of deep red, behind her ears and arched a professionally plucked eyebrow dubiously. "It's a repulsive habit and you better not be puffing away in my car. Charlie will kill you."

"What else is new?" The waitress appeared. "Saved by the bell." Elizabeth smirked. "Can I get a Coke? I wouldn't drink this crap if you paid me." She pushed the iced tea toward Charlotte, causing it to splash onto the table. The waitress balked at the spilled liquid and smacked a handful of napkins on the table. "Well, maybe if you paid me. But it would have to be a lot."

Charlotte often considered how two such different people could be derived from the same genetic cloth. Sure, Elizabeth had changed significantly since the tragedy, but hadn't she always been somewhat rough around the edges, a bully of sorts, even though she was the little sister?

There'd been more than a dozen occasions through the years, at least that Charlotte could recall, when she'd been both mortified by and in awe of her sister's gumption. Like when Charlotte was in fifth grade and Elizabeth was in fourth and Peter Becker—the meanest and also cutest boy in Charlotte's class—had told everyone that Charlotte had showed him her boobies behind the gymnasium bleachers. And that she was as flat as a board. Unbeknownst to Peter, he'd picked the wrong girl—and the most prudish—to mess with. Not because Charlotte had been prepared to defend herself or, really, to do anything but cower behind the very same bleachers Peter had cited, crying her eyes out from utter humiliation. Of course she hadn't shown him her boobies— nor would she ever show any boy her boobies until she was married—but who would believe a loser like her over the perennially popular Peter Becker? Only Elizabeth.

So during recess that day, in front of all of the fourth, fifth, and even sixth graders, Charlotte's scrappy little sister had marched over to Peter, standing on her tippy-toes so their faces were a mere two inches apart. She'd pointed her index finger right at him and shouted, so everyone could hear, "Your penis is so small, I bet you have to search for it when you wanna pee." It hadn't necessarily been the most clever or well-conceived attack, but it had done the trick. Their fellow classmates had burst into a chorus of derisive laughter, rendering Peter Becker shocked and woefully shamed. He'd been put in his place by a girl, and a pint-sized one at that. Charlotte had cringed. Not in a million years would she have stood up to Peter or said the word *penis* aloud in front of half the school. But she'd also been beset with pride. Elizabeth had defended her honor, impervious to the notion that confronting Peter could have destroyed her as yet untarnished elementary school reputation. More than that, Elizabeth knew who she was. She knew what she wanted. And she didn't falter in pursuit of it. Something Charlotte had never been able to do.

"So listen." Charlotte readied herself to deliver the speech she'd rehearsed the night before, in the shower that morning, and then again on the car ride over. "I need your help."

"*You* need *my* help? That's rich." The waitress returned with Elizabeth's soda. "I'll take the pancakes. Tall stack. Don't skimp on the syrup." Elizabeth squinted to read the name tag on her uniform. "Heather." Heather nodded sardonically. Charlotte imagined Heather recounting the story of her "bitchy customer" later that night to her similarly pierced and inked boyfriend over beers at a local dive bar, the invasive shrieks of a Z-list cover band drowning out her trifling grievances.

"I'll just have a house salad with grilled chicken. Dressing on the side, please. Actually, oil and vinegar will be fine." Elizabeth scowled at her. "On the side." She turned back to her sister. "So, as I was saying."

"You need my assistance. . . ."

"Right. One of us has to go to Florida to help Mom deal with Dad." Their father had recently suffered his third heart attack in three years, and this time he hadn't bounced back the way he had in the past. He was practically immobilized, forcing their mother—who by her own admission was hardly the poster child for a healthful lifestyle—to work overtime caring for him. Charlotte had offered to pay for a full-time nurse, someone to whom cleaning bedpans was as commonplace as scratching her head, but her mother had obstinately declined, declaring that it was their house and she didn't need some "meddlesome intruder" with her nose in their business.

"Okay?" Elizabeth wasn't going to make it easy. She never did.

"So can you do it?"

"By myself?" Elizabeth scoffed.

"Yes, by yourself." Charlotte added, "I'll pay for your plane ticket."

"Oh, wow, thanks!"

"Fine, pay your own way."

"I would, but I'm not going." They both knew she wouldn't, even if she was amenable to making the trip. Was it really so much to ask of a grown woman to hop on a prepaid flight from New York to Fort Lauderdale to take care of her sick father? How many times had Charlotte done the very same thing? The fact was, it was expected of Charlotte, not of Elizabeth. Nothing was expected of Elizabeth.

"Lizzy, Gia starts school tomorrow. I have a million things going on, and for once, I can't handle everything."

"What's that supposed to mean?" The waitress arrived with their lunch, and Elizabeth immediately drenched her pancakes in syrup. Like aunt, like niece. In turn, Charlotte sprinkled vinegar on her rabbit food.

"It means I'm always the one to go. I'm sorry, but it's true."

"You're sorry?"

"You know what I'm saying, Lizzy." She took a bite of her salad. "Do you have something specific going on that hinders you from going? I'm sure Mom and Dad will happily accommodate your schedule." The whole notion that Elizabeth even had a schedule was preposterous. Her hours working as a salesgirl at the Posh Teen in town were sporadic at best and seemed to correspond directly to how empty her pockets were. Aside from that, there were scattered therapy sessions, which—as evidenced by that week's appointment—could easily be postponed.

"Do you?" Elizabeth countered.

"I just told you that Gia's starting school and I have other stuff to deal with."

"What stuff?"

"Who cares?"

"I do."

"Fine. Guess what? I'll go. As usual. I'll do it all." Charlotte threw her hands up in the air. "I've lost my appetite." She stood to leave. "You know, you should really be a better daughter to Mom and Dad. They've supported you through everything. *Unconditionally.*"

"Whatever you say, *perfect child.*" It was what Elizabeth had called her for the better part of their high school career.

"As if you listen to a thing I say." Charlotte swung her purse onto her shoulder and folded her jacket into the crook of her arm. "I'll talk to you later." She stalked off.

"Um, big sis." Charlotte swiveled back around to find Elizabeth's smug expression. "You forgot to pay the check."

Chapter 4

"Are you excited for your first day?" Allison thrummed her long, delicate fingers on the steering wheel to the fitful pulse of her heartbeat.

"Mom, you've asked me that, like, a million times." Logan grinned broadly, revealing a mouthful of metal. Not a flattering look, but to her he was still the most handsome little boy in the world, even with braces. And even if he wasn't that little anymore. "I'm really excited." He patted her on the shoulder reassuringly.

"Good, me too." Allison smiled and stroked the top of his head, ignoring the involuntary tautening of every muscle in her body as their car fell in line with the others bordering the busy street for school drop-off. She couldn't help but feel that, in some ways, it was her first day too. She'd been up at four in the morning, unsure whether to feel exhilarated or anxious. Somehow, healing in her new surroundings seemed easier than being exposed to daily reminders of Jack. On the other hand, she was terrified she'd lose those cherished memories. Save for Logan, they were all she had left.

"It's cool that I'm going to the same school you went to. Don't you think?" Logan blew his bangs out of his eyes and took a generous bite of the warm cinnamon raisin bagel he was clutching in both hands. A glob of cream cheese dribbled down his chin, landing on his blue jeans. In one swift motion, he scooped it up with his index finger and deposited it directly into his mouth, delightfully unaware of the chalky white blotch it had left behind.

Allison had decided to mail-order a dozen bagels from Sammy's in New York City in an attempt to inject some familiarity into Logan's new routine, which had prompted him to ask, "Don't they have bagels in Wincourt?" Of course they had bagels in Wincourt. But they didn't have Sammy's. Sammy's had been *their* bagel place. Hers and Logan's. Just as she and Jack had had *their* bagel place on the Upper West Side, which they'd rolled into on Sunday mornings wearing scarcely more than their pajamas. Luigi's. She'd never forget that name because each and every time they'd gone there, Jack had mused about how silly it was to name a bagel place after an Italian guy, even if he was the owner. Couldn't he have pretended to be a Jonah or a Noah for the sake of tradition?

In many ways, it was as if she'd lived two separate lives in New York. One with Jack. And one with Logan. But there were no crossed paths. No shared experiences among all of them. There was just Allison. The common thread that entwined their splintered family of three into one patchwork tapestry of memories.

"Huh?" Lost in thought, she turned into the Wincourt Elementary School parking lot.

"I said it's cool I'm going to the same school that you went to when you were my age." Logan looked up at her expectantly. "Mom, are you listening to me?"

"Yes, I'm listening." She laughed, putting the car in park. "Now you listen to me." She cupped Logan's face in her hands and kissed him on the forehead. "You have the best first day of school ever, okay? And remember I love you—"

"—to the moon and back." Logan finished her sentence and hopped out of the car, as if the fact that his whole world had been turned upside down was no big deal. Why was it that kids were so much more resilient than adults?

Allison skulked outside Logan's classroom, careful to remain incognito. No matter how many times he'd sworn up and down that he'd be fine, she still couldn't manage to vacate the premises. Being back at Wincourt Elementary School—the site of her own second- through sixth-grade career—felt like coming home in a way she hadn't anticipated. For starters, everything was exactly the same, only on a smaller scale. Or had it always been that way? Upon walking through the front door, she'd suddenly become a giant in a midget's world. Narrow hallways. Miniature chairs. Pint-sized people. It was tantamount to Munchkinland in *The Wizard of Oz*, minus Glinda, the Wicked Witch of the West, and the Yellow Brick Road.

She hadn't bothered to make the trek up for parents' night, having been focused solely on the myriad details of their move. And also because, traditionally speaking, parents' nights were risky—the beaming fathers asking questions they'd never actually need the answers to, just so they could be part of the process, if only for a night. After that, the mommies and nannies would be in charge of things like books, lunches, permission slips, and name tags sewn into every piece of clothing—that is, if you planned on seeing it again. Allison had become accustomed to dealing with all these things herself, but there was something about watching the dads on parents' night, well aware of the profound void in her life and in Logan's life, that she preferred to eschew. Of course the administration at WES understood her "situation," as they referred to it, and had assured her that they'd do everything in their power to make sure Logan's matriculation went smoothly. They'd even suggested a meeting between Logan and the school psychologist—an emotional security measure—which Allison had declined. There was no reason to single him out, she maintained, unless absolutely necessary.

"It never gets easier, huh?" Allison diverted her eyes from peering through an opening in Logan's classroom door to find an attractive woman neatly turned out in expensive-looking black slacks with a crisp cream linen shirt and a powder blue cardigan tied over her shoulders.

"I know, right?" Allison smiled absently.

"Which one's yours?" The woman crept up behind her and tilted her head so she too could get a glimpse into the classroom.

"The little boy over there with the red and blue plaid button-down." Allison pointed to where Logan was kneeling on the ground next to a chubby girl decked out in leopard-print leggings and a hot-pink T-shirt emblazoned in silver sparkles with the message *I'm a Princess.*

"Oh, that's my daughter, Gia." She frowned. "The not-so-little one he's working with."

"She's adorable. I'm Allison, by the way." She extended her right hand, still aware of Logan's every movement.

"Charlotte." The woman shook her hand weakly. "You're new here?"

"Kind of." Allison turned her back to the room for the first time since saying good-bye to Logan. "I grew up in Wincourt, but after college I relocated to Manhattan. I just moved back here."

"That's exciting!" Charlotte's face brightened, as if returning to Wincourt were the equivalent of winning Mega Millions.

"I guess." Allison raked her fingers through her long, wavy blond hair, gathered it at the nape of her neck, and twisted it into a tight bun, releasing it once she realized she'd left the ponytail holder she usually wore around her wrist at home. She'd also left Logan's lunch on the kitchen counter, where, quite intentionally, she'd placed it as a reminder. "I mean, yeah. It is. Exciting."

"I'm sure it's overwhelming too." Charlotte nodded meaningfully.

"You could say that."

"Is your husband . . . Are you . . . ?" Charlotte fidgeted with the tassel on her purse.

"I'm not married." It was all Allison could manage in the moment. It had taken her long enough just to be able to say those words. *I'm not married.*

After all, it wasn't like she'd gotten divorced. Or hadn't found someone she wanted to spend the rest of her life with. One second she'd been a wife. The next she'd been a widow. How was one supposed to digest that, much less become accustomed to informing strangers? She'd given little thought to what she was going to say to people in Wincourt, assuming that news of the widow and her son joining the Wincourt Elementary School family had preceded her. It'd been such a long time since she'd had to explain her "situation" to anyone.

"I see." Charlotte nodded soberly, and Allison surmised that being a single parent in Wincourt was considered a handicap of sorts, kind of like having one leg. Or one home. Or one car. "I'm just waiting for my husband. He's in the restroom," Charlotte confirmed and then, aware that her declaration might be perceived as inconsiderate, added, "Don't worry. You'll never see him here again! He only shows on day one. And I have to drag him kicking and screaming for that. But, you know, it's important. To Gia." She mumbled the last part, as if she wasn't convinced.

"Gotcha." Allison smiled politely, sensing Charlotte's awkwardness.

"That must be him now." The men's bathroom door swung open to reveal a tall, handsome man impeccably dressed in a charcoal gray suit and polished black leather dress shoes. He walked toward them briskly, focused intently on his iPhone, his fingers stabbing at the keyboard furiously.

"Charlie?" Allison's eyes widened and he looked up. "Charlie Crane?" His hard expression softened instantly.

"Ali? Holy shit!" He wrapped his arms around her, hoisting her into the air in his sturdy embrace. "What the hell are you doing here?"

"I live here now." She motioned to the ground. "I mean, not right here." She giggled. "But in Wincourt. And my son, Logan, goes to school here. What the hell are *you* doing here?" Allison beamed, digesting the strange and amazing coincidence that was standing in front of her.

"Same deal. Wow. I can't believe it. How long has it been?"

"So I take it you two know each other?" Charlotte interrupted, having been completely sidelined by the main event.

"Yes. Oh God, I'm so sorry. Yes." Allison looked back and forth between the two of them. "Charlie and I are old friends. Very old friends." She saw a dark cloud shroud Charlotte's face. "Oh no, nothing like that. Charlie was my husband's best friend from summer camp. We all met there when we were what? Ten?"

"Oh." Charlotte appeared visibly relieved. "Wait, I thought you said you weren't married."

"I'm not."

"About that." Charlie's buoyant mood became subdued. "I'm so sorry, Ali. I should have—"

"It's okay." Allison took a deep breath and then exhaled before turning to Charlotte. "My husband, Jack, was killed in a bus accident eleven years ago. He was on his way to Stowe for a ski trip."

"Oh God." Charlotte pressed her left palm to her chest. "That's . . . awful. I had no idea. How insensitive . . ."

"It's really okay," Allison assured them both. "There was no way you could have known."

"I wanted to reach out to you, Ali. I just . . . I didn't know what to say." He shook his head and hunched it toward the floor. Allison knew the drill. It was practically impossible for people to look her square in the face and offer their condolences. Even eleven years later.

"I promise it's fine." She hadn't done this dance in a while. "I'm just happy to know someone up here. It's been a while."

"You're remarkable, Ali. You always were." Charlie stared at her intently and then snapped out of his haze. "I can't believe it, but I have to run. I have a nine thirty conference call at work. Can we exchange info? I'm *dying* to catch up. I mean, wait, that came out—"

"It's okay!" Allison laughed. It never ceased to amaze her how perfectly pulled-together, exceptionally articulate people could deteriorate into bumbling fools when forced to deal with the subject of death or loss. Specifically when it wasn't their own loss.

"I host a little get-together every week or so for a few of my girlfriends," Charlotte interjected again, quite clearly desperate to insinuate herself into the conversation. "I call it a Wine and Whine." She twisted her mouth uncertainly, checking with Charlie for confirmation. He nodded. "We eat a little, drink a little more, and whine about our—"

"Husbands."

"Well, yeah, but lots of other stuff too, so it wouldn't be . . . ," Charlotte sputtered.

"That sounds great. I'd love to come." It wasn't strictly the truth. Generally speaking, Allison shunned female husband-bashing fests. She'd never understood the appeal of sitting around and complaining about the person you were voluntarily married to. Maybe she'd be in the same boat if Jack were still alive. Maybe he'd be grating her last nerve every minute of every day the way she knew most women's husbands did. Whether it was throwing their dirty clothing on the floor just inches from the laundry basket or not coming home from work early enough to pay their wives and kids the attention they deserved. Or, even worse, not listening absorbedly to every word that came out of their mouths. To Allison, these gripes cast an insignificant shadow on a world she'd never known and perhaps never would.

"Oh good." Charlotte clapped her hands together. "It's settled, then. And you and Charlie can catch up afterward."

"Perfect." Charlie grinned and kissed Allison on the cheek. "I'll look forward to it."

Twenty minutes later, following an animated phone call to her mother about running into Charlie Crane, Allison found herself standing in front of a tantalizing selection of sandwiches at a new-to-her gourmet shop in the center of town. On the heels of the morning's events, however, it felt unfeasible to focus on anything, namely, which sandwich to pick up for Logan's lunch. She'd promised his teacher she'd be back within the hour so Logan didn't have to eat a stale peanut butter and jelly sandwich courtesy of the school's limited culinary offerings or the tuna sandwich from home, which had been basking in the morning sun on their kitchen counter for the last two hours.

"Can I help you with something?" Allison looked up to find a man with wavy dark brown hair and fetching blue eyes watching her from behind the counter. Caught off guard first by his presence and then again by how cute he was, she felt her cheeks warm and a blush creep up the nape of her neck.

"Um, definitely." She smiled demurely. "I'm debating between the roast beef and the chicken salad." She pointed to two hearty sandwiches made with thick slices of French baguette. When they'd lived in the city, there was nothing Allison had enjoyed more than sharing a fresh-from-the-oven Zabar's baguette with Logan, while they sauntered up and down Broadway window shopping. If it was a nice day, they'd wander back to the East Side through Central Park, taking their time to absorb the sights, sounds, and even smells of Manhattan's heart and soul.

"I see." He raised an eyebrow. "That's a tough one. Those are my two favorites."

"I bet you say that to all the girls."

"Mmmm. So that's what you think of me." He laughed. "How about you buy one and I'll throw in the other for free?"

"Oh, that's so sweet, but you really don't have to do that."

"I insist."

"Won't your boss be upset if you give free food away to all your customers?"

"Why don't you let me worry about that?" He lifted both sandwiches from the case and started wrapping them in paper. "And, for the record, I don't give free food to *all* the customers."

"Well, thank you," she replied coyly, aware that he was flirting with her. It wasn't the first time since Jack had died that a man had come on to her, and it probably wouldn't be the last. She couldn't lie. It felt nice. But that was the extent of it.

"My pleasure." He rang up one of the sandwiches, slipped both of them into a plastic bag, and handed it to her. "Come back soon, Ali."

"I will, thanks." She turned to walk away. "Wait, how did you know my name?" She swiveled back around.

"I guess you don't remember me?" He smirked, and she searched his face, narrowing her eyes on each and every feature in the hope that something would jar a memory. There'd been a time when she could recall everyone she'd ever met. Their names. Their stories. Even what they'd been wearing when she was first introduced to them. But after Jack had died, there'd been a decade of people who'd passed through her life in a blur.

"I'm so sorry. I'm usually really good with—"

"Dempsey. Dempsey James. We went to high school together." He nodded. "I was the loner with the rockin' mullet. I think we were both in Ms. Lorman's biology class. Actually, I know we were. You were the only thing worth concentrating on for an hour."

"Of course. Dempsey." Allison tilted her head. "You look different."

"You have no idea who I am." He laughed.

"I do!" She laughed with him.

"Nah, you don't." He shook his head, still smiling. "Not to worry. We can change that."

Chapter 5

"This doesn't look right." Charlotte sighed, rearranging the blocks of Brie, smoked Gouda, and Camembert on her grandmother's sterling silver cheese platter—her fifth and final attempt. "Janna, can you please come in here?" she called out, endeavoring to manipulate the olive-oil-and-rosemary-infused crackers she'd picked up at the gourmet shop into a fanlike pattern lining the rim of the platter. To her dismay, the result was no less chaotic than before. "Janna!" she bellowed with mounting urgency.

It was baffling to Charlotte how there never seemed to be anyone within shouting distance except when she wanted to be alone. Then it felt like everyone in the house was huddled in one section of one room, pestering her with their needs, wants, and have-to-haves—even if Charlie, of able mind and body, was right there. For example, why would Gia ask her father—who was standing next to the refrigerator—to get her some juice when she could just as easily summon Charlotte from the other side of the kitchen? More mind-boggling still was the fact that Charlie had become accustomed to the same treatment. He'd once told her that he spent five days a week at the office taking orders from entitled clients and the very last thing he wanted to do on the weekends was take orders from his entitled daughter. *Join the club,* she'd thought but hadn't said.

Sometimes, Charlotte wondered if Charlie actually liked being a father, which was ironic given that *he'd* been the anxious one all those years ago. Shortly after they'd first met, Charlie had professed to her—over two Sashimi Deluxe Specials and three pitchers of hot sake at Sushi Samba—that he wanted to start a family before he turned thirty. He'd explained that his own parents had been young when they'd had him and that he felt strongly about following suit. "I don't want to be the old man on the playground who can't kneel in the sandbox." This declaration had endeared him to her immediately. What man confessed on a second date that he was ready for daddyhood ASAP? At twenty-four years old, most of her girlfriends were struggling to find a guy who'd pay for dinner and, if they were lucky—no less than a year into the relationship—vaguely commit to the idea of getting married. Someday.

Charlie's attitude had been such a departure from anything Charlotte had experienced that by date number four, she'd found it impossible to picture her life without him in it. She'd yearned to fall asleep in his warm embrace every night and wake up there every morning, their bodies and minds dovetailing, yin and yang. And the fact that their names were practically the male and female versions of each other, well, that, according to Charlie, was serendipity.

Before long, they were finishing each other's sentences and guessing, with surprising accuracy, what the other one was going to order from any given menu, at any given meal. "You're thinking about the eggs Benedict, but you're going to pick the French toast," Charlie would announce, grinning like the Cheshire cat.

"You're thinking about the western omelet, but you're going to have the granola. With a side of apple-smoked sausage," she'd counter, pleased with herself for getting it right. And extra-pleased that she and this gift of a man knew each other so intimately, so immediately.

Charlie had proposed two months later, with a stunning four-carat, cushion-cut diamond that, back then, had seemed the size of a cantaloupe. Now, more than a decade later, her ring paled in comparison to those of her friends in Wincourt, most of whom were older and had gotten married in their thirties.

But the ring had never been important to her. All she'd cared about was him. All she'd craved was him. Charlie's scent had been an aphrodisiac, his gaze a suggestion, and his touch an overture. She'd been captivated by his prowess for living life to the fullest and the unrestricted passion he'd exhibited toward his job, his friends, what little family he had, and now her. Charlotte loved to be loved by him—an unpredictable emotion for her, since she'd spent the majority of her formative years avoiding physical affection.

It wasn't like she was a virgin or anything that drastic. She'd had a boyfriend in high school who'd been her first. They'd done it one time and one time only on a pullout couch in his friend Jerry's partially finished basement. Jerry's parents had been out of town, and Jerry had been upstairs in the living room watching *Die Hard with a Vengeance*. If the sex had been anything beyond pitiful, the frequent explosions reverberating through the drainpipe-covered ceiling might have provided an appropriate soundtrack.

After that, Charlotte had met Billy during her sophomore year at Cornell and they'd become fast friends. With benefits. Billy was a junior and her go-to guy for sorority functions or a lonely Saturday night. She was his go-to girl for Budweiser-induced booty calls at two in the morning. There was nothing romantic about it, which suited them both just fine. Last year, Billy had sent her a friend request on Facebook, which she'd accepted excitedly, her stomach doing a little flip. She was eager to see where he'd ended up and whom he'd ended up with. And wasn't it always flattering to hear from an old flame, even through social media?

She'd expected to find a matured version of the Billy she remembered, sporting fresh tufts of gray hair and, most likely, an ample beer gut—Billy had been a heavy drinker. Instead, she'd been confronted by an attractive and exceptionally fit-looking man whose profile boasted that he was married, had two adorable little boys, and had recently achieved his lifelong goal of completing the Ironman triathlon. Huh? She'd never seen Billy run so much as a block, unless the corner store was low on six-packs and smokes. Even more surprising was that his wife was one of those all-American, Neutrogena-ad-evoking beauties—the type with skin so luminescent you wanted to head straight to the drugstore and buy every magical face-clearing serum on the market.

Charlotte had pored over every photo, searching for one where the entire family didn't look airbrushed-perfect, but she'd come up empty-handed, which had unsettled her. It wasn't that she wanted to be with Billy. She hadn't particularly wanted to be with him in college. Still, he looked happy, and even though she didn't begrudge him that, something about his flawless existence was a jagged pill to swallow.

"I here, Mrs. Charlotte," Janna, her devoted Filipino housekeeper, whispered, startling Charlotte. Janna had an untrained talent for sneaking up on people, which Charlotte had once told her would make her an excellent spy. Janna had giggled nervously at the suggestion, probably because she had no idea what that meant.

"Oh, thank God." Charlotte motioned to the platter and then secured the two large Velcro rollers in her hair. "I'm hopeless."

"I fix it for you." Janna set to work shuffling cheeses and crackers while alternating skewered slices of strawberry and pineapple from the refrigerator with a flourish of fresh flowers, until the presentation was Martha Stewart–worthy.

"Thank you." Charlotte smiled gratefully, marveling at the way domesticity came so naturally to Janna. "I have to run upstairs and take these out." She pointed to the rollers. "Please set everything up on the table in the great room."

"Yes, Mrs. Charlotte. I make everything lovely for you."

And lovely it was when Charlotte came downstairs twenty minutes later with her naturally wavy hair wrestled into a long, straight bob, just the right amount of volume at the roots, thanks to the rollers. She'd taken extra time on her makeup and selected an outfit that conveyed casual chic—dark-washed blue jeans, black Gucci ballet flats, and a powder blue Ralph Lauren cable-knit sweater layered over a white T-shirt. She wasn't sure why she felt the need to impress Allison. Maybe it was that Allison and Charlie were old friends. Or that she was new to Wincourt and Charlotte wanted to stake her claim before Allison had a chance to meet the other moms at school. Either way, there was something different about Allison that appealed to her, and more than anything, Charlotte wanted Allison to like her. And for Charlie to notice.

The bell chimed and Charlotte rushed to answer it. She'd actually considered whether or not to have Janna greet her guests, but Sabrina and Missy—who practically let themselves in these days—would have balked at the pomp and circumstance. Even though they both let their housekeepers and nannies deal with everything.

"Helllllloooo!" Sabrina and Missy chorused, standing in the doorway proffering matching bottles of prosecco.

"Can you believe we brought the exact same thing?" Sabrina rolled her eyes. She'd confided in Charlotte years earlier that she was convinced Missy wanted to be her and had pointed out every circumstance since that time that evidenced her claim.

Like when Missy had shown up to Parker Gresham's Fabulous Fifth birthday party wearing the same Dolce & Gabbana sunglasses that Sabrina was *certain* Missy had seen her sporting in a Facebook photo from their trip to Turks and Caicos three weeks earlier. Or, nine months later, when Missy had hosted a fund-raiser to benefit the Wincourt

Museum, decked out in a sleeveless gold Carolina Herrera cocktail dress, which Sabrina was *certain* she'd earmarked in the most recent copy of *InStyle* magazine. Which she'd lent to Missy. "Obviously, imitation is the highest form of flattery. But at some point, get your own identity, girl!" Sabrina had remarked time and time again. And time and time again, Charlotte had nodded in agreement, well aware that if this was the way Sabrina talked about "one of her two best friends in the whole wide world," then she ought to be at least a little wary. Not that Missy was an innocent. Charlotte had spent entire lunches listening to her bad-mouth Sabrina. But when the three of them were together, the only targets of their slander were those not present. Belong or beware.

"As if we won't drink it." Missy chortled, surveying Charlotte from head to toe. "Cute jeans."

"Thanks." Charlotte smiled and noted the compliment, which very well may have been veiled disapproval. "Let's move into the great room. Janna set up a gorgeous spread. Wine?"

"Obv." Sabrina rolled her eyes again and they both followed Charlotte. Missy had once commented that no one's eyeballs got a better workout than Sabrina's—up and down, round and round—they revolved more often than the door at a Bergdorf Goodman shoe blowout.

"So where's the new girl?" Missy settled into a white linen club chair by the granite-rimmed gas fireplace, crossing her toned, albeit stubby legs before reaching for a carrot stick. No matter how hard Missy worked at it, she'd never be stick skinny like Sabrina or most of the other women in Wincourt. And it wasn't for lack of trying. Every morning after dropping her daughter, Miley, at school, she headed directly to the sports club for an hour-long spin class, followed by another hour of free weights with her personal trainer. She shunned gluten, sugar, wheat, and dairy—basically anything with more calories than a stalk of celery. Her only vice, which she insisted she couldn't sacrifice, was alcohol. "It helps me forget how hungry I am," she maintained. Charlotte could understand. She too had tried countless diets to no avail, always returning to the weight her body seemed most comfortable at, which—as it happened—was thirteen pounds of comfort she could do without.

She could also appreciate Missy's unwillingness to forego her nightly glass of wine, or two. Or three. There'd been a time when Charlotte barely drank anything, save for when she and Charlie were celebrating a milestone. And she'd often wondered why so many of her parents' friends, including her own father, "needed" their nightly scotch, whisky, gin, vodka, whatever their pleasure, to take the edge off. What edge? That was until she and Charlie had started bickering, then fighting, and finally parenting—while bickering and fighting. Nothing tasted better, then or now, than a chilled glass of sauvignon blanc at six p.m.—no earlier and certainly no later.

"She should be here any minute," Charlotte replied, just as the doorbell rang again. "Speak of the devil." She started to walk toward the foyer, until she heard Janna's muffled voice and then Allison's.

"I'm so sorry I'm late." Allison appeared, smiling reticently, her dewy complexion and light gray eyes glistening under one of Charlotte's thoughtfully aimed recessed spot-lights.

"Not at all. Come join us." Charlotte ushered Allison to-ward them, kissing her on the cheek and half hugging her awkwardly. "Allison, this is Sabrina. And this is Missy. Sa-brina is Gabriella's mom and Missy is Miley's mom."

"Hi." Allison waved. "I guess that would make me Lo-gan's mom." Sabrina and Missy nodded knowingly.

Charlotte had told them Allison's story. Part of her had wanted to keep it private out of respect for Allison and Lo-gan, but she'd been unable to hold it in for more than a day. She'd tried to impart the information in the empathetic manner she'd rehearsed. Unfortunately, Sabrina had rushed it out of her, citing an imminent waxing appointment, which she'd subsequently canceled in order to feast on the fodder. Within seconds, Sabrina had conferenced in Missy and the two of them were haranguing Charlotte for not tell-ing them the moment she'd found out. Then the line of ques-tioning had commenced. *How did he die? Did he drown? Did they find his body? Did she know she was pregnant? Did he know she was pregnant? Did he leave her any money?* Charlotte had attempted to answer their litany of queries, mainly Sabrina's, but their thirst for the nitty-gritty details had been insatiable.

"Well, aren't you gorgeous?" Sabrina grinned broadly. Charlotte had speculated that Sabrina would be instantly envious of Allison's undeniable physical beauty. That she would view it almost as a personal affront. Charlotte had also speculated that, for that reason alone, Sabrina would be desperate to befriend Allison.

"Yeah, right." Allison sat down next to Charlotte on her tan Ultrasuede sofa, draping her gauzy orange-and-white-patterned maxidress over her tanned legs. "I swear I look better with a little makeup!"

"I was serious." Sabrina nodded, visibly captivated by Allison's presence. "If this is you without makeup, we better watch our husbands, ladies." Charlotte widened her eyes at Sabrina. "What?"

"I love your dress!" Missy smiled.

"Thanks." Allison sliced a sliver of smoked Gouda and reached for a cracker.

"Richards?" Missy watched Allison covetously as she took a bite.

"Excuse me?"

"It's a clothing store in Greenwich," Charlotte explained. She felt inexplicably protective of Allison.

"The *best* clothing store," Missy elaborated.

"Definitely not Richards, then." Allison laughed breezily. "More like Gap."

"Oh, you shop there for yourself?" Sabrina asked interestedly. "I've never even looked in the adult section. I can barely get Gabriella to wear their pajamas anymore. Such a spoiled little thing. I'll have to check it out."

"It was cheap and it's easy to throw on. Can't go wrong with that combo, right?"

Charlotte hid a smile. Most people were intimidated by Sabrina's imposing personality, but not Allison.

"I suppose not." Sabrina turned to Missy and Charlotte. "So, as you guys know, Craig is out of town. Thank God."

"Jealous!" Missy affirmed. "Isn't it the best when they go away?" Her eyes locked with Charlotte's and she looked down shamefully.

"The best," Sabrina acknowledged. "Right, Charlotte?"

"I guess." She fidgeted with the stiletto charm dangling from the stem of her wineglass. Why was it such a challenge for these two to spare a little sensitivity?

"Oh, please, just last week you were telling us how blissful it was without Charlie around. You said, and I quote, 'Is it terrible that I want him to stay in Chicago for another week?'"

"You did say that." Missy nodded.

"Does anyone want more wine?" Charlotte shot up from the couch.

"Might as well." Missy's wineglass tottered between her fingers.

"I'll take a refill too," Sabrina offered, clearly reluctant to relinquish control of the conversation.

"Allison, are you sure I can't get you anything other than water?"

"I'm fine with this for now, thanks."

"Anyone home?" Charlie's voice reverberated from the entryway, followed by the thud of the front door and Lolly's paws clambering down the marble staircase.

"What's he doing here?" Sabrina's face warped into a guise of disbelief.

"He said he'd be early, but . . ." Charlotte shrugged. Over the years, she'd become accustomed to tacking on two hours to whatever time Charlie had sworn he'd be home. In the beginning, he'd been effusively apologetic, often presenting her with a bouquet of white calla lilies, her favorite, as a peace offering. Though, as time had passed, her unadulterated desire to be with him as many hours and minutes of the day as humanly possible had been crushed by her drive to hold him accountable for every second he was delayed.

"Hey, ladies." Charlie strode into the room.

"Hi, honey." Charlotte pecked him on the cheek, and his eyes scanned the room, landing on Allison.

"Ali!" He walked toward her determinedly, lifting her into a bear hug. "I still can't believe this." He shook his head. "How are things? Are you settled in? Remind me where you guys are exactly."

"We're on Rover Lane. Number fifteen."

"I know it well. I used to shoot hoops with some of my buddies at the park on Weaver."

"Yup, Turtle Park. Logan's already been there a handful of times with my dad."

"That's right; I forgot you grew up around here. Well, that makes more sense. How are your parents?"

"Great. Thrilled. It's their dream come true to have their grandson within walking distance."

"I'm sure." He took his jacket off, tossed it onto a vacant chair, and sat down on the couch next to Allison, oblivious to anyone else in the room.

For the next fifteen minutes, Sabrina, Missy, and Charlotte were a captive audience as Allison and Charlie chatted animatedly, the conversation spanning from "that summer at Camp Tawana" to "when I heard about Jack" and finally landing on the long fix-it list thumbtacked to a corkboard in Allison's art studio. A broken knob here. A leaky faucet there. The nagging nuisances that came with owning a house.

"I can help you take care of that stuff." He patted her arm. "Don't let it stress you."

"You don't even own a tool set." This was Charlotte's opportunity to cut in. She couldn't remember the last time she'd seen him so much as hammer a nail.

"I do so." Normally he would've shot her a dirty look, but tonight he was on his best behavior. Charlotte could tell that Charlie cared what Allison thought and that they shared a common connection, even if that connection was a ghost.

It was easy to see why Charlie liked her. In many ways, Allison was the friend Charlotte had originally envisioned before moving from Manhattan to the suburbs. Instead, she'd fallen in with the "rich bitches," as she'd heard some of the other moms refer to Sabrina and Missy. And probably to her too when she wasn't around. But Allison was different. She was the type of person you wanted to confide in, drop your defenses with, and open up to without reservation. The type of person who you hoped would be the keeper of your secrets, because you knew she wouldn't let them go or, worse, promulgate them.

"That would be great, Charlie. Thank you." Allison smiled easily.

"My pleasure." He smiled back, checking his watch. "Ugh. I've got to run upstairs to my office for a conference call with China. But I'll see you on Saturday?"

"You got it!"

"Excellent." Charlie stood up, waving his hand cursorily behind him as he walked out. "Good seeing you, ladies."

"I'll let you know when dinner is ready," Charlotte called after him, but he was already gone.

Chapter 6

"I am man. Hear me roar!" Charlie poked his head into Allison's art studio, where she was sitting in front of a large canvas, wholly absorbed in the new piece she was creating. Typically, she had a plan, a clear vision for the final outcome of her design, but this time she was pleasantly unsure of where the journey would take her. Somehow, this endeavor felt different. She felt different.

"Huh?" Allison looked up, wearing a distracted expression on her face, which was full of paint smudges.

"Everything on your list is done." He walked toward her, flexing his muscles good-humoredly and grinning all the while. He handed Allison the crumpled sheet of yellow legal paper she'd jotted her multiplying to-dos on.

"You are a god." Allison laughed as he continued to grunt and pose like the bodybuilder he was not. She'd advised him to dress down for the occasion, promising dirt and dust mites in nooks and crannies she'd yet to have an opportunity to scour. Unfortunately for Charlie, his idea of casual was a pair of expertly pressed chinos and a pinstriped button-down shirt, both of which were now smeared with grease. "Look at you. You're a mess!"

"I could say the same for you!" He motioned to one of the half dozen splattered old white T-shirts that had become her work uniform. "It's really no big deal."

"Come on. That shirt looks nice." Allison swept her hair into a loose bun.

"This old thing?" Charlie pointed to himself. "Had it since last I saw you."

"Yeah, right." Allison tilted her head and made a face. "At least let me take it to the dry cleaner." She got up, dunked her paintbrushes in a cup of water, and led him into the kitchen.

"You know they have someone for that these days. It's called a—"

"Assistant?" Allison finished his sentence.

"I was going to say wife, but okay." Charlie smirked.

"Chauvinist pig." She wagged her finger in his direction. "You should be ashamed of yourself."

"I am." He hung his head in mock disgrace. "Seriously, though, don't worry about it. I've got about a dozen identical shirts in my closet." He sat down on one of the barstools surrounding the center island and washed his hands in the copper farmhouse sink.

"I bet you do." Allison snapped a dish towel in his direction and stood on her tippy-toes in a futile attempt to pull a platter from the top cabinet.

"Can I help you?" He watched her, visibly amused by the effort.

"Nope. You've exerted yourself enough already today."
She hoisted herself onto the counter for better leverage. "All
those years of gymnastics classes are finally paying off."

"Are you crazy? You're going to kill yourself." Charlie
rushed around the island to spot her. "Get down from there."

"Okay, Dad." Allison sat back down and hopped off herself, even though he insisted on supporting her to be safe.

"I hope you don't do that kind of thing all the time. You
could fall and break your neck." His expression was stern.

"Only out of necessity," she replied breezily, gripping the
oversized white Wedgwood platter in her hand and then
placing it on top of an antique wooden cutting board she
and Jack had received as a wedding gift from his now late
aunt Sylvia. "By the way, how'd you manage to fix the drawer
in Logan's room? I struggled with it for hours." Allison was
no Bob Vila, but she did know her way around a hammer
and a power drill. Being handy was a skill she'd involuntarily developed over time, given the absence of a man around
the house. Still, her capabilities were limited.

"Sheer talent." He parked himself back on the barstool.
"Do you have any water?"

"Oh my God! How rude am I? I've just put you to work for
hours without so much as a cold beverage." She opened the
refrigerator. "We've got Evian, Pellegrino, apple juice, OJ,
and . . ." She shuffled a few things around. "Corona."

"That sounds great." He wiped his sweaty brow with his
already soiled shirt.

"Lime?"

"Even better."

Allison knelt to open the crisper. "I think I'll join you."

She grabbed two beers and set them down on the counter, fishing through a few different drawers for a bottle opener and the right knife. Her mom had unpacked most of the kitchen accessories. "Coming right up." She popped off the tops and pushed a lime wedge into each. Adeptly, she covered the mouths of the bottles with her thumbs and flipped them upside down in either hand.

"What are you doing?" Charlie narrowed his grassy green eyes.

"You've never seen this trick?"

"Can't say that I have. What's the trick?"

"Good question." She tried to keep a straight face. "I can't divulge all of my secrets, but it's definitely something to do with the lime getting all in there."

"Ah, I see." He laughed. "Very technical."

"The technical-est." She turned the beers over and passed one to him. "Let me at least give you some lunch."

"I could be convinced to eat."

"Excellent!" Allison rubbed her hands together. "We've got turkey, bologna, salami, roast beef, and various kinds of cheeses and breads. My mom's a little neurotic about keeping us well fed." She went back to the refrigerator, calling over her shoulder, "If you're really adventurous, I've got leftover beef chili and chicken wings from last night."

"From Anthony's?" His stomach growled on cue.

"Nope, Allison's." She'd made a big batch of each the day before, putting both her new crockpot and the oven to use for the first time since moving in. There'd been no need to cook until all her mom's prepared meals had been devoured by one very hungry ten-year-old boy.

"You cook?" He looked dubious, and something told her that the kitchen was not Charlotte's realm.

"Only when my personal chef is off."

"Very funny." Charlie raked his fingers through his strawberry blond hair. "Forgive my incredulity, but finding a woman who cooks around here is like expecting it to snow in June. Improbable at best."

"Well, ordering in every night in Manhattan wasn't an option. So I guess I learned somewhere along the way. I'm not half bad. I swear!"

"I'll take your word for it, but only if you join me."

Ten minutes later, Allison and Charlie were sitting opposite each other on the couch with vat-sized bowls of chili and two plates of crispy chicken wings on the coffee table. She'd offered to set places for them along the breakfast bar if he preferred, but he'd said the sofa was fine. He'd even kicked off his brown leather Sperry boat shoes.

"Does this please your gourmet palate?"

"It's amazing." He spoke with his mouth full. "Can't you tell? I'm practically shoveling it in." Allison guessed that comfort food was not a staple in the Crane household, given that Charlie was slim and fit and Charlotte had mentioned something in passing about always having to watch her weight and Gia's.

"Good. They're Logan's favorites."

"Well, don't let me near the rest of it, then, or there'll be none left."

"I can always make more." Like her mother, Allison took great pleasure in feeding people. Nourishing others nourished her in a way she couldn't explain.

"So how is it being back in Wincourt?" Charlie ladled a hearty bite of chili into his mouth. "Are you missing the city?"

"Strangely, not that much. In a way it's like that was a separate life." She'd written practically the same thing in her journal the previous evening. "I know that sounds ridiculous, since we've only been here for a week and a half."

"No, I get it." He thought for a second. "It must have been hard for you."

"What?"

"Being a single mom. Doing everything yourself." Charlie set his bowl on the coffee table and wiped his mouth with the blue linen napkin in his lap.

"It wasn't always a picnic," she admitted. "Thankfully, Logan was an easy baby."

"Lucky you. Gia was a terror." He grimaced. "She still is."

"Girls are typically more difficult."

"Have you met Gia?"

"Only briefly at school and then at your house."

"Let's just say 'difficult' is a walk in the park compared to how I'd describe my daughter."

"I'm sure it'll get better."

"From your mouth to God's ears." He shook his head. "Either that or I might die of a heart attack at forty." His face flushed. "Shit, sorry."

"Okay, you seriously need to get over this or we can't be friends."

"Over what?" Charlie feigned ignorance.

"The fact that every time you mention death, you're worried I'm going to be offended or injured, whatever it is.

People die, Charlie. It's okay." She nodded. "It's actually really nice to have someone close by—other than my parents—who knew Jack."

"He was one of the good ones."

"Yes, he was." Allison curled her legs under her. "And, like most men, he was also a pain in the ass sometimes. So let's not get too sappy here." She smiled warmly, well aware that in some strange way, she was more comfortable talking about Jack than other people were.

"Do you remember that time at camp when he sprayed shaving cream under the covers of every bed in bunk nine?"

"How could I forget!" She giggled. "Whose shaving cream do you think that was?!"

"No wonder it smelled so pretty." He laughed with her. "Man, I thought he was going to get kicked out for that. The look on Brenda's face . . ."

"You're telling me."

Brenda and Arnie had been the owners of Camp Tawana back in the day. They'd sold it about a decade after Allison, Charlie, and Jack had gone there, by which time they must have been well into their sixties. The camp had been in Arnie's family for ages, and since neither Arnie nor his only sibling, Steve—also one of the owners and the tennis director—had any kids of his own, there'd been no reason to hold on to it. Everyone there, from the juniors to the seniors to the counselors, had been terrified of Brenda. Allison had never given it much thought at the time but years later had wondered if Brenda had been bitter about being tethered to Camp Tawana. When she'd first married Arnie, apparently he'd been an investment banker, and his father and mother had been the ones spending their summers in Maine gathered around the flagpole each morning and falling asleep to "Taps" as early as nine o'clock every night. Wrangling seven hundred boisterous kids day in and day out for two straight months had to be exhausting.

The only person, to Allison's knowledge, who had not quaked in their Nike high-tops at the mere thought of having to answer to Brenda was Jack, even on the heels of "the Shaving Cream Incident," as it had come to be known by generations of campers to follow. Allison and Charlie, on the other hand, had feared for Jack's life when Brenda had summoned him to her office. Now, of course, it seemed preposterous. What really could she have done, short of sending him home? It wasn't like she could have raised a hand to him. Or crossed the line past gently reprimanding him. Maybe she'd docked him a week of candy from the canteen—who could remember? But when Jack had resurfaced, after what had felt like hours, all his friends—and he'd had many—had been collectively relieved. Allison, for her part, had been so relieved she'd gone to second base with Jack an hour later on a musty green wool sofa in the counselors' lounge, which they'd snuck into, despite her attempt at convincing Jack that breaking yet another rule might not be in his best interest.

"I wonder where Brenda is today," Charlie mused, dunking a chicken wing in blue cheese dressing.

"Divorced from Arnie."

"Really?" Charlie seemed surprised.

"Are you kidding? They despised each other."

"You think?" Men could be so clueless.

"I know." Allison took a swig of beer. "She clenched her fists and gritted her teeth every time he spoke at the morning meeting. And the only time Arnie looked relaxed was when Brenda went home for a weekend to see their cats."

"People with more than two cats can't be trusted," Charlie declared.

"We agree on that." The phone rang and Allison grabbed the cordless receiver off the side table next to her. She checked the number before answering. "Hi, Mom. . . . Yup. . . . Logan would love that. . . . Lasagna is perfect. . . . Six thirty is great. . . . Okay, sounds good . . . Love you too." She hung up. "Family dinner tonight."

"You mentioned they're really happy to have you here." Charlie gestured toward the phone with his chin, as both hands were occupied—one with beer, one with chicken.

"You have no idea."

"Makes me miss my folks."

"They don't live around here?"

"They passed away."

"I'm so sorry."

"Yeah. My dad three years ago. And my mom about six months after that. I think losing him was too much for her."

"I can understand that."

"We were really close. Like you and your parents."

"What about Charlotte? Does she have family nearby?"

"Just her sister, Elizabeth." He rolled his eyes. "Don't get me started on her. And their parents live in Florida, which is just as well."

"Got it." Allison stood to take their plates to the sink. "I hate to rush you, but I promised I'd meet my dad and Logan at Turtle Park in twenty minutes. You and Charlotte and Gia are welcome to join us."

"Thanks, but they went shopping today." He sighed. "Because neither of them has enough clothing."

"Will I see you at the next Wine and Whine?" Allison raised an eyebrow.

"I try to stay away. Sabrina and Missy aren't exactly my favorite people." He stood up and gathered the rest of the plates and utensils. "It'll be nice for Charlotte to have someone like you around."

"She seems great." Allison smiled softly. She barely knew Charlotte. What else could she say?

"Yeah, definitely." There was an awkward silence.

"Okay, well, thank you again. So much. For all of your help." She hugged him. "I owe you at least a few more lunches."

"Don't be ridiculous. I wouldn't have it any other way." He held her at arm's length and shook his head. "Allison Parker. I still can't believe you're here in Wincourt."

Chapter 7

September came and went in a whirlwind of books, binders, and backpacks, every crisp page and freshly sewn monogram beset with the promise of cultivating bright young minds. The longer days, which typically commenced at seven a.m. with a mildly grouchy Gia fighting to wear an outfit that was age inappropriate, ended with an arms-belted-across-her-chest-fists-balled-and-a-scowl-on-her-face Gia refusing to go to bed before ten p.m.—and that was on a good night. By the time October was threatening to slip into November and the leaves were changing colors like a chameleon, Charlotte felt as though she'd been trudging through wet cement for weeks on end. Soon the leaves would be tumbling into heaping piles for kids to cavort in until being swept away in advance of the first snowfall.

Charlotte could barely tolerate northeastern winters. Having grown up in central Florida, she felt allergic to the freezing temperatures and bulky clothing. Forget about the wind, hail, and, heaven forbid, a real storm. If she could have hibernated like a bear from early November until mid-April, she would have. Her first semester at Cornell University had been an unwelcome shock to her system. She'd been warned that it was going to be cold and had purchased what felt like a full wardrobe of clothing to accommodate her new environment. Unfortunately, she'd grossly miscalculated just how freezing it was going to be and somewhere around December had been forced to buy a better-late-than-never, full-length down coat in a gleaming shade of white, which was so puffy she'd looked like a swollen marshmallow waddling around campus. Charlotte had pleaded with the salesgirl to check in the back for another color, any other color, but she'd just shrugged sympathetically enough and said, *Sorry, sweetie. Out of stock. This is what you get at the end of the season.*

During the first months, even years, of her relationship with Charlie, they'd talked about moving somewhere warmer. She'd suggested San Diego. He'd countered with San Francisco, citing a long-standing fascination with the Golden Gate Bridge. They'd even mulled over the Carolinas and Texas. *I'd look killer in a pair of brown lizard cowboy boots and a Stetson,* Charlie had joked, and she'd laughed effortlessly, thinking that, to her, he'd look killer in anything. Better yet, nothing at all. But the years had gone by, one colder than the next—or so it seemed to Charlotte—and Charlie had become further ensconced in his career as a hedge funder and she in the Wincourt social scene. Every now and then, in the depths of winter, when the frigid temperatures were almost too much to endure, Charlotte would resurrect the conversation, but Charlie would just laugh and say something like, "Where would you get your hair and nails done in South

Carolina?" or "How would you survive without Sabrina and Missy in Dallas?"

Those were the things he thought mattered to her most?

Charlotte placed a large hand-painted salad bowl filled with arugula, sliced mushrooms, and slivered almonds in the center of the kitchen table, feeling particularly buoyant about today's lunch. She'd invited Allison weeks earlier, but with both of their hectic schedules, it'd taken this long for them to settle on a free afternoon—the last Saturday in October and possibly one of the few remaining days evocative of spring. The air was light and sweet, like a wisp of cotton candy on your tongue, and the warmth of the sun enveloped you like the tender cradling hands of a first-time mother.

Quite intentionally, she hadn't invited Sabrina and Missy to join them. She was intent on getting to know Allison without the other ladies around. Charlotte suspected Allison just might be the kind of friend who cared more about the latest life was dishing out than your latest designer shoe purchase. But she hadn't figured her out yet. And there was still the obstacle that was Charlie to factor into the equation. It was silly, she knew, to view her own husband as an impediment. After all, she and Allison might never have made it past pleasant smiles exchanged in the school hallways if not for him. Either that or Sabrina would have gotten to her first, deciding whether "they"—as a group—were going to accept or alienate the new girl on the block. Still, Charlotte couldn't help but feel cheated. She wanted Allison all to herself, and she couldn't put her finger on why.

The doorbell chimed and Charlotte instinctively tossed the salad, hurrying to answer the door before Layla—their weekend babysitter—could beat her to it, not that Layla had a fighting chance, seeing as she and Gia were tucked away in the outermost wing of her ten-thousand-square-foot house. "No disruptions, please, unless there's an emergency," Charlotte had politely requested of Layla that morning when she'd arrived promptly at eight to find the kitchen in turmoil from Gia's prebreakfast temper tantrum. "Mr. Crane will be working in his office, so once you've cleaned up in here, please take Gia to the playroom until lunchtime. Sorry for the mess."

Reliably, Layla had nodded and offered a soft-spoken, "Yes, Mrs. Charlotte."

"Just a second. I'm coming . . . ," Charlotte called out, as if Allison could hear her through their impenetrable iron door with copper patina finish.

Before Charlie, Charlotte had never considered the fact that one could customize so many details in a home. She'd have been just as happy with the wooden door that was there when they'd purchased the place five years ago. And the light fixtures in every room. And the hardware in all the bathrooms. Who really knew the difference between pewter and brushed nickel anyway? Apparently Charlie did. He'd once told her that he'd always dreamed of being an architect but he didn't have the brain for all the geometry that went with it. At some point he'd figured that if he earned enough money, it would be equally gratifying—not to mention a lot less time spent studying—to renovate an already existing property that he could puff his chest over being able to afford.

"Hey!" Allison beamed over the rims of two brown bags

overflowing with a cornucopia of fruits and vegetables. "These are for you."

"Oh my gosh. Let me take those from you."

"No, no, I've got them balanced. One false move and your foyer will be aisle one at Whole Foods. Just lead the way." Allison followed Charlotte into the kitchen and set the bags down on the counter. She was dressed in her uniform—cork wedge sandals and a billowy maxidress, this one an almost-sheer, chiffon-like fabric swathed in a maelstrom of turquoises and pale yellows.

"What is all this stuff?" Charlotte started unpacking vibrant orange peppers, baseball-bat-sized cucumbers, and Ziploc bags stuffed with unidentifiable green herbs. "It looks and smells amazing."

"Logan and I picked it from our garden this morning. The previous owners moved out in June. I guess they were good friends with our Realtor, so they let my mom in to plant. It was her surprise to us, and I think she went a little overboard!" She smiled and Charlotte noticed for the first time that Allison's nose was slightly crooked in the most flattering way. Somehow the awkward curvature, which would have been unbecoming on anyone else, complemented Allison's naturally flushed cheeks, her light gray eyes, bee-stung pink pout, and long, beachy blond waves, which always looked elegantly and effortlessly tousled, even at school drop-off early in the morning. Charlotte couldn't tell if she wore any makeup at all, but if she did it was scarcely more than some lip balm and a coat of clear mascara on her offensively long, butterfly-like lashes.

"Well, we're thrilled to be the recipients of your mom's exuberance. What's in these?" She lifted six Tupperware containers packed with a thick greenish-brown substance from one of the bags and wrinkled her nose, which was not at all crooked, thanks to Dr. Morton Rosen, and still was not as well-suited for her face as Allison's.

"That, my friend, is the best pesto you will ever eat. Our backyard may have been overtaken by a jungle of basil if not for that pesto. It's a little brown because the olive oil settles at the bottom, but once you mix it . . ." Allison closed her eyes and licked her lips. "Heaven."

"Did you make it?" Charlotte was kind of hoping she'd say no.

"Of course! But it's my mom's recipe. Thus the accolades. Honestly, it's easy. I can give you the recipe."

"Oh, okay, thanks." Charlotte nodded. "Are you hungry?"

"Starved." Allison rubbed her belly.

"Excellent. Have a seat." She motioned to the kitchen table, which was draped in a burnt orange silk tablecloth and adorned with candles wrapped in cinnamon sticks and corn husks and lumpy gourds in varying shapes, sizes, and colors. The centerpiece was a hulking carved and seeded pumpkin stuffed and overflowing with vibrant leaves, each one at least the size of Allison's hand. Even the salad matched the décor.

"This is spectacular." Allison sat down at one end of the long table. "You really have a talent." She leaned forward to smell one of the cinnamon sticks. "Yummy."

"Oh, please, you think I did this?" Charlotte laughed. "I don't have a creative bone in my body." It wasn't strictly the truth. When she'd worked in advertising, albeit briefly, she'd often been praised for her inspired ideas. Still, she hadn't massaged those muscles in years, and anyway, concocting campaign slogans had come naturally to her, unlike domesticity.

"I doubt that." Allison swept her hand in front of her. "Look at this place."

"Yeah, I can't take credit." Charlotte shook her head and set a Gruyère and broccoli quiche, which Layla had left warming in the oven, in front of Allison—the browned and bubbling cheese was so fragrant Charlotte was almost tempted to indulge in a slice. Almost. "We have an amazing interior decorator. I can give you her name if you want. All I did was tear pictures of rooms I liked out of magazines and occasionally a lone piece of furniture. As for the table, I swear my housekeeper, Janna, is the Filipino version of Martha Stewart. What can I tell you? She changes the theme with every season."

"That's convenient." Allison took the silver knife from the quiche plate. "Shall I?"

"Oh, absolutely. Let me get us something to drink. Iced tea good?"

"Great."

"Help yourself to salad too."

"This looks delicious." Allison smiled. "I won't bother asking if you made it."

"Now you're catching on!" Charlotte returned to the table with two tall frosted glasses filled with iced tea and decorated with a skewer of fresh blueberries tangled in fresh mint. "Oh, no quiche for me." She dismissed Allison's attempt to serve her even a small piece.

"You're a better woman than I am!" Allison put the slice on her own plate and gave herself some salad as well, passing the bowl to Charlotte. "You do eat lettuce, right?"

"Oh yes. It's a favorite!"

"Well, I'm definitely in awe of your willpower."

"It's either that or fat thighs." Charlotte smacked the side of her leg. "So tell me, how's everything going? I wish we could have done this sooner. I've been dying to hear how you're settling in. Is Logan liking school?"

"He is. And the house is shaping up really nicely. Lately I've been holed up in my studio working on a new project. It feels nice to be inspired to paint something of my own again. Something I'm not being commissioned to do."

"I can imagine." Charlotte nodded. "Have you made any . . . friends?"

"Aside from you and Charlie, not really." She took a bite of salad. "Can I be honest?"

"Of course!" Charlotte let herself relax for the first time all day. This was exactly what she'd been waiting for. Girl time alone with Allison.

"I haven't found the other moms in the class to be that *welcoming*. I know that sounds awful, but I was sort of hoping there'd be a few more women I could relate to. I guess it's still early days."

"Yeah, it's a tough crowd. But you have me. And Sabrina and Missy."

"True." Allison tilted her eyes downward.

"You don't like them, do you?" Charlotte had noticed Allison wince more than a few times during the Wine and Whine. And Charlie had been over to Allison's sporadically in the past few weeks to help out with this or that. God only knows what he'd said to her about Sabrina and Missy. She only hoped he had the sense not to say anything negative about her.

"Oh no. They're sweet. I just . . ."

"Sweet? Ha!" Charlotte hooted. "Not necessarily the word I'd use. You can be straight with me. I know they're my friends, but I'm not really like them." There. She'd said it. But wasn't she like them? If you asked most of the other moms at school, they'd probably say the three of them were one and the same. Still, in her heart, she knew that Sabrina could turn on her faster than spoiled milk if someone more appealing came along. It had almost happened three years back when word had gotten around that Ben Affleck was going to be filming a major motion picture in Wincourt and that Jennifer Garner and their kids might be moving there with him. Sabrina had very nearly dropped Charlotte and Missy on the spot.

It wasn't that Sabrina and Missy were bad people. They were fun to hang out with, especially when Sabrina was in a good mood, and there had been times when they'd come through for her in a pinch, but still, Charlotte remained cautious about letting her guard down entirely. She feared that if she was too forthcoming about her problems and frustrations, it could come back to bite her. That was why meeting Allison felt like such a gift, especially since Charlie used to be her outlet from the superficial social circle in which she roamed. Not in a "girl chat" sort of way, but he'd been her partner—for better or worse—which, sadly, they seemed to have lost. And once they'd started drifting apart, she'd found herself desperate to rely on someone more genuine, someone to whom she could open up without reservation. She'd considered trying to befriend a few of the other mothers at school, ones who seemed slightly less shallow, but she knew that Sabrina was territorial when it came to her, and at the end of the day, it was easier to sit comfortably on the boat than to rock it.

"Okay, well, since you put it that way, I guess they're probably not the best buddies I envisioned." Charlotte wondered if *she* was more like the best buddy Allison had envisioned, but she wouldn't dare say something that desperate.

"Fair enough!" The doorbell rang and Charlotte sighed, resentful of the interruption just as she was finally getting somewhere with Allison. "Let me go get that." She placed her neatly pressed linen napkin on her chair and rushed out of the room.

Two minutes later, Charlotte walked back into the kitchen with an irritated expression on her face and her sister trailing behind her.

"Oh, hi." Allison stood up. "I didn't know you were expecting someone else."

"I wasn't." Charlotte frowned at Elizabeth. "At least, not for another two hours."

"Sorry, sis. Must have gotten the times mixed up."

"Right, whatever." Was it really so much to ask her sister to buy a desk calendar, or—heaven forbid—use the brand-new iPhone Charlotte had given her to schedule appointments? *Like the rest of the world.* "Allison, this is my sister, Elizabeth. Elizabeth, Allison. She grew up in Wincourt and just moved back with her son, Logan, who's in Gia's class. Coincidentally, she and Charlie are old friends from summer camp." Charlotte deliberately left out the part about Allison's dead husband. That was Allison's information to share, if and when she felt comfortable.

"It's so nice to meet you." Allison extended her hand and Elizabeth shook it somewhat reluctantly.

"Yeah, you too." Elizabeth forced a smile just as the phone rang.

"For God's sake, is there never any peace and quiet to be had around here?" Charlotte picked up the receiver. "Hello . . . Hi, Sabrina . . . I'm just tied up. . . . You're kidding. . . . Okay . . . Hold on. . . ." She covered the mouthpiece with her hand and whispered to Elizabeth and Allison, "I have to take this. I'll be super quick."

Charlotte slipped out of the room, loath to leave them alone together, and twenty minutes passed before she returned to find Allison and Elizabeth sitting at the kitchen table engrossed in a lively conversation—Elizabeth in Charlotte's chair, eating her salad and a slice of quiche. Why not?

"We thought you'd skipped town." Elizabeth smirked. She was sitting cross-legged on Charlotte's elegant linen chair, coiling Gruyère cheese around her fork like a toddler.

"Nope, I'm here." She bristled, hoping Elizabeth would get up. Or move over. Or, better yet, come back later. She turned to Allison. "I'm so sorry. Sabrina and I were supposed to go on this girls' trip to Canyon Ranch after Christmas and now she can't make it. I doubt the resort will give us a full refund. Not to mention that I could *really* use a few days away. The whole thing is a nightmare."

"*Nightmare,*" Elizabeth deadpanned, and Charlotte glared at her.

"That's a bummer. A spa trip does sound really nice," Allison empathized.

"Why don't you come?" The words fell out of her mouth before she could even think about what she was suggesting. But it really was the perfect solution. "It's not a long drive and it's only a few days. What do you think?" Charlotte smiled sanguinely.

"Wow, I don't know. . . ." Allison looked at Elizabeth and then again at Charlotte, who realized she was probably wondering why she hadn't asked her sister first.

"Come on! It'll be so much fun. . . ." *And it'll drive Sabrina completely mad.*

"The thing is, my parents leave for their house in California after New Year's, and they're there into March. I know my mom has to come back for a few days for a friend's surgery, but it's not until the end of January. I don't have anyone to watch Logan."

"He can stay with me." Charlie strolled into the room sporting a bathrobe and an unshaven face. Charlotte couldn't help but wonder how long he'd been eavesdropping or notice how cute he looked in his bathrobe. She blushed on his behalf. "Sorry for the casual attire. I had a six a.m. conference call." He kissed Allison on the cheek. "How are you, Lizzy?"

"So much better now that you're here," she mocked, and he ignored her.

"I could never impose in that way." Allison shifted awkwardly in her chair, likely waiting for Charlotte to weigh in. But what could she say? The shock of Charlie offering to care for someone else's child when he barely managed to care for his own had unexpectedly sidetracked her.

"Don't be ridiculous. It'll be fun! I need some more testosterone around here anyway."

"I'd have to ask Logan. I don't know what to say."

"Say yes," Charlie urged.

"Is it okay with you?" Allison turned to Charlotte.

"I guess." She nodded her head vaguely. "I mean, yeah. That's great."

"Then it's settled. Allison will go on the trip with you." Charlie picked a mushroom out of the salad with his fingers. "And I'll play Mr. Mom for the weekend."

Chapter 8

"Honestly, I'm not sure what to make of the whole thing." Allison reached across the table to pluck a hard-boiled egg from her mom's chef salad. "Charlie's great. He's really been going out of his way to help me out. And Charlotte's certainly been the most welcoming of any of the moms at Logan's school. It's just that there's this weird vibe whenever they're in the same room together."

"What do you mean by 'weird vibe'?" Allison's mother narrowed her light gray eyes in contemplation and pierced a hunk of cucumber with her fork.

"I can't put my finger on it. I haven't really spent much time with both of them, but the little time I have spent . . . I don't know. It's like there's a tension in the air. Maybe it's just me, but it's like he barely acknowledges her existence. And I think she's insecure about it."

"You can't blame her for that." She lifted the cucumber to her mouth and Allison watched her nibble at it like a gerbil. Her mother was possibly the most refined person she knew.

There was no shoveling food, like the gentleman at the next table who was inhaling the Italian Combo in the manner of a starved puppy dog, lapping up the oil and vinegar trickling down his chin after every ambitious bite.

Far from it. Caroline Taylor, born Caroline Harper in Kennebunkport, Maine, to a reverend and a schoolteacher, never left the house without makeup, though you'd never know she was wearing any. Her hair was always neatly styled, nary a gray strand in sight. And her outfits were unfailingly age appropriate and typically designer. She never spent money unnecessarily, but she did appreciate the finer things. Good food, luxurious fabrics, and a home appointed with antiques that together were worth more than Allison's house itself. She'd always been of the mind-set that shopping sprees were ridiculous, insisting that a smaller closet full of items that might be more expensive but would stand the test of time was far more valuable than a large closet packed with junk. She also subscribed to the theory that you should never shop for a specific event, unless it was your wedding. If you saw something you liked and it fit you well, you should purchase it without regret. Then, when an engagement did come along, you wouldn't have to buy something at the eleventh hour that wasn't right.

"Yeah, I suppose. Maybe it's hard for me to understand because Jack and I were never like that. Sometimes I think about where we'd be today. Ya know?" Allison smiled politely at the lady lunching on the other side of them, who was, quite clearly, eavesdropping on their conversation— unfortunately for her, it was odds-on the least salacious dialogue within earshot.

"Of course. Though I hardly think you'd be like Charlotte and Charlie. You and Jack had something very special, Ali. Like your father and me. Most people don't have that. Or if they do, they eventually find a way to destroy it."

"You know what's funny? I feel like all of my friends' parents were married when I was growing up here, and now it seems like every mom in Logan's class is either divorced or already on husband number two. Or three."

"It's ridiculous. People split up these days like they're throwing out the trash." Her mother shook her head. "Marriages take work. They're not always easy street."

"I've never once seen you and Dad have a real fight."

"Ha!" She laughed. "Then you must not have been paying attention. We've fought plenty, believe me. Oh, how we've fought. But remember, love and hate are closer than love and indifference. Not that I could ever hate your father, but you get my point. If someone doesn't stir up passion inside you—both the good kind and the bad—then it's not a true relationship. At least in my opinion."

"I guess that's what it is with Charlotte and Charlie. It's not like they're going at each other." She took a bite of her tuna fish sandwich and finished chewing before continuing. Among the many things her mother had taught her, proper manners were at the tippy-top of the list. "It's more like they're strangers."

"That's unfortunate."

"Should I feel weird being friends with both of them?"

"I don't think so. As long as you don't get caught in the middle. I know Charlie is an old friend and that he's a connection to Jack. But girlfriends are important. Do you like this Charlotte? Is she someone you see yourself becoming closer with?"

"I definitely like her, and I think there's a lot more to her. Under the surface. I told you she invited me on this trip to Canyon Ranch, so I'll see how that goes." Allison sipped her cold lemonade, savoring its tangy bite. "That's the other thing. When she invited me, her *sister* was sitting right there. I mean, how awkward is that? And then when Charlie said he'd take Logan while we're gone, I thought Charlotte was going to keel over from shock. Very quickly, the whole thing reached an unrivaled level of get-me-the-hell-out-of-here."

"Sounds like she could use a real friend." Allison's mother crunched a piece of yellow pepper. "This salad is enormous. Do you want some?"

"Sure." Allison handed her mother her plate. "Taste the tuna. It's delicious. I wonder what they put in there. The flavors are amazing."

"Carrots, onions, and sweet relish. Now you have the secret." Dempsey appeared at the side of their table, seemingly out of nowhere. "Are you ladies enjoying yourselves? Mrs. Taylor, may I say you look beautiful as always?"

"You may." Allison's mother blushed like a teenager in the face of her first crush. "And I've told you to call me Caroline, what, a million times now?"

"Wait, you two know each other?"

"Of course. I come in here three times a week. Dempsey is a gem. This is my daughter, Allison. She and our grandson, Logan, just moved back to Wincourt."

"Ali and I go way back." He pushed his wavy dark brown hair out of his beguiling blue eyes. "We went to high school together."

"You never told me that!" Allison could see her mother's wheels start to spin.

"To be honest, I didn't make the connection until now. Taylor's not exactly an uncommon last name."

"Right." She looked back and forth between the two of them. "Ali and I were just talking about how nice it would be if she had more *friends* up here."

"Mom! I'm sure Dempsey has plenty of friends."

"Actually, no. I'm kind of a loser." He laughed easily. "I'm kidding. But I'd love to get together sometime."

"Um, sure, yeah. Maybe once I'm settled in." Allison fidgeted with her straw, poking at the bobbing ice cubes in her lemonade.

"Whatever works. You know where to find me." He took Allison's mother's hand in his, dotting it with a kiss. "Caroline, always a pleasure. If you ladies need anything, give a shout."

"Thank you." Her mother smiled bashfully and watched as Dempsey disappeared behind the counter.

"What happened to 'girlfriends are important'?" Allison whispered, leaning across the table so no one else would hear.

"I didn't say a few handsome and single men in the mix could hurt, did I?"

"I'm not ready for that." Allison waved her hand dismissively.

"Ali, I'm not suggesting you marry him. Dinner wouldn't be the end of the world, though. We don't mind babysitting."

"Don't *mind*?" She sniffed. "You'd have me out every night if it was up to you!"

"Can I help it if my grandson is scrumptious and perfect?"

"Well, we agree there." Allison picked at the homemade potato chips next to her sandwich. "I can't believe you and Dad are leaving for California in early January and you won't be back until the middle of March."

"I know. But remember I'll be back in late January for Loretta's procedure, so that'll break it up a bit. We thought about cutting it short—"

"No, don't be silly. It'll be good for me to have time to concentrate on painting. I've started a new piece. But aside from that, I've been so busy with the house and back-to-school stuff that I've been ignoring the bread and butter. Actually, yesterday I got commissioned by some Brazilian billionaire's wife to do—in her words—an 'interpretive portrait' of them and their kids. I'm not sure what that means exactly. Anyway, I'm sure we'll survive while you're gone."

"But will *we*? Finally we have Logan next door and now I have to be without him for so long. I told your father we can always come back early if we want. That's what airplanes are for." She paused in advance of her next thought. "You don't think he's adorable?"

"Who?"

"What do you mean 'who'? The pope." She flailed her arms in the air. "*Dempsey.* He's more than easy on the eyes, if you ask me."

"Mom."

"What? I'm just saying . . ."

"I know what you're saying!" Allison crinkled her nose. "But he works at a sandwich shop."

"I know I didn't teach you to think like that."

"That came out wrong. It's not that there's anything wrong with working in a sandwich shop. It's just that he was so smart in high school. I looked him up in the yearbook after running into him last time. He had a three-point-nine GPA. He went to the University of Pennsylvania for undergrad and then to Wharton business school. Don't you think there's something off about going through all of that schooling only to work behind the counter slicing turkey?"

"Did you happen to notice the name on the awning outside?" Her mother smirked meaningfully.

"Yeah, DJ Gourmet. So?"

"*So,* that 'DJ' stands for 'Dempsey James,' my darling daughter. He has six other locations within a sixty-mile radius. I'd say his years at Wharton were well spent."

"Oh wow. I had no idea."

"Not that it should make a difference."

"I know—" Allison started to speak and her mother interrupted.

"Shhh. He's coming back over." She put a finger to her mouth, which instantly curled into a wide grin as soon as Dempsey arrived.

"These are for you." He set a frothy cappuccino in front of each of them. "I know it's your mom's favorite, but I wasn't sure about you, so I took a little liberty." He beamed at

Allison and a flush inched up the back of her neck, slinking its way to her cheeks.

"Thank you." Instinctively she batted her eyelashes, which—apparently—was cue enough for her mother.

"You know, I really have to run." She shot up from her chair. "I can't believe Thanksgiving is next week and there are so many preparations to be made. It would be a shame to waste the cappuccino. Dempsey, if it's not too much of an imposition, maybe you'll take my place?" She nudged him toward her chair. And before he or Allison could get a word in edgewise, they were seated on either side of the table smiling awkwardly at each other. "I'll call you later, sweetheart." She dipped down to kiss Allison on the cheek and, on her way out, mouthed, "You'll thank me later," over Dempsey's shoulder.

"I'm so sorry." Allison rolled her eyes.

"Sorry for what?" he asked breezily, tipping back in his chair. "Your mom's the best."

"True. It's just that sometimes her best intentions aren't best for *everyone*."

"I think that's what mothers are for. The very reason why they were put on this earth."

"I guess." She laughed, feeling the tension release from her body. "So you make a killer cappuccino, huh?"

"Only one way to find out." He motioned to her cup and she took a small sip.

"Oh my God, that's . . ."

"Killer?"

"Something like that."

"I aim to please."

"I bet you do." The words fell out more flirtatiously than she'd intended. "I didn't mean it like that."

"Ali, relax." He put his hand on hers. "It's just coffee."

"I know." She nodded nervously.

"With any luck, the first of many." He picked up his cup and clinked it against hers. "To friends."

She smiled and for the first time, their eyes locked. "To friends."

Chapter 9

"*What is going on in here?*" Charlie burst through the door whispering urgently and gesturing frantically. Charlotte flinched, sighting the pulsing blue veins threatening to rupture his temples.

"I'm *trying* to get everything together, okay? I don't understand why this turkey isn't done yet." She checked on the twenty-pound bird again, despite the fact that every recipe she'd read online—and she'd pored over at least three dozen, panicked at the prospect of a dreadful Thanksgiving—had strongly recommended *not* opening the oven door unless absolutely necessary. *Define absolutely necessary,* she thought, standing in the middle of the kitchen helplessly and questioning why oh why she'd ever dreamed she could manage it all herself. In years past, she'd ensured that Maria, Janna, or Layla, or some combination of the three, had been in place to help her. Unfortunately, "the help"—as Charlie referred to them—were all with their own families tonight.

When each of them had approached her to request the

day off, she'd thought, *Why not?* Certainly they could organize everything for her in the days leading up to the main event and all she'd have to do was implement their handwritten instructions, which she had. I mean, honestly, how hard could it be to place an already stuffed turkey in the oven and wait for the timer to pop? Beyond that, she'd just have to heat up the side dishes and desserts. It wasn't rocket science. She'd gone to an Ivy League school, for God's sake.

Only now, in the heat of the moment, Charlotte wasn't sure if she'd ever felt more defeated. Elizabeth, Nick, and Gia were already seated at the table. Charlie was rushing in and out of both rooms, clearly irritated. Gia was whining. Elizabeth was whining. Nick was on his fourth beer. She was on her third glass of wine. And her blood pressure was about to shoot through the facade of their "perfect" existence.

"I knew this was going to happen." Charlie sighed, massaging his brow with the tips of his fingers.

"Thank you, that's very helpful." Charlotte's eyes stung as she willed herself not to cry. That would come later. With any luck, much later.

"*Helpful?* Do you know what's not *helpful*? Leaving me out there for an hour to entertain your sister, who's so goddamn rude to me in my own house that it's taking all my willpower not to kick her out. And, you know, Nick and I have so much in common. So that's going swimmingly. But the best part is that Gia has now taken to throwing all the gourds on the floor, so she can watch them smash to pieces. I'm literally wrestling them out of her hands."

"Charlie, what do you want me to do here? I told you I'm trying. If you'd like to take over, be my guest." Charlotte darted from here to there and back again, pulling things from the refrigerator and alternately trying to translate Janna's extensive, though barely legible, notes. The last thing she needed was to have to placate him.

"No, I don't want to take over. I work hard enough during the week, thank you."

"And I don't?" She regretted the question immediately. She knew the answer. His answer.

Unless you went to an office every morning and didn't return home until the evening, in Charlie's opinion, you didn't have a *real* job. It didn't matter if you cared for six kids with no help. Or if you sat on the board of ten different charitable organizations, devoting your time to those less fortunate. Or, even if, like Charlotte, you had only one very obstinate child who sucked the life out of you when your ungrateful sister wasn't doing the same *and* you took care of everything for the house *and* you were on the planning committees for two annual galas, one to raise money for children with cancer and the other to secure funds for the Wincourt school system. So what if she had help? Who wouldn't if they could? There was plenty of "work" to go around.

"I didn't say that." He exhaled. "This is why I told you not to take on everything yourself."

"I don't want to get into this now."

"Then you shouldn't have started it."

"I didn't start it. You're the one who came in here, remember?"

"Because there's no dinner on the table!" He flapped his arms in the air. "Jesus, Charlotte, the kitchen looks like the entire supermarket exploded in here, there are three starving people out there who'd probably rather order a pizza, and we've barely seen a morsel of food save for the bread basket and hunk of cheese Gia's plowing through."

"I'm sorry, okay? I'm sorry." She turned away just as hot, salty tears welled in her eyes and began streaming down their familiar path. She hated that he had this kind of power over her. Some days it felt like too much to handle. And then, once in a blue moon, he'd do something nice. Never a grand gesture, but something, and she'd tell herself that *that* was the real Charlie. The Charlie she'd once been desperately in love with and, below the surface, hoped she still was.

"Don't do this. Come on." He walked toward her, cupped his hands over her shoulders, and turned her in his direction. "Crying is only going to make it worse."

"I can't help it, okay? I'm upset."

"About what?"

"About this! I'm ruining everything and you're yelling at me."

"I did not yell." His hands fell to his sides, balling into fists, and he backed away. If there was one thing Charlie hated more than anything else, it was feeling like a bully.

After a particularly hellacious fight they'd had a year ago—one in which Charlie had really dug into her, calling her pathetic, among other character-assassinating adjectives, and telling her to shut up when she'd tried to come back at him—Charlotte had made the near-fatal-to-their-marriage mistake of calling him verbally abusive. In an instant, he'd packed an overnight bag and stormed out the door, declaring that he wanted a divorce and that he'd return when he damn well pleased. Charlotte, in turn, had run to her bedroom, locked the door, and hidden under the covers, sobbing and texting him pleading messages to come home. Perhaps she was pathetic after all.

"Fine. I'm sorry. It's me. It's my fault." *Isn't it always?* Because why would Charlie ever be wrong? Why would he ever apologize? Or, at the very least, take ownership of his mistakes, admit that maybe, just maybe, at some point in time, he'd played some small role in the unraveling of their relationship.

In the end, Charlotte was always the one to express regret. How many times had she gone so far as to solicit forgiveness when she'd done nothing more than sit silently while he'd berated her about this or that? She'd learned her lesson through experience. If she fought back, things escalated. If she spoke to him the way he spoke to her, all hell broke loose. Eventually, she'd realized it wasn't worth it. She could stay or go. She'd thought about the latter. She'd thought hard about it when things got really bad. But she always landed at the same conclusion. She'd be alone without Charlie. Even worse, Gia would have to grow up with divorced parents living in separate households. And likely spend years in therapy righting the wrong they'd inflicted on her.

Thirty minutes and a vat of burned stuffing later, Charlotte stumbled into the dining room wearing a stained apron and a taut smile. She'd chugged half a bottle of red cooking wine to lull her anxiety, on top of the three glasses of white she'd downed in quick succession earlier in the evening. At the time it'd seemed like a good idea—a little liquid courage to cue her inner resourcefulness and to ease the added tension from bickering with Charlie. Now, as she teetered on the four-inch heels she'd slipped back into before hoisting the platter of carved turkey into her jittery arms, it was clear to everyone but her and Gia that she was trashed.

"Let me take that from you." Charlie rushed over and grabbed the platter from Charlotte, setting it down in the center of the table and then steering her to her seat.

"We thought you drowned in a pot of gravy," Elizabeth teased.

"Wouldn't you like that?" Charlotte slurred in return.

"Hey, say it, don't spray it." Elizabeth brushed Charlotte's spit off her shoulder while Gia giggled at the expression.

"What happened here?" Charlie was staring at the mangled turkey.

"I carved it." Charlotte smiled woozily and nearly fell off her chair.

"Whoa, there." Nick caught her and propped her back up. "How much did you drink, little lady?"

"Just a glass or two . . ." Charlotte started counting on her fingers. "Or was it three?" Her eyes widened suddenly. "I forgot the rest of the food!" She hiccupped. "Oops, 'scuse me!"

"Don't go anywhere. I'll get it." Charlie shot up from his chair before Charlotte could attempt to make a move. "Can you help me, please?" He gave Elizabeth a stern look.

"Sure, put the guests to work." She rolled her eyes and followed Charlie into the kitchen. They reappeared seconds later.

"Uh, Charlotte, I don't see anything else but some blackened stuffing." Charlie was visibly bemused.

"Huh." She twisted up her face. "It's hard to remember what I did with it."

"Okay, I think we've all had enough. How does pizza sound?"

"Pizza!" Gia cheered.

"We're gonna blow this joint. We have pizza in the hood too." Elizabeth signaled to Nick. "Let's go." He followed obediently. "Thanks for, uh, everything." She walked past Charlotte, ruffling her sister's hair. "Good luck dealing with three sheets to the wind over here."

"Yeah, thanks." Charlie frowned. "You're a big help, as always." He muttered under his breath as the front door slammed behind them, and then turned to Gia. "It's time for bed."

"You said we were getting *pizza!*" she wailed, folding her chubby arms across her chest.

"There's no possible way you could be hungry, Gia. I watched you eat six rolls and a block of cheese." He pointed up the stairs, leaving Charlotte sitting silently, staring at nothing, while he tucked his daughter in and read her a story. When Charlie crept out of her room and walked back downstairs, he found Charlotte in the same place he'd left her.

"That was a complete disaster." She spoke softly, her eyes fixed in front of her.

"I wouldn't say it was a success." He piled the clean plates into a stack.

"Do you hate me?" Involuntarily, tears started tumbling down her cheeks again, but she still couldn't look at him.

"Of course not." He sighed. "I'm worried about you."

"You are?" She turned to face him with a glimmer of hope in her eyes.

"You didn't need to take this on by yourself. You could have asked someone to help you."

"If I can't pull together a simple family dinner . . ." She trailed off, unable to formulate a cohesive thought.

"Thanksgiving isn't a simple dinner, Charlotte. For example, Elizabeth might have lifted a finger, or even Nick. It really burns me how unappreciative they are. You do more for them than anyone." He shook his head.

"I know."

"Let's get you to bed, okay?"

"Okay." Charlotte nodded vaguely as Charlie lifted her into his arms and carried her up the stairs. She nuzzled her head into the side of his neck, finally allowing her heavy eyelids to surrender, and whispered, "I love you."

He exhaled and kissed her clammy forehead. "I love you too."

Chapter 10

The holiday season had whirred past in a fluster of food comas and flickering lights. Since childhood, Allison had relished the tradition and ceremony of it all, from her father's boisterous turkey call as he carved the Thanksgiving bird with the precision that only a surgeon's hands could achieve, to the tearing, shredding, and discarding of red, green, gold, and silver wrapping paper on Christmas morning. The first December after Jack had died, her mother had procured a modest tree, setting it up next to the couch in Allison's living room and draping it in white lights only and no more than a dozen ornaments judiciously scattered. It didn't feel right, she'd said, to overembellish, and everyone had agreed. Allison had no memory of that day—the pot roast her mother had since told her she'd cooked, or receiving the heart-shaped locket carrying a photo of Logan, with the inscription *For My Precious Girl. Love, Daddy*, which her father had steadily clasped around her neck.

This year, Allison had been invited to two New Year's Eve

parties, one at the Wincourt Country Club, hosted by her parents' billionaire friends the Browns. Everyone knew Harold Brown had made his money in vodka and strip clubs. And the other was at Charlie and Charlotte's—their annual End-of-Year Extravaganza, as she'd referred to it. Allison had tactfully declined both, opting instead to clink glasses of sparkling apple cider with Logan while he fell asleep in her arms, struggling to keep his eyes open long enough to watch the ball drop in Times Square—a battle he'd unwittingly lost. Two days later, they'd driven her parents to LaGuardia Airport, where they'd reluctantly waved good-bye from the curb, her mother reminding her she'd be home for three days in just a few weeks. Before long, Allison was on her way to meet Charlotte for their girls' getaway, a cocktail of mixed emotions hissing from within.

"I can't believe it's taken me this long to do something like this." Allison lay back on a cushy chaise lounge in the Serenity Room at Canyon Ranch with a mud mask hardening on her face and thin slices of cucumber shielding her eyes from the temperate mood lighting.

"Me neither." Charlotte was reclining next to her with a thick layer of some gooey seaweed concoction smeared across her forehead, cheeks, chin, and nose. The aesthetician had sworn it would decrease the appearance of fine lines and possibly—depending on her skin's natural elasticity—even some of the deeper creases. Allison had watched as Charlotte had fallen hook, line, and sinker for her sales pitch. She didn't say as much, but she wondered, as she had so many times before, why someone as attractive as Charlotte was so observably insecure. "You've really never left Logan for even a night?"

"Nope." Allison shook her head, not that Charlotte could see her. "Honestly, I had no place to go."

After saying yes to the trip, Allison had driven straight home and immediately regretted it, vowing to call Charlotte first thing in the morning and graciously back out. Her mistake, or so she'd thought in the moment, had been telling her mother, who'd been adamant about her taking the time for herself, to relax. "This is precisely what the doctor ordered," she'd said. "I don't want to hear another word about you not going. I only wish we could be here for Logan." She'd offered *again* to delay their departure for California or stay behind and meet Allison's father there after her friend Loretta's surgery, but Allison had, *again*, insisted that they keep their plans, especially since they had nonrefundable tickets. Not surprisingly, Logan had been thrilled at the prospect of staying with Charlie and Gia. Allison knew in her heart that her sweet little boy craved the attention of a male role model and that, while his grandfather was a more than suitable placeholder, he was undeniably much older than the dads in Logan's class. She wasn't sure whose smile had been wider when she'd dropped him off at Charlotte's house the previous morning—Logan's or Charlie's. Charlie seemed to need her son in the same way Logan needed him.

When Charlotte had first described Canyon Ranch, calling it a "healthy-living facility," Allison had been wary. It wasn't that she had anything against being healthy, but she certainly didn't need to lose weight or want to spend her first vacation in more than a decade working out and worrying about eradicating her cellulite, what little there was of it. "Just look at the website," Charlotte had urged, sensing her apprehension. "I guarantee you won't be disappointed."

Touché. Canyon Ranch, it turned out, was way more than grass smoothies for breakfast, wrinkle shrinking for lunch, and dimple zapping for dinner. Way more. On their website, they called it "a unique spa vacation experience," and even that hardly did it justice. The sprawling property, which was located in the bountiful Berkshires, in the heart of western Massachusetts, centered around a dramatically renovated mansion, which—their tour guide had informed them—had once been a private home and then a seminary and boarding school after that. Although that was hard to imagine now.

Beyond the streaming list of spa treatments, which ran the gamut from massages to facials to full-body wraps promising you'd not only feel lighter, but actually shed a pound or two (at least!), there was Pilates and Gyrotonics, dancing and yoga, biking and hiking, and skiing and snowshoeing, not to mention the saunas, indoor and outdoor swimming pools, state-of-the-art cardio and weight rooms, exercise studios, and indoor tennis, racquetball, squash, and basketball courts. An extensive and expert staff was on hand to cater to your every whim—they'd even called Allison in advance of the visit to prebook services and learn more about her likes and dislikes in the way of, well, everything. Meals were prepared by their accomplished chefs and were billed as nutritious and delicious, which instantly made Allison regret the comfort food she normally fed her body. There was something for everyone and far too much to conquer in one visit. It was no wonder Charlotte returned year after year.

"I find it hard to believe that *you* had no social invitations. You're *gorgeous.*" Charlotte flattered her for what felt like the zillionth time, not that it was tiresome to be continually praised.

"I suppose I didn't really put myself out there, you know, after Jack died. And then it kind of became the status quo." Allison stretched her mouth open to loosen the mask, which she could feel cracking on her skin. "The idea of doing anything but having dinner with my little man and curling up on the couch to watch TV before reading him to sleep seemed impossible." She paused. "No, that's not the right word. Maybe more like uncomfortable."

"I can understand that."

"I guess somewhere deep down, I felt like the last thing Logan needed was to watch me walk out the door and wonder whether that would be the last time he'd ever see me." Charlotte didn't say anything. "Sorry to be a downer."

"No, no, I'm glad you're talking about it."

Allison smiled to herself. Charlotte, despite her sometimes pretentious posture, was actually very easy to confide in, and there was something about her, though Allison couldn't identify it, that made Allison want to reveal otherwise suppressed elements of her life and how those elements had shaped her into the person she was today. In the past— with other women she'd met through Logan's nursery school or kiddie classes—it had always felt like a risk to divulge too much—anything, really. A risk she hadn't been willing to take for fear of being spurned.

"So you never thought about dating at all?"

"Of course I thought about it. It would have been hard not to, especially with my mom nudging every month or so after the first couple of years had passed. She was as gentle as one could be about it, but still."

"Yeah." Charlotte was quiet for a moment. "How long did it . . ."

"Did it what?"

"Take you to get over him?"

"I haven't."

"Really?"

"Not entirely. And I probably never will. I know this sounds so cheesy, but Jack was the one for me. As much as I hate to say it, he was my soul mate. I couldn't see beyond him. I still can't."

"Wow." Allison wondered if Charlotte was calculating how long it would take her to get over Charlie, which, from the sound of it, wasn't eleven years.

"I still write to him." Her sudden admission surprised even her.

"What do you mean?" Charlotte was intrigued.

"I write him letters in my journal. At first it was every night, sometimes twice a day, if I was really down. When my therapist suggested it, I thought it was a ridiculous idea, but honestly, it really helped. In many ways it saved me."

"So you have a whole journal of letters to him?"

"Not exactly. I write about lots of stuff. Sometimes I even sketch things when I'm inspired. But the letters were what helped keep me sane from the start."

Allison thought back to the last note she'd written to Jack. She'd confided in him that packing up her apartment in

Manhattan alone had been draining. She'd said that her parents had offered to help but that she'd wanted to do it herself. There'd been so much of his stuff, *their* stuff. For starters, the cheesy ivory leather wedding album with the tacky gold trim Jack *had* to have, because he thought it looked more official than the modern, stylish options. And the scrapbook Allison had made him for his twenty-first birthday, which had reminded her of his perilous penchant for Sour Patch Kids. Perilous because he used to eat so many of them at once that the sides of his tongue would become raw from the sugar. She'd also had a good laugh over finding the certificate for the star Jack had "purchased" and named after her. She'd reminded him how she'd thought it was *so* romantic at the time. (But seriously, what a racket!) Allison had even come across old photos of them from Camp Tawana, cringing at her larger-than-life eighties hairdo, which had been frozen in time thanks to Aqua Net.

Finally, she'd reiterated to him what she wrote so often: that wherever he was, she hoped it was nice there. That she hoped they had ice hockey on TV all the time for him. And corn muffins. He'd loved corn muffins, toasted with butter. She'd made one for him every morning for about a month after he was gone. Just in case he came home.

"And then you never stopped?" Charlotte probed, puncturing Allison's reverie.

"Never stopped. As I said, it's become more infrequent over time, but I still need it. I know this may seem strange, but it's kind of like a drug, and it lifts me up faster than any real drug would. Well, maybe not, but I'm not willing to be one of those people who walks around in a permanent haze."

"So you never took anything?"

"Oh no, I took everything under the sun the first year. Prozac, Valium, Zoloft, Ativan, Xanax. It was necessary, or so the psychiatrist in my therapist's office said, but I didn't feel right when I was on them. The misery felt better. It was authentic, ya know? At some point, I didn't want to numb the pain. I wanted to wade through it to the other side."

"You make it sound so easy." Charlotte sat up, removing the cucumber slices from her eyes, and Allison did the same, each of them giggling at the other's plastered face.

"Ha! If only you'd seen me then, in the same pair of ratty, stained, smelly pajamas for weeks on end, unwashed hair, and if you think I'm skinny now . . ."

"There's a diet I haven't tried." Charlotte's hand flew to her mouth. "Oh my God. I didn't mean that how it sounded. I'm so sorry. I . . ."

"Don't apologize. It was exactly the right thing to say to lighten the mood!" Allison laughed. "Now, should we get someone to wash this crap off and sneak out for some ice cream? Yes, I'm well aware it's, like, thirty degrees!"

"I can't imagine anything better." Charlotte smiled. "And I know just the place."

Later that evening, they were reclining once again, only this time on the king-sized bed in their shared suite. Sabrina had canceled her room, oblivious to the fact that Allison was planning to go in her place, a fact that Charlotte had deliberately failed to convey until Sabrina had practically dragged the information out of her. Despite her wealth of outward confidence, to know Sabrina was to realize that, underneath, she was no less insecure than everyone else. She was just more adept at obscuring it with bravado.

"Why did you let me eat so much?" Charlotte sighed, rubbing her belly in a circular motion.

"Seriously? You had a salad." Allison arched one of her meticulously groomed eyebrows, which Svetlana—a robust blond woman of Slavic descent—had skillfully waxed and plucked that morning in one of the spa's many treatment rooms smelling of hibiscus and vanilla extract.

"Yeah, with a shovel of bacon bits on top."

"I'm pretty sure that wasn't bacon. I don't think they do fried pork here."

"That doesn't make me feel better." Charlotte propped herself up against a heap of pillows. "Plus, you're forgetting the predinner dessert." They'd driven into town at around four o'clock to hit the Scoop, formerly Bev's, on Church Street in Lenox, which Charlotte had insisted was home to the best hand-churned ice cream on the planet.

"Don't you mean frozen yogurt?" Allison had lapped up a double cone of mint chip and butter pecan, while Charlotte had watched enviously, taking microscopic bites from her kiddie cup of sugar-free, fat-free, *taste-free* swirl.

"It's all the same." She moaned. "And it all goes straight to my butt and thighs."

"Oh, please. You really shouldn't be so down on yourself."

"Says the woman with the size-zero figure."

"Size two."

"Poor thing."

"Right, because you're what? A six?"

"On a good day." Charlotte closed her eyes, and they sat

quietly for a few minutes, leaving Allison unsure if Charlotte had fallen asleep. "I was thinking about what you said earlier." Charlotte opened her eyes again and stared up at the ceiling.

"About what?"

"Jack. How he was the one for you. Your soul mate."

"Yeah?"

"What if Charlie isn't my soul mate? What if there's someone else out there, married to another woman, and we're both navigating life unhappier than we should be? You know, because we never found each other." Allison kept quiet, allowing Charlotte to muse. "What if the day, or the week, or even the month after Charlie and I met, I was supposed to inadvertently brush up against this man on a crowded subway car and we were supposed to ride to the next stop together, holding hands through every dark tunnel, realizing in an instant that we were meant to be?"

"You ride the subway?" Allison smiled and Charlotte swatted her arm.

"You know what I mean."

She did. Allison had asked herself so many what-ifs over time that she could hardly begin to tally them. *What if* she hadn't let Jack go on the ski trip? *What if* he'd landed the new job he'd been interviewing for and had been forced to bow out of the trip himself? After all, he'd been practically certain that everything had gone perfectly and they'd both been shocked and disappointed when the firm had decided to "go in a different direction" at the last minute. *What if* she'd rebuffed his advances in bed the night they'd conceived Logan? The litany of supposing was endless.

"I do, but I don't have the answers you're looking for." Allison rolled onto her side to face Charlotte, who was surrendering her uncertainty to exhaustion. "Let's talk more tomorrow, okay?"

"That sounds good," Charlotte mumbled, barely lucid. "Good night . . ."

"Good night." Allison closed her eyes and, for the first time in months, let herself dream about Jack.

Chapter 11

Charlotte and Allison had both woken up with nagging cricks in their necks, moaning about how preposterous is was for two grown women to have to sleep in the same bed, even if it was king-sized. "Good thing we have massages at eleven!" Allison had declared, shimmying toward their shared bathroom before calling out, "Dibs on first shower!" Charlotte had protested frivolously, delighting in how much closer she and Allison had become in just over twenty-four hours. Then she'd thought about how proud it was going to make Charlie that Allison liked her too.

After their morning treatments and a late lunch of hummus with whole wheat crackers, marinated tofu, seasoned brown rice, and a medley of fresh steamed vegetables followed by guava sorbet for dessert, Charlotte had insisted that they head back to the spa for manicures and pedicures and to spend half an hour in the sauna to "sweat out all the toxins." Allison had agreed without question, leaving Charlotte to wonder if she was always so laid-back.

"You are the loudest snorer ever, by the way." Allison coiled her hair into a topknot and secured it with an elastic band.

"I am not!" Charlotte objected. "Anyway, you're a cover hog. I'm asking for an extra blanket tonight."

"I'm sure that won't be a problem, unless it has calories!" She opened her mouth and covered it with her hand, feigning horror.

"Very funny." Charlotte adjusted her towel to make sure it didn't slip, while Allison discarded hers. "You're naked." Her eyes widened.

"Well, look at that, I am." Allison smiled mischievously. "Go on, take yours off."

"No, thanks." Charlotte shook her head like a two-year-old refusing to eat her Brussels sprouts. "I don't do public nudity."

"Public nudity!" Allison scoffed. "You're too much. First of all, I swear to you I've seen what you've got. Secondly, I'd hardly say we're in midtown Manhattan. Throw caution to the wind. Walk on the wild side. You get my drift. . . ."

"That's easy for you to say. Your body is perfect."

"Would you stop? You look great, Charlotte. Seriously. And don't worry, I have my own insecurities. Every woman does. And probably every man too; they just don't analyze it the way we do or judge each other." Allison leaned back on her elbows, closing her eyes and allowing the penetrating heat to slacken her sore muscles. "I mean, have you ever heard two men gossiping about their friend's cankles?"

"No, I have not." Charlotte dabbed at the beads of sweat dripping down the side of her neck. "Believe me, I work my butt off to look like this. And no matter how hard I try, I still can't work my actual butt off!" She thought back to how many diets she'd been on over the years. Cabbage soup. Weight Watchers. Jenny Craig. Nutrisystem. Medifast. Blood type. Atkins. There'd been one where she'd consumed only specially prescribed cookies for a week. And another that had required her to eat by color: green one day, orange the next, and so on right over the rainbow. Not to mention the many juice fasts she'd endured, during which time she'd been so starving that "bitch on wheels" had been a euphemism for her swaying moods.

"That's because your body is happy at this weight."

"Well, what if I'm not?"

"I think that's got more to do with up here." Allison tapped her index finger on her forehead. "And the crazy moms at school who SoulCycle themselves into skeletons in skinny jeans. Honestly, they look prepubescent, if you ask me. I can't imagine any man would be attracted to that."

"I don't think it's for the men."

"Pretty sad, huh? That women are so competitive that they're willing to waste away to nothing in order to be two pounds thinner than their supposed best friends."

"It's the way of the world, I guess. Or at least the Wincourt world."

"Well, it's a stupid way, if you ask me. And we're not helping generations of women-to-be, which is even more pathetic."

"I know. Charlie hates the way Gia looks." Charlotte tilted her face down, toward her freshly painted pink toenails. She wasn't sure how much she could or should say to Allison.

After their conversation about Jack the day before, Charlotte had been ready to spill everything to Allison about her troubled marriage to Charlie. How every day she asked herself where she'd be in five years. Ten years. Would he walk out on her the day Gia left for college? Or would they both stay, firmly planted in unhappiness, unwilling to admit the failure that was their relationship? In some small way, selfishly speaking, Charlotte wanted her to know the man Charlie could be, had become, when he wasn't being his old self around Allison. But above all, she wanted and desperately needed someone to rely on, because more often than not, she was the shoulder everyone leaned on.

"Gia's not even ten years old yet. She's beautiful."

"She's also chubby. Charlie wants her on a strict diet, which in some ways I can understand. I've struggled with my weight all my life. And I don't want Gia to have to go through that too. But it's still hard." Charlotte sighed. "He's the one that doesn't want her eating pancakes or chips or ice cream. I'm the one that has to say no. How can I expect her to eat a fruit plate when the other kids are inhaling macaroni and cheese and chicken fingers?"

"You can't. And you shouldn't. I'm surprised at him." Allison shook her head disapprovingly, and Charlotte took that as an indication that she could divulge more.

"It's not the only thing we fight about." Allison didn't say anything. She just nodded, giving Charlotte the room to expand. "It could be anything. On any given day. I'm pretty sure he hates me at this point." She swallowed a lump in her throat.

"He doesn't hate you. Marriages are hard work. Or so I've been told."

"Did you and Jack ever fight?" Charlotte looked up, the pain evident in her eyes.

"We certainly had our disagreements."

"No, I mean did you ever completely have it out? You know, name calling and all."

"No, we didn't. Jack wasn't a name caller. I can't imagine Charlie is either."

"Ha!" Charlotte snorted. "I know he's your friend, so I shouldn't . . ."

"Anything you say to me in private is between us, Charlotte."

"It hasn't always been the way it is now. When we first met, it was like he was addicted to me. And me to him. You know when you're in that stage when just dropping the person's name into a conversation gives you a burst of adrenaline that could get you through even the worst of bad days?"

"Absolutely." Allison wrapped her towel around her again.

"That was us. Totally head over heels. He used to bring me white calla lilies from the Korean market across the street every single day. They're my favorite."

"It's always that way in the beginning."

"I know. But it doesn't always take the turn it did in our case."

"What do you think happened?"

"That's the thing. I wish I knew." A lone tear escaped from the corner of Charlotte's eye. "There wasn't one defining moment or even two. We just grew further and further apart until the distance became so great that we were practically strangers. You haven't noticed?" Charlotte could only speculate about what Charlie had already told Allison, though from the sound of it, it wasn't much, if anything at all. He was probably less intent on making Charlotte look bad than he was on ensuring he remained the good guy, at least as far as Allison was concerned.

"A little," Allison admitted. "But I never thought it was this bad."

"You have no idea."

"He's never . . ."

"Hurt me? God, no. He'd never do that. Still, words can be damaging."

"Without a doubt."

"I know I'm not perfect." She sniffed, wiping her runny nose with the corner of her towel. "I hate who I am when I'm around him. And how I treat him sometimes. There's just so much bottled-up resentment. I used to tell myself, 'Today is going to be a good day. I'm going to be really nice to Charlie when he gets home from work.' And then he'd walk in the door, already irritated about something, and my well-intentioned plan would crash and burn. I do know how to push his buttons when I want to."

"I'm so sorry. I had no idea." Allison liberated her hair from the ponytail holder, allowing it to tumble loosely across her bare shoulders.

"It's nice to have someone to talk to about it for a change."

"What about your sister?"

"My sister." Charlotte rolled her eyes. "Where do I begin?"

"She seemed really cool when we met at your house." Allison fanned herself with her hand. "Though I did notice you didn't invite *her* to come to Canyon Ranch."

"It's complicated. Elizabeth used to be very cool. In fact, that's just the word I would have used to describe her before . . ."

"Before what?"

"She lost her baby girl."

"Oh my God." Allison looked genuinely stricken. "What exactly do you mean by *lost*?"

"It's not something we talk about anymore, so . . ."

"I understand. You don't have to tell me."

"No, it's okay." Charlotte paused, feeling somewhat guilty that the tragic circumstances of Elizabeth's life were now fodder for securing her newfound bond with Allison, but she continued. "About ten years ago, Elizabeth and her ex-husband, Rob, had a little girl named Cossette."

"Pretty name."

"One night while Rob was out of town on a business trip, Elizabeth put Cossette to sleep on her back, but at some point she found a way to roll onto her stomach. She was only three months old."

"Oh no." Allison's eyes watered. "Not SIDS?"

"Yes, SIDS. You never think it'll happen to your child, you know?"

"Of course."

Charlotte could remember it like it was yesterday, though an entire decade had elapsed. They'd both been pregnant at the same time, which had been a blessing. They'd never been terribly close growing up, and for the first time, they'd had common ground to unite them. Elizabeth had been thrilled when Charlotte had told her she too had a bun in the oven. They were both destined to be young mothers, Elizabeth had said, even going so far as to suggest that they should try to coordinate any and all future pregnancies! Charlotte had been equally ecstatic, having been certain previously that she and her sister would never have a meeting of the minds on anything.

"And it wasn't her fault. It could have happened to anyone."

"Without a doubt." Allison concurred wholeheartedly.

"Unfortunately, Rob didn't see it that way. He walked out on her within two weeks."

"Just like that?"

"Just like that." Charlotte shook her head. "To this day, she hasn't heard from him. They communicated completely through lawyers. He's remarried with three kids now."

"How do you know?"

"Facebook."

"Right."

"I guess because of that or for whatever reason, Elizabeth blamed herself too. She's struggled with depression ever since. It took a huge toll on our family. That's why we all kind of tiptoe around her." Charlotte sighed. "It also factors into why Charlie and I fight so often."

"I don't get the connection."

"Elizabeth depends on me, maybe a little too much. Charlie says it's unnatural. He thinks I never say no to anything when it comes to her. Including giving her money."

"She's your *sister*."

"That's what I tell him, but—if I'm being honest—he's right in some ways. He just doesn't have the best delivery in saying so." Charlotte pulled her hair back into a bun. "The thing is, how can I not feel guilty?"

"Why guilty?"

"I had my own gorgeous, healthy baby girl one month

later. Talk about pouring salt on the wound. I may as well have ground it in."

"It's not your fault you were pregnant too."

"It doesn't matter whose fault it was. It was, as my mother put it, an unfortunate coincidence. I'm fairly certain Charlie felt the same way, even worse, liked he'd been stripped of the joys of first-time parenthood."

When Gia had been born, there'd been subdued happiness from the entire family. Elizabeth hadn't been able to come to Charlotte's baby shower, or to visit her in the hospital. She hadn't even been able to meet Gia for the first few months. Elizabeth had gotten a free pass on everything, understandably, even though it had still hurt Charlotte on some level. Gia represented the child Elizabeth had lost and everyone knew it. And, after that, Elizabeth had become sort of like Charlotte's second child. Sure, she loved her niece, but there was always an underlying sadness mixed with a measure of bitterness and entitlement.

"Can you guys go to counseling? You and Charlie . . ."

"He thinks therapists are for crazy people."

"I used to feel the same way, until Jack died. My mother literally had to drag me into my therapist's office and sit in the waiting room during the first six months of appointments, until she and I were both confident I could make it there alone."

"Can I borrow your mom?" Charlotte laughed feebly.

"Anytime. Free of charge!"

"So, not that I don't want to talk about my problems all day, but—off subject—I wanted to ask you about something."

"Okay . . ."

"Charlie and I cochair the Wincourt school fund-raiser every year. Which, you know, means he gives money and I work my ass off!"

"Right." Allison smiled.

"I have a meeting next week to discuss this year's theme, and I thought, wouldn't it be amazing if you could donate a piece of artwork that we can display and auction off at the gala, to raise money for the new baseball field and computer center."

"Hmm." Allison scrunched her nose. "I don't know. I'm kind of shy about my art. I usually work with private collectors. Although I am crafting something now. It's still early days and I'm not sure where it's going, but it could be a good fit. I think."

"Pretty please!" Charlotte clapped her hands together in a prayer position. "With a cherry on top . . . it's for a good cause."

"I'll think about it." Allison relented.

"So that's a yes?" Charlotte pressed.

"Maybe." Allison laughed. "Okay, fine, yes. But the theme better not be erotica!"

"In Wincourt?" Charlotte chirped. "I don't think you have to worry about that!"

Chapter 12

Allison had returned from Canyon Ranch radiating a refreshed and rejuvenated glow. She'd spent the majority of the week painting prolifically while Logan was at school, completing three commissioned pieces by day and pouring her heart and soul into her new—and still persistently evolving—personal creation by night. She wasn't sure if she'd have nerve enough to donate it to the annual Wincourt Gala and Fund-raiser quite yet, but one thing was for certain: it was compelling her out of bed in the wee hours. She'd find herself wide awake at three a.m. so eager to return to it—to add even the smallest touch for fear of it fleeing her mind by morning—that falling back to sleep had become delightfully unfeasible.

Finally, Allison felt inspired. And at peace, a sensation that had been impossible to achieve while living in New York City. It was hard to believe that all you had to do was drive forty-five minutes north of Manhattan to inhale unpolluted air. Or to wander for miles devoid of the deafening sirens of fire engines and police cars intruding on your meandering thoughts.

When she'd dropped Charlotte off at home and picked up Logan, he'd bounded into her arms and allowed her to give him a good, long squeeze in front of Charlie and Gia, which he rarely did now that he was a "big boy." Charlie had reported that all had gone smoothly and had reminded Allison that he was planning to stop by over the weekend to attend to a few more things around her house. Charlotte, Allison noticed, had appeared somewhat apprehensive at the prospect of them being alone together, after all that she'd confided to her on their trip. So before leaving, Allison had pulled her aside and whispered, "What happens at Canyon Ranch stays at Canyon Ranch," and then winked in an effort to comfort her. Charlotte had nodded, smiling cautiously. If she was still anxious, at least Allison had tried.

"I can't believe what great bones this place has." Charlie walked into the kitchen, wiping his forehead with the sleeve of his heather gray Camp Tawana sweatshirt. "I've always wanted to say that, by the way."

"And I can't believe you still have *that*." She motioned to his sweatshirt and handed him a tall glass of ice water with a wedge of lemon affixed to the rim. "And so casual. Who are you?"

"I'm glad you noticed." He grinned proudly. "I got it at one of the reunions and wore it just for you. And as a shout-out to Jack, of course." He motioned to the ceiling. Or heaven. Either one.

"I'm sure he heard you." She laughed, wrapping her arms

around her torso, as a shiver shimmied up her spine. "Any chance you can do something about the heat? Or lack thereof." December had been brutally cold and January wasn't promising to thaw the arctic chill.

"Unfortunately, that's beyond my skill set." He sat down on one of the barstools at the counter. "But I'll ask Charlotte who we use and get back to you with a name."

"Excellent." She opened the refrigerator. "Now, what can I offer you?"

"I'm fine." He shook his head, taking a sip of water.

"Seriously, what have you done with Charlie Crane?" She turned to face him, holding the door open to reveal shelves swollen with bundles of vibrant fruits and vegetables, thick hunks of hard and soft cheeses, and containers filled with hearty leftovers that she knew Charlie would devour greedily but gratefully if she insisted, which she would. It was their unspoken agreement. He worked. She fed. And everyone came away satisfied.

"Really, I don't want you to feel like you have to prepare a meal for me every time I come here to help you out with something. If anything, I owe *you*." He looked away momentarily.

"Why would you owe me?" She arched an eyebrow.

"It's just, you know, Jack was my friend."

"I'm sorry, we don't accept pity for payment at Chez Parker." Allison let the refrigerator door swing shut on its own.

"Oh no, I didn't mean it like that," he fumbled.

"Great. Then how does turkey meatloaf sound? Side of mashed potatoes?" She spun back around before he could answer, gathering the fixings in her arms. It was nice, after so much time had elapsed, to finally be able to cook for a man again. Sure, there was Logan's bottomless pit of a belly to satiate, but it hadn't been until recently that he'd really started appreciating her epicurean talents outside of plain pasta with butter and macaroni and cheese from the box. And still his preteen taste buds were prohibitive.

Allison would never forget the time that Logan's first-grade teacher, Ms. Kotter, had told her how he'd bragged to everyone in his class that his mother made the best cereal for breakfast. Initially she'd been mortified, swearing up and down that she'd tried to entice him with eggs, pancakes, French toast—even homemade granola—but all he'd eat was either a bagel with cream cheese or a heaping bowl of Cinnamon Toast Crunch. Ms. Kotter had giggled, informing Allison that she was probably one of the few moms at school who actually made her child breakfast and that she should take it as a compliment rather than a critique.

"You spoil me so." Charlie washed his hands in the sink next to her and sat back down. "I keep meaning to tell you what a delight it was to have Logan last weekend. He's such an amazing kid."

"Thanks. I try." She smiled, knowing full well it had little to do with her. Logan had been a unique, compassionate, and easy child practically from day one.

"Seriously, most of Gia's friends are total brats. Logan was so polite, I think I finally had to tell him he didn't need to thank me for making him an apple. I was like, 'Dude, I swear, all I did was take it out of the bowl and hand it to you.' And Gia was much better behaved when he was around. I think he shamed her into submission with his charming disposition. I wish Charlotte would take a page from your book."

"I own no responsibility for Logan's fabulousness." Allison dolloped a generous mound of mashed potatoes on top of a thick slice of meatloaf and slipped it into the microwave to heat up.

"Well, you should."

"I'm telling you. He's always been that way."

"Yea, but nurture definitely plays a big part."

"Or is it nature?"

"Can we agree it's a little of both?"

"Fine, I'm mother of the year," Allison teased and set the tantalizing plate of food in front of Charlie, who licked his lips appreciatively. "But so is Charlotte."

"She's a total pushover."

"Hey." Allison waved her index finger. "Until you've walked a mile in her shoes . . ."

"You mean the five-hundred-dollar shoes I buy every other month?"

"Very funny."

"By the way, this is ridiculously delicious." He spoke with his mouth full, and Allison caught herself before reprimanding him. "I wish Charlotte would take a page from your cookbook too!"

"Jeez, you're tough." Allison handed him a napkin, wondering if everything Charlotte had said about Charlie was true. She'd listened to her litany of gripes, thinking that, while she imagined Charlie wasn't perfect, he couldn't be anything but the easygoing guy she'd spent so many summers with and shared so many happy memories with, some bittersweet. Sure, people changed. But could his personality really be that different behind closed doors? Allison had never been anything but transparent, possibly to a fault, and Charlie hadn't given her any indication that he'd transformed so drastically. Possibly until now. "I'm sure Charlotte possesses plenty of gifts that I don't. For one, she's very intuitive. Have you noticed? She understands people. You know, how and why they operate. I, on the other hand, am typically surprised as hell when someone does something out of character."

"Interesting . . ." He didn't seem all that interested. "Well, she's also stubborn. There's more to Charlotte than meets the eye. And I'm *always* the bad guy." Charlie was visibly agitated for the first time in Allison's presence.

"Whoa, there. No one said you were the bad guy. It's not black-and-white." Allison took a step back, literally and figuratively. "In fact, I shouldn't have said anything." Could Charlotte have told Charlie that she'd divulged so many personal details about their relationship to Allison? It seemed highly unlikely, but in the heat of the moment, people often said and did things they couldn't control and would later regret.

"No, no. It's just . . . I . . . we . . . there are problems."

"I see." She nodded, quieted by the awkward position of figuring out whether to lie—to pretend that she didn't know about their deep-seated issues—or to admit that Charlotte had opened up and then some. After all, hadn't Charlie been her friend to start? But then again, so much time had passed, and for whatever reason, Allison felt a sudden allegiance to Charlotte.

"It's a lot of fighting." He put his fork down next to the unfinished slice of meatloaf, an immediate indication that he was off-kilter. "And the thing is, I work hard all day. Really hard. Then it's always a battle over something or other when I come home. Like why I didn't take the trash out that morning or why I was three minutes later than I said I was going to be. I can't be held to impossible standards. It's exhausting."

"I'm sure." She refilled his glass with more water, reminding herself that there were always three sides to every story. His. Hers. And the truth.

"I hate to say this, but when I come here it's so . . . simple. If I asked Charlotte to heat me up some food in the microwave, like you just did, she'd do it, but not without making me feel lazy or guilty."

"It's different."

"How so?"

"I'm not your wife. You don't have to live with me, and I don't have any bottled-up resentment. Plus, I don't think it's fair to compare her to anyone else."

"I'm telling you. She's not the same person when she's around other people as she is at home, with me."

"Sorry, I didn't mean to make you feel like I was defending her. Honestly, it's probably better that I stay out of it altogether." Allison attempted a compassionate smile but suspected it came off as awkward at best. The last thing she needed or wanted was to be caught in the middle of Charlie and Charlotte's rancorous game of he said, she said, or worse, become an unwilling pawn in their warfare.

"No, it's okay. I'm sorry. It gets me worked up. I didn't mean . . ." He smiled sheepishly. "It's nice to have someone to talk to about it is all. In case you haven't noticed, I don't have a lot of friends."

"Well, I guess you're in luck." She laughed. "Because neither do I!"

"It won't be long before everyone in town wants a piece of you. So I'm staking my claim now!"

"Claim staked." The doorbell rang. "That'll be my mom." Charlie stood up. "Don't worry. She'll let herself in."

"Hi, sweetheart," Allison's mother called out on cue. "I've got a car full of groceries." Allison had urged her mother, during her short time home before heading back to California, to concentrate on her friend's recovery—the sole reason for her return—but as expected she'd already been to the supermarket twice and had taken any and every opportunity to stop in to see her grandson. Poor Loretta was probably being sidelined.

"I'll go help." Charlie rushed toward the foyer and minutes later returned lugging four brimming brown paper bags with her mother trailing behind him, offering direction.

"Where can I find one of these?" Allison's mother pointed to Charlie. "What a gentleman."

"Your wish is my command." Charlie smiled beguilingly.

"Ooh, I like him even more now."

"Mom, Charlie. Charlie, Mom." Her mother's perma-grin wilted. As Allison had figured, her mother had thought—more like hoped—that Charlie was a love interest. Not a married man and the former best childhood friend of her dead husband. Even to Allison, who knew better, it sounded like a *Jerry Springer* segment.

"Nice to finally meet you."

"What? You don't remember me from Camp Tawana visiting day?" he joked.

"All I remember about Camp Tawana visiting day is her father carrying twice as many grocery bags as you just did. God forbid you kids had gone eight weeks without junk food."

"That's right!" Charlie turned to Allison. "And then, do you remember, we'd run around hiding chips and candy all evening, thinking we were smarter than the counselors?"

"How could I forget?"

"Steven Jones!" They shouted his name in unison.

Their last summer at Tawana, Steven Jones had concocted the seemingly revolutionary scheme of digging holes in the woods and burying the leftover spoils in the ground. The staff would never bother to look there, he'd maintained. And he'd been absolutely correct in that assumption. What he had not considered, however, was that the squirrels, coyotes, foxes, raccoons, and bears would. They'd had to evacuate the entire camp for twelve hours, until all of the buried food had been unearthed and the wildlife commission had declared the property kid-safe once again.

"What an idiot." Allison started unpacking a sack of potatoes.

"That idiot is now a partner at Goldman Sachs with about a billion dollars in the bank."

"Fine. So he's a rich idiot."

"Fair enough." Charlie looked at his phone. "That's weird. I have fifteen missed calls."

"Sorry, I should have told you cell reception is terrible here." She handed her mom can after can of crushed tomatoes and white beans to fill the pantry. "If you want to listen to your messages or make a call, you'll probably want to step outside on the porch." He nodded, walking in that direction, with the phone already glued to his ear.

"He's adorable." Allison's mother mouthed, even though Charlie was well out of listening range. "Too bad he's taken."

"I'm not so sure about that. The 'too bad' part, I mean."

"Oh, right. I forgot they're the ones with the issues."

"I think it's much worse than I originally thought."

"Don't get involved," her mother warned.

"I'm trying not to, but—"

"But nothing. I promise you it'll end up blowing up in your face if you do."

"Excellent, thanks."

Charlie came back into the kitchen, his brow knit into an overall vexed expression. "I've got to run."

"Is everything okay?"

"Yeah. I mean, no. Charlotte is pissed." He groaned. "I was supposed to meet them at Gia's dance recital and it totally slipped my mind."

"It happens," Allison's mom reassured him. "I can't tell you how many times Allison's father missed this or that because he was tied up at work."

"It was a pleasure to see you again, Mrs. Taylor." Charlie kissed her and then Allison on the cheek. "And thank you for saying that. I'm not sure Charlotte will be as forgiving, but I'll take my lumps on this one." He offered a feeble wave and left with his tail between his legs.

After the front door closed, Allison's mother turned to her. "What did I tell you? Stay out of it."

Chapter 13

"So did you give it to him good?" Sabrina smirked. "I would have."

"I think he knew I wasn't pleased, but he was apologetic." Charlotte uncorked a bottle of pinot grigio and pulled three white wineglasses from the uppermost kitchen cabinet, setting one each in front of Sabrina and Missy and the other at her place, standing across from them at the breakfast bar. "Although he did say something about how 'things happen' and that I should 'lighten up' after that."

The problem was, "things" always "happened" when it came to Charlie. Whether it was something as innocuous as missing Gia's dance recital or something unforgivable, like the time he'd been two hours late to his daughter's second birthday party. Charlotte, to her eventual horror, had tried to spin a sordid tale about how he'd been deathly ill from food poisoning for three days and that she wasn't sure if he was going to make it at all. The last part had been true. Unfortunately, Charlie had waltzed in just as Gia was about to blow out her candles, informing everyone he'd been stuck on the eleventh hole at Wincourt Country Club. Even worse, when some of the guests had asked him how he was feeling from the food poisoning, he'd been unwilling to corroborate Charlotte's white lie—which, as she'd pointed out later, had been to cover for him. In turn, he'd said, "Don't pretend like you did it for me." This had sent her into a tailspin. She'd accused him of not caring about his child. Of putting extracurricular activities before his flesh and blood. He'd countered, insisting that it wasn't extracurricular. That it was for business. And that Gia would never know the difference nor would she have any memory of his absence. Their heated discussion had then bourgeoned into an out-and-out crusade, in which they'd exchanged nasty invectives across a Dora the Explorer–themed table littered with juice boxes and paper plates with smeared icing over Diego's and Boots' faces.

"Well, did he at least offer an excuse?" Sabrina tapped the rim of her wineglass to indicate she wanted it filled. Charlotte complied.

"Yeah, seriously, what was so important?" Missy chimed in.

"He was helping Allison fix some things around her house."

"Uh-huh." Sabrina narrowed her eyes disapprovingly at Missy when Charlotte wasn't looking.

"What?" Charlotte didn't need to see Sabrina's expression to detect the condemnation in her tone.

"Nothing." Sabrina raised her hands in the air, palms facing outward, and turned her head to the side in mock defense. Stirring the pot came as naturally to her as putting one foot in front of the other.

"Well, it's obviously *something*. So just spit it out," Charlotte snapped, refilling the glass of wine Missy had chugged and watching as Sabrina's eyes widened in surprise.

Rarely did anyone speak to Sabrina so directly. She was accustomed to people tiptoeing around her, "yessing" her every whim, and cowering when she gave even the slightest signal that they'd done something she didn't approve of. Which could be just about anything, depending on Sabrina's volatile mood. But, now that Allison was in the picture, Charlotte was beginning to care less and less what Sabrina thought.

"Excuse me?" Sabrina scoffed, motioning to Missy for backup. "Forgive me for trying to be a friend."

"Seriously, Charlotte," Missy echoed. "Sabrina's got your best interests at heart. We all do." She nodded conclusively, nibbling the edge of a carrot stick.

Charlotte chided herself for assuming the worst. After all, until Allison had showed up, she'd had no issues with counting Sabrina and Missy as her closest friends. Hadn't she always turned a blind eye to their catty behavior in the name of self-preservation?

"Sorry, I'm just on edge lately. What were you going to say?"

"Well, correct me if I'm wrong, but Charlie has been spending a lot of time at Allison's house *fixing* things." Sabrina's face was stern. She wasn't one to forgive and forget that easily. Quite the opposite. She was probably cataloging Charlotte's outburst in the portion of her brain reserved for those who'd wronged her. "I'm just saying. I don't want you to get hurt."

"They're old friends. I don't think there's anything to worry about on that front." Charlotte waved her hand dismissively, careful to sound breezy enough that Sabrina wouldn't be roused again.

"Maybe not, but there's nothing wrong with being vigilant," Sabrina cautioned. "I'm sure you remember what happened to poor Lucy Sloane."

PoorLucySloane. It had become one word shortly after the entire school and town had gotten wind of her husband's affair with their son's kindergarten teacher, Miss Biggones a regrettably suitable name, given that she'd been a buxom blonde with assets the size of watermelons.

"I'd hardly say that's what we're dealing with here." Charlotte laughed. Although if she was being completely honest, she had been a little annoyed that Charlie had been with Allison instead of at Gia's recital. Not because it had ever crossed her mind that he'd *been with* Allison, but rather that he could have gone back to her house any day and anytime to help her with things. Of course she didn't like it when he was late or absent at all, but typically his excuses were work related. Even the day of Gia's birthday when he'd been on the golf course, it'd been with international clients.

"If you say so," Sabrina offered glibly. "But Allison is gorgeous and single. And I bet she plays the 'lonely widow' card all the time."

"For sure," Missy agreed. "Men love a damsel in distress."

"She's not in distress," Charlotte avowed, turning her back to them before making a face. "And they've known each other since they were kids. Charlie was best friends with her husband, for God's sake."

Sabrina considered this for a moment. "Exactly. There's a long history between them."

"Allison's going to be here any minute. Can we please change the subject?"

"Whatever you say." Sabrina's lips stiffened into a straight line. "Just don't come running to me when you find out they're banging each other in the janitor's closet." That was where PoorLucySloane's husband and Miss Biggones had been caught in the act.

"I won't."

"Boy, am I ready to wine and whine!" Fifteen minutes later, Allison waltzed into the kitchen, blissfully unaware of the pronounced tension in the air. "You would not *believe* the day I've had." She enveloped Charlotte in a warm embrace and handed her an aluminum-foil-covered plate. "Brownies. I got the recipe from *Cooking Light*, so you better eat them."

"Thanks." Charlotte beamed, inwardly chastising herself for permitting Sabrina to plant her wicked seeds of doubt. Of the two of them, Allison was definitely not the one she should be wary of.

"Hey, Sabrina. Hey, Missy." Allison waved and they offered taut smiles in return. "Ooh, I'll have what they're having." She pointed to their wineglasses, both of which had been refilled twice and were empty again.

"Well, don't you look darling as always," Sabrina remarked, appraising Allison's worn blue jeans and chunky cable-knit sweater.

"I was painting all day."

"Of course. Charlotte mentioned you dabble in art."

"I do a little more than dabble. It's my career."

"That was not the word I used," Charlotte mumbled, and Sabrina shot her a dirty look.

"Can one really make money at that?" Sabrina questioned. "I mean they did coin the term *starving artist* for a reason, right?" She laughed at her own joke. Or whatever it was.

"I don't know who *they* are. But yes, I can tell you first-hand that it can be quite lucrative. Like anything, it's up and down."

"Well, I wouldn't say *anything*. You don't hear people saying, 'There goes that starving lawyer,' do you?" She giggled again, visibly tipsy.

"Can I help you with something?" Allison ignored Sabrina and instead turned to Charlotte, who was busying herself by wiping down her sparkling granite countertops. Whatever it took to fly under the radar of Sabrina's second shakedown of the night. Even for Sabrina, this was rare form. Charlotte was sensing more and more that there was something about her newfound friendship with Allison that really got under Sabrina's skin.

"Oh no. I'm good, thanks. Instinct," she lied. There was nothing instinctual about cleaning up, at least not to her.

"Well, we'd love to see some of your work sometime. Isn't that right, Missy?"

"Absolutely. We'd *love* to." Missy eyed the plate of brownies Allison had baked for Charlotte. "Can I have one of those?" she asked covetously.

"I thought you were on a diet," Sabrina reprimanded Missy as Charlie would Gia.

"She said they were light."

"I think each one has about a hundred calories, though don't hold me to it, because I did adapt the recipe a bit so they wouldn't taste chalky." Allison bit into one herself.

"She bakes *and* paints. How very Renaissance woman."

"Actually, Allison agreed to let us auction off a new piece she's working on at the school gala," Charlotte announced. "I was going to bring it up at the meeting next week."

"I see." Sabrina nodded. "Not that I'm opposed, per se, but isn't that something the committee should vote on?" Sabrina and her husband, Craig—a quiet man whose sole purpose, it seemed, was to sign checks and pay credit card bills when he wasn't conciliating his wife—had been cochairs of the event for five years before handing over the reins to Charlotte and Charlie. In other words, Sabrina still thought she was in charge.

"Not really."

"Is that so?" Sabrina was visibly taken aback by Charlotte's flippant attitude, which—to Charlotte's dismay—only fueled Sabrina's fiery temperament. "I was under the impression that we operated within a democratic system. But what do I know? I was only the chair for half a decade."

"I can't imagine there's anyone who wouldn't want Allison's work represented at the gala." Charlotte intentionally put Sabrina on the spot. "I thought it would be nice to display it as part of the décor that night, and then we can also have people bid on it. Definitely for the live auction, not the silent. I'm sure it'll be a big-ticket item."

"Bigger than the use of our vacation home in Aspen for a week?"

"That's very generous of you." Charlotte hid a smile. She

refused to give Sabrina the satisfaction, since she'd never once offered to donate their ski chalet before.

"I mean, I'll have to check with Craig."

"Sure." Charlotte shrugged.

"But it's not like he'd dare say no to me."

"Who would?" Missy gobbled up the second half of her brownie and reached for another. "These are amazing."

"Thank you. They're so easy. I'll e-mail you the recipe."

"She doesn't cook." Sabrina interjected.

"That's no big deal. A child could make these."

"Oh, that's good. Miley can help you, then." Sabrina was nothing if not quick with a clever retort.

"Is Charlie around?" Allison asked, unaware of the heavy burden inherent in her question.

"Not yet." Charlotte checked her watch. It was only seven o'clock. He was unlikely to materialize for at least another hour.

"I wanted to thank him for the muffins."

"Oh?" Charlotte wasn't sure what Allison was referring to, but she noticed Sabrina perk up.

"He must have dropped by this morning before we were up. He left a big box of them in front of our door. I guess Logan had them while he was here and raved about them."

"Well, isn't that special." Sabrina appeared quite obviously satisfied to be the recipient of such a juicy nugget of information.

"I'll let him know you appreciated the gesture." Charlotte smiled broadly in order to quash Sabrina's smug mien and to conceal the truth, which was that it irritated her a little.

She couldn't remember the last time Charlie had picked

up breakfast, or any meal for that matter, for his own family. Of course, if she mentioned as much to him, he'd say something like, *Well, I know you'd never actually eat a muffin. And that's just about the last thing Gia needs.*

"Thanks." Allison skirted around the kitchen island. "I'll be right back. Today was so hectic I don't think I've gone to the bathroom since before lunch!" She hurried out of the room.

And before Charlotte could say anything in Charlie's defense, Sabrina whipped her head around. "Muffins, huh?"

Chapter 14

Allison had been both surprised and delighted to hear from Elizabeth, especially when she'd proposed a lunch date. The one and only time they'd met at Charlotte's house, there'd been an immediate chemistry—a circumstance that had visibly peeved Charlotte and subsequently fortified Elizabeth with a rise of satisfaction. Another enigmatic relationship that Allison's mother would advise her to steer clear of. But for whatever reason, Allison was drawn to these people. And not just because Charlie was an old friend. After all, if she took everything Charlie said as bible, she'd be left with little reason to associate with either Charlotte or her sister.

In a sense, she supposed, it was obvious. They were all vulnerable in such radically different yet patently tender ways, herself included. Maybe—selfishly speaking—investing in their pain was a means of easing her own. Or maybe it was just morbid curiosity. Kind of like watching a train wreck in progress and knowing that if you tried to help, you'd risk being run over, flattened like a pancake on the proverbial track to enduring desolation.

Allison had suggested DJ Gourmet as their meeting spot. For one, the food was the best in town. And, if she was being honest, she looked forward to seeing Dempsey. This morning she'd brushed a hint of blush across the apples of her cheeks, had smeared her naturally pink lips with a trace of shimmery gloss, and had stroked her eyelashes with two coats of clear mascara, curling them in advance. *There's nothing wrong with wearing a little makeup every now and then.* She could hear her mother's urging refrain buzzing in her ear as she opted not to prime her skin with a layer of opaque foundation. She didn't want him to think she was trying too hard, because—the truth was—she had no idea if she wanted to be trying at all. And even if she did, what she was trying for?

What she did know was that Dempsey made her feel giddy in a way she hadn't since *before*. Not just because he was weak-in-the-knees sexy. Actually, that wasn't it at all. It had more to do with the way he looked at her and spoke to her, like he valued every second of time she was willing to afford him, which hadn't been much. *Baby steps,* she told herself, despite the fact that she was still learning to crawl.

A year after Jack died, the first wedding invitation had arrived. But it wasn't any old invitation. It was from a woman she'd met through a mutual friend. A woman who, like Allison, had lost her husband in the bus accident. Only, was she like her? Because if that was the case, as Allison had thought it was, then she wouldn't have been remarrying *twelve months* after her husband had died. In a torrent of anger, Allison had shredded the thick, embellished ivory stock with her own hands, allowing a rainstorm of paper to trickle down to the carpet, where she'd left it until she'd summoned enough strength to wield her trusty Dustbuster. And just like that the pieces had been gone, as had any thought of the wedding and the friendship, if you could have called it that in the first place. She'd never bothered to RSVP, which under normal circumstances would have been uncharacteristic. But at the time, Allison had been fueled with rage, disappointment, perhaps even envy, though she'd considered that only in hindsight. How *dare* this woman move on with her life when Allison had barely been able to move from pajamas to blue jeans without racing home to change as soon as she was finished with whatever forced activity she'd reluctantly engaged in? How *dare* she walk down the aisle in church, in front of God and hundreds of friends and family, when Allison couldn't make it down the aisle of the supermarket, in front of perfect strangers, without bursting into tears because she'd caught sight of Jack's favorite chocolate chip cookies out of the corner of her eye? It had felt like the worst kind of betrayal.

The thing was, there had been other weddings to follow. Some in quick succession, some three or four years later. She'd read about them in the newspaper or heard about them through one of the mothers at Logan's nursery school, who'd assumed she'd want to be privy to anything and everything to do with that fateful day. How wrong they'd been. What she'd wanted was to forget. To erase it from her memory altogether. To pretend that Jack had passed away peacefully in his sleep, blissfully unaware that he was about to be swallowed by a ball of fire as the bus he was riding in plunged off a bridge and came crashing to the ground in a heap of metal.

Why was it, then, that eleven years later, when most of these women had new families—with multiple children unrelated to their perished husbands—Allison still couldn't get through a single night without instinctively reaching over to Jack's side of the bed, only to endure a lesser, but still very tangible, pang of loss? If anyone could understand, it would be Elizabeth. While Jack's death had felt insurmountable in those first days, weeks, and months *after*, Allison couldn't fathom the agony inherent in losing a child. Without Logan, she was certain her life would be meaningless. There'd be no reason to get out of bed in the morning, to put one foot in front of the other. Because where would there be to go? Perhaps Elizabeth had seen a kindred spirit in Allison, as she had in her.

"Hey, pretty lady!" Elizabeth appeared with a healthy flush on her face, her auburn hair swept back into a loose chignon. It looked like she too had applied a little makeup in advance of their meeting, undoubtedly for a different reason.

"Hey!" Allison stood up, tucking the gardening book she'd been reading back into her purse. It was never too soon to start planning. "Wow, you look nice."

"Job interview." They sat down across from each other. "Don't tell Charlotte."

"Why?" Allison crossed her legs, leaning forward so the couple next to them couldn't eavesdrop. The close proximity of the tables was the only downside to DJ Gourmet's layout, but there was no avoiding it. While the space as a whole wasn't tight, there was always a line out the door in the mornings and at lunchtime. "That sounds like something she'd be happy about."

"Oh, for sure, but she'd also nudge me about it every five

minutes." Elizabeth glanced at the oversized chalkboard above the prepared-food case. "What's good here?"

"*Everything.*" Allison had already decided on the Asian chicken salad. Or was it the grilled cheese with oozing fontina and apples pressed between two thick slices of peasant bread? "Numbers three and nine are my favorites." Jack would have offered to share, even if neither of them had been his first choice.

"Yum. Wanna split those?" A smile reached Elizabeth's probing blue eyes, as if she'd read Allison's mind and she knew it.

"Yeah, I do!"

"I like a woman who enjoys her food. In case you haven't noticed, my sister eats like a rabbit."

"I have. She said it's hard for her to stay slim. A problem I, fortunately, do not have."

"Same here." Elizabeth looked around for a waitress. "Do they come take our order?"

"Oh, you've *never* been here."

"I don't think so. I live on the other side of town. Maybe once for a muffin or something."

"You have to go up to the counter and then they bring it to the table when it's ready." Allison pushed her chair back. "I'll go."

"Don't worry about it. I got it." Elizabeth hopped up. "Drink?"

"Just water."

"Pellegrino?"

"Nah, the good old-fashioned tap variety is fine."

"*Thank you.* I honestly don't understand why people pay

five dollars for bubbles." Elizabeth stalked toward the counter in her scuffed black leather boots, which didn't look entirely appropriate for a job interview, unless she was applying to be a hooker, but Allison decided to keep her opinion to herself. She and Elizabeth weren't there yet.

Allison thought wistfully about the time in college when her best friend, Melanie, had come out of the closet—literally, not figuratively—dressed in the most hideous, mismatched getup she'd ever seen. Allison hadn't said a word. She'd just pointed back toward the closet, belly laughing and shaking her head, while Melanie had tilted hers downward in mock shame. She'd resurfaced seconds later in plain blue jeans and a black sweater. There were just certain relationships where verbalizations weren't necessary. A simple look or motion could say it all. Allison missed that.

"Success?" She swiveled in her chair as Elizabeth approached the table.

"Um, yeah, but—excuse me—who is the fucking hot-as-hell guy standing between the cakes and the coffee machine? You know, the one who looks like Johnny Depp post–*21 Jump Street*. He's been ogling you like a dog in heat and you're a fine piece of meat."

"That's the first time I've heard that one." Allison laughed.

"You like it? I just made it up." Elizabeth grinned complacently. "But seriously, do you know him? Because if not, you should."

"I do, actually. We went to high school together."

"And?"

"And nothing. We barely knew each other. We still don't. He seems nice. I mean, it's not like there's anything going on . . . or . . . that I want anything to be, you know, whatever. . . ." Allison stumbled through her weedy explanation, which she could tell Elizabeth wasn't buying.

"Uh-huh." Elizabeth smirked.

"Enough about me. Tell me about your interview," Allison deflected as a neatly dressed twentysomething woman with a pleasant smile diverting attention from her crooked teeth appeared with two overflowing plates of food and a side order of frizzled onion straws.

"That was fast!" Elizabeth motioned to the onion straws. "But I don't think we ordered those."

"Compliments of Mr. James."

"Thank you." Allison nodded, catching sight of a grinning Dempsey in her peripheral vision. She'd swooned over them last time she was in with her mom and had begged for the recipe.

"You are *totally* blushing." Elizabeth waved at Dempsey, who saluted in return.

"You were going to tell me about the interview," Allison reminded her.

"I was?" Elizabeth feigned ignorance. "Okay, fine. It's just a temp firm, but they send people out for some good stuff. Short-term, no more than six months at a time. Still, it beats working as a salesgirl at the Posh Teen. Those kids are such entitled little brats."

"That sounds promising." Allison took a sip of water, nearly choking on a partially melted ice cube as a hauntingly familiar figure walked through the front door of the café. At first she couldn't place his face, but then it hit her like a frying pan to the skull. Instinctively, she dipped her head toward the ground, praying he wouldn't spot her and, if he did, that he wouldn't recognize her. No such luck.

"Well, look who we have here," Buck Baird bellowed, sauntering over to her table, a grossly bloated version of the rakishly handsome star of Wincourt High School's undefeated soccer team. He'd scored so many goals his freshman season that he'd been labeled "Lucky Bucky" from then on. The name had transcended his good fortune on the field—one of the main reasons Allison had resisted his persistent overtures. That and the fact that he'd been something of a meathead. A hot meathead, but still.

The summer after their sophomore year, she'd finally relented, agreeing to one date, for lack of anything better to do on a random Saturday night. He'd driven her, in his father's beat-up Cadillac—which had reeked of chewing tobacco, Old Spice cologne, and dark rum in one pungent brew—to Hideaway Hill, where he'd expected to feel up *her* hills. To his obvious disappointment they'd been more like bug bites. He'd tried to go further. "The kids" were calling it third base at the time, but she'd resisted his advances. If there'd been less of a crowd, he might have been more forceful. She could tell he had it in him, especially when he was further motivated by a very large boner pressing against his too-tight Levi's. Instead, he'd grumbled something about blue balls and had taken her directly home without even the remotest suggestion of food or drink. Some date.

Not that she'd cared. She'd been overcome with relief the minute she'd slammed the dented Caddy door behind her and run into her house without looking back. What she hadn't expected was that he'd intended on having a second "date," one that would entail her putting out. Everything. When she'd graciously declined his calls and dodged him in the hallways at school the following year, he'd promptly spread the rumor that she was a slut who'd "jumped him like a car battery." His words, not hers. But she'd never forget them. How could she when they'd been etched into the door of every bathroom stall in Tillingheimer Hall?

"Hi, Buck. How are you?" Allison tried to give Elizabeth a warning look, but Buck's swollen brown eyes were fixed on hers.

"Not as good as you, apparently." She watched as he took stock of her merchandise like the horny old man he probably was. Even though they were the same age, he looked to be about ten years her senior, at least.

"I'm just in the middle of a meeting with my colleague, here." She motioned to Elizabeth, who'd caught on without needing a signal.

"That's right. Important business."

"You wouldn't be blowing me off, now, would you?" His voice grew louder as Dempsey sprinted to Allison's side.

"I hope you're not bothering these ladies, Buck." Dempsey's abundant wavy brown mane and invitingly fit form only served to highlight Buck's receding hairline and distended beer gut.

"Buzz off, Dempsey." He shooed him away with a beefy hand, refusing to divert his gaze from Allison. "I'm not bothering you, am I?" He smiled at her roguishly.

"Um, I . . . ," Allison stammered awkwardly.

"We did say we're in the middle of a meeting. So maybe you can come back another time?" Elizabeth offered. "Or preferably not."

"This one's a spark plug. I like that. Kind of like you, Ali." He reached out to stroke her shoulder and Allison recoiled.

"Okay, that's enough. I'm going to ask you to leave." Dempsey put a hand on Buck's back to guide him toward the door.

"Dude, get the fuck off me." He shoved Dempsey.

"I'm not going to ask you again." Dempsey's voice was even as he positioned himself between Buck and Allison.

"What? Are you two some kind of item now?" He glared at Allison. "You know she's a little whore, right?" Elizabeth's hand went to her open mouth as Allison's eyes filled with hot, bulbous tears and her heart beat rampantly against her chest.

"Aaaaand . . . we're done. If you don't leave now, I'll remove you myself." Dempsey's face was red and his jaw tight.

"As if you could." Buck unleashed a raspy chortle, which turned into a coughing fit. "You may think she's a good girl now, but Buck knows better. Isn't that right, Ali?"

Allison flinched as a repulsed expression registered on Dempsey's face. What if he believed Buck? He'd probably read it on the bathroom wall when they were in high school too. Who hadn't?

"Let's go." And with that, Dempsey took hold of Buck's arms in a death grip and dragged him away by force.

When he returned moments later, Allison and Elizabeth had already slipped out the back.

Chapter 15

Charlotte dashed around her bedroom frantically, back and forth from her gargantuan walk-in closet to her pristinely adorned king-sized bed, tossing shirts, shorts, pants, and various pairs of shoes—flip-flops, wedges, even high heels—into her oversized Louis Vuitton suitcase. Next it was into the bathroom for an array of essential toiletries, her hair dryer, Velcro rollers, and a gel eye mask for the plane ride. After that, she'd select jewelry and, finally, throw in the extras, like chargers for her cell phone and iPad, along with a stack of fashion magazines to peruse on the beach. If they ever got to the beach.

Despite having planned the trip to visit her parents in Florida more than three weeks earlier, with the best intentions of packing in advance, Charlotte had been consumed by preparations for the Wincourt school fund-raiser in addition to her usual appointments and errands. It was hard to understand how anyone had the time to commit to a real job, especially without help. So often she found herself running around like a chicken with its head cut off, until she glanced at the clock, only to realize it was already time to pick up Gia from school.

Gia. Sigh. She'd wailed this morning when Layla had taken her for a playdate at her friend Marcy's house, armed with the knowledge that Charlotte would be gone by the time she returned home. Even though, most often, it felt like Gia could give or take her in favor of a television show or trip to the ice-cream shop, Charlotte knew that her daughter needed her. That, at the end of the day, being with Mommy was always Gia's first choice. She loved Charlie, sure. Her sweet little face always lit up when he entered the room; she craved his undivided attention, which she rarely got. Not that anyone did. He could certainly be an adoring father when he wanted to be, when he had a spare hour or two to play dolls with her or to chase her around their three-acre property, causing Gia to giggle boisterously as Charlie called out, "I'm gonna get you!" Those were the moments when Charlotte would stand at the door to the playroom or crack a window in the kitchen so she could watch them play and hear the infectious sounds of a daughter who worshipped her daddy, even though he didn't necessarily comprehend the extent of it.

"Aren't you only going for three days?" Charlie walked into the bedroom, still in his pajamas, with his tortoiseshell reading glasses perched on his nose and his strawberry blond hair ruffled. She'd always liked the way he looked in glasses. Something about it turned her on.

"Yup." Charlotte spoke in a clipped tone. She was still irritated that he'd come home late the previous night, especially since she'd told him she needed to pack without having to deal with Gia putting her two cents in. He'd blamed it on a business call. Of course.

"Seems like a lot of stuff." He sat down on the bed, leaning back against the pillows and lifting his feet up too. "I doubt you'll need any dresses to sit around your parents' condo."

"You're on my Loro Piana cardigan." Charlotte tugged it out from under his leg. "Anyway, since when did you become the authority on fashion?"

"I'm just saying." He lifted his hands into a defensive pose. "I know you don't like to carry a heavy bag through the airport. That's all."

"Well, it's a good thing it has wheels, then." She didn't bother to look at him.

"Are you pissed at me?"

"No." *Yes.*

"Well, you seem it." For a fleeting moment she was flattered that he'd noticed.

"I'd rather not get into it now," Charlotte said dismissively, rolling her underwear into cylinders so she could arrange it around the perimeter of the suitcase. She had a system for this, as she did for everything else.

Charlie had once told her he was pretty sure she suffered from obsessive compulsive disorder. She'd been instantly offended, recalling an episode of *Oprah* that covered OCD. One segment had featured a woman who couldn't leave her house without driving around the block a zillion times to check and recheck that she'd closed the garage door. The next segment had been about a man who did everything in threes. If he tapped his pencil on his desk, he had to tap it two more times. If he smiled at a passerby—guess what? Another smile, smile. So she liked everything to be in its place. What was the big deal about that? It was better than being a slob.

"There is an 'it,' then." He exhaled and folded his arms behind his head.

"If you must know, I didn't appreciate the fact that you waltzed in at eight o'clock last night when I'd specifically told you I wanted time to pack without Gia harassing me."

"I'm sorry, but I couldn't get out of work. You know I would have been here if I could have been." His mea culpa sounded authentic, but Charlotte knew better.

"Do I?" She heard her own acerbic tone but couldn't manage to curtail it. Anyway, what was the point? They'd had this same fight over and over through the years, and it always ended the same way. With Charlie walking away and Charlotte left stewing.

"From the sound of it, I guess not."

"I don't know what to tell you." She shrugged.

"Charlotte, I don't think you comprehend that I can't just get up from my desk and walk out of a meeting because you need peace and quiet to put some clothing in a bag. It's not like you're jaunting off to Paris. You're going to Daytona Beach to care for your sick parents. What could you possibly need beyond the basics?"

It had actually been Charlie who'd taught her how to pack like a pro. He'd been on so many business trips that he'd mastered the art. She'd been in awe as he'd pointed to a heaping pile of clothing and then a small carry-on bag and said, with a knowing smile creeping from his lips to his twinkling green eyes, *Bet you don't believe I can get all that in there.* She hadn't. But he had. He'd showed her how to roll her socks and smaller items to stuff into shoes and even bra cups—he'd been excited to discover that option, having never traveled with bras himself. He'd watched and advised patiently as she'd learned how to stack her sweaters, skirts, shirts, and pants, alternating them like blocks in a game of Jenga. Charlotte had delighted in seeing how satisfied he was with her progress. After that they'd pushed the suitcase onto the floor and made love for what had seemed like an eternity.

"I wouldn't expect you to understand."

"Fine. You know what? If you want to stay annoyed, there's nothing I can do about it." He stood up. "I'm going to make some breakfast."

"Why not? I just spent twenty minutes cleaning the kitchen."

"What? I'm not allowed to eat a meal in my own house?"

"I didn't say that."

"You might as well have." Charlie marched over to his own walk-in closet, pulled a sweatshirt over his head, and slipped into a pair of boat shoes. "I'm going out for a bagel."

"Fine." Running away was always his answer. "Will I see you before I go?"

"Do you want to?"

"Whatever."

"Okay, Charlotte." He stopped to give her a kiss on the cheek. "Have a safe flight."

"Is this seat sticky?" Charlotte pressed her fingers against the cheap leather. "This seat *is* sticky. Excuse me? Excuse me?" Her voice grew louder and more agitated as she tried to summon one of the flight attendants, who was busy hoisting another passenger's suitcase into the overhead compartment.

"Would you shush? People are staring at us." Elizabeth pushed past Charlotte. "I'll sit there. You take the aisle."

"I don't like the aisle. I need to be able to see out the window during takeoff and landing. You know that."

"Well, would you rather sit by the window in the sticky seat or in the nonsticky aisle seat? Your call." Elizabeth stood hunched over, waiting for Charlotte to make a decision, until she sat down, resigning herself to a viewless ride. "What the hell has gotten into you today?"

"What's that supposed to mean?" Charlotte snapped. Fine, so she was a little cranky. Who wouldn't be after the morning she'd had?

Shortly after she'd sparred with Charlie, he'd returned with a bagel for himself and one for her. When she'd nearly bitten his head off, insisting that if he really knew her he'd be well aware of the fact that she hadn't eaten a bagel since 1998, he'd stalked out of the room, mumbling expletives under his breath: *You try to fucking do something nice for someone . . . and that's what you fucking get.*

A few minutes later, Gia had come home from her playdate prematurely, citing a sour stomach, which she'd suggested might feel better if Charlotte didn't go on her trip. Layla had apologized profusely, swearing up and down that she'd had no other choice and that she'd even driven around the block five or six times in the hopes that Charlotte would have left already. This had impelled Charlotte to glance at

the clock, only to realize she was running twenty-five minutes behind schedule. And she did not like being late. It only
made her more anxious than she normally was. On the car
ride to the airport, Charlotte had gazed out the window at
nothing, while Elizabeth had prattled on and on about this
or that. Some new job Nick got. The fact that they were
thinking about getting a puppy. How she was pretty sure
she'd gotten food poisoning from the new Indian place in
town. All Charlotte had been able to do was sit quietly, looping the events of the morning in her head as her blood pressure soared.

Once they'd finally reached the Delta terminal—there'd
been hideous traffic on I-95—Charlotte had felt like a caged
animal, ready to leap on anyone who so much as looked at
her the wrong way. Which they had. Starting with the attendant at curbside check-in. Then it had been the pleasant lady
behind the ticket counter who'd committed the cardinal sin
of forgetting that they'd been upgraded to first class. Lastly,
Charlotte had glared at an innocent elderly woman who'd
taken too much time in the bathroom stall.

"You've been a crazy bitch since you picked me up."

"Bad morning." Charlotte closed her tired eyes and opened
them to the same reality.

"Do you want to talk about it?" Elizabeth reached for the
copy of *SkyMall* in the back pocket of the seat in front of her
and started leafing through the pages aimlessly.

"Not really." Charlotte summoned the same flight attendant who'd ignored her before. "Can I please have some
water?" Her mouth was parched and she could feel a sting-
ing in the cavern of her throat. Just what she needed now

was to get sick on top of everything else. Though the irony of falling ill on the way to take care of her already ill parents wasn't lost on her. In fact, it wasn't an altogether bad idea. She could lie in bed all day with no one to badger her with needs, wants, or have-to-haves. And Elizabeth would be forced to shoulder the burden of caring for all three of them. *Right*.

"Okay, well, I'm all ears if you want to vent."

"You wouldn't understand." Charlotte shook her head, refusing to let her sister see how upset she really was. Even if she tried to explain it, it wouldn't make sense. The events of the morning weren't nearly enough to drive anyone to the edge. But the cumulative effort of years' worth of power struggles was.

She'd never forget her first fight with Charlie. It had been both unexpected and unsettling. They'd bickered over a rug she'd bought for the living room of their first apartment in the Chelsea neighborhood of Manhattan. Charlotte had thought it was spectacular in all its glory of vibrant blues and greens with a floral pattern around the border. She'd been so excited to show it to him when he got home from work. Charlie had hated it. But that wasn't what had set him off. Rather, it had been the hefty price tag. Charlotte had relied on ignorance as her defense. How was she supposed to know it wasn't a fair price for a quality rug? The salesperson at ABC Carpet had told her it was a steal. Charlie had questioned how she could be so gullible and had called her irresponsible when she'd said it was nonreturnable. Charlotte had cried. Charlie had comforted her and apologized for being "mean," as she'd called him. And that had been that. The wound had been opened and closed in the matter of a half hour. The wounds had continued to open and close with every further dispute until—at some point—they'd ceased being mended. Now all Charlie had to do was sprinkle in some salt to achieve the desired effect.

"Whatever." Elizabeth continued flipping through the magazine, pausing to admire a fluffy, midnight blue dog bed, monogrammed in white with the name Prince. "So I had lunch with Allison a couple of weeks ago."

"What?" Charlotte came to attention.

"Yeah, she took me to this great gourmet place in town. She's awesome." Charlotte had noticed that Elizabeth and Allison had hit it off at her house and it had annoyed her at the time. But she'd hardly expected her sister to pursue the relationship. Elizabeth didn't pursue anything, much less anyone, Charlotte chose to associate with. She wondered who'd initiated the lunch. Probably Elizabeth. Just to get under her skin. Still, it was throwing her off balance to know that Allison actually enjoyed her sister's company.

"I know. She's *my* friend, remember?"

"Wasn't she kind of Charlie's friend first?"

"What's the difference? Can't you just—" Charlotte stopped herself, realizing she was about to come off sounding like a ten-year-old, if she hadn't already.

"Can't I just what?" Elizabeth knew exactly how to press her buttons.

"Nothing."

"Just say it, Charlotte."

"Can't you just find your own friends to hang out with? You've never been interested in any of mine before."

"Who? Sabrina and Missy? No mystery there."

"What's wrong with Sabrina and Missy?" Charlotte didn't really need the answer.

"Let's see. Where should I begin?"

"Forget I asked."

"Good idea."

"I'm going to take a short nap," Charlotte said, eager to squelch the conversation. She closed her eyes again, this time drifting off into a restless sleep.

The next thing she heard was the pilot's voice booming over the intercom. "Folks, I'd like to welcome you to the Sunshine State. It's seventy-four degrees and partly cloudy. Thanks for flying with us today, and don't forget to take your belongings. Cheers!"

Here we go, she thought, glancing over at a peacefully sleeping Elizabeth. And for the first time in as long as she could remember, Charlotte felt a twinge of genuine affection.

Chapter 16

"Hi. I'm here to pick up an order. The name is Parker." Allison smiled politely at the young man behind the counter, craning her neck to see whether Dempsey was working in the open kitchen toward the back of the shop.

She hadn't seen or spoken to him in the two weeks since her confrontation with Buck. But when she'd arrived home that evening, on the heels of a long afternoon of running unwelcome errands—her mind still whirring and her heart still hammering—there'd been a spectacular bouquet of white dendrobium orchids spraying from the top of a hand-painted clay vase sitting on her doorstep. The note had read:

> *A,*
> *I'm so sorry about today. Please come back soon.*
> *—D*

She'd beamed and then scolded herself for having worried all day about what Dempsey must think of her. After she and Elizabeth had slipped out the service exit into the rear parking lot of DJ Gourmet, Elizabeth had stopped Allison, who was practically hyperventilating by that point, and assured her that Dempsey wouldn't believe a word of what Buck had said. She'd insisted that Dempsey was one of the good ones. She could tell. And anyway, who in their right mind would listen to a bonehead like Buck? Still, Allison hadn't been entirely convinced. Plus, what about the twenty or so other people who'd been members of the captive audience? They could have been mothers at Logan's school or friends of her own mother and father. Certainly, Allison was no stranger to being a spectacle—the tragic widow—but she wasn't accustomed to being the target of such blatant profanation.

Elizabeth had called her that night to check in, and her empathetic posture had surprised Allison yet again, based on what she'd heard about Elizabeth from Charlotte and Charlie, who relied on adjectives such as *selfish*, *bratty*, *lazy*, and *inept* when describing her. It was a strange thing about this town, or at least this group of people she'd fallen in with. No one was what they seemed or what they were supposed to be, not as far as Allison could tell. Again she thought about her best friend, Melanie, and their college days—a time that was so much simpler in the way of making friends and forging meaningful relationships. She'd never questioned ulterior motives or wondered if she was being manipulated like a pawn on a suburban chessboard.

"Hey, you." Dempsey came up behind her, squeezing her shoulder gently and folding her into a hug when she turned to face him. "I was wondering when I'd see you again."

"Sorry. I guess I was a little gun-shy about coming back here so soon. Seeing Buck again isn't exactly at the top of my wish list."

"Don't worry about that." Dempsey led her to a private table tucked into the hindmost corner of the café area. "I took care of Buck. He won't be bothering you anymore."

"My hero." She pressed her hands to her heart and giggled softly. "Seriously, though, thank you so much for the stunning flowers. You really shouldn't have."

"Why not?" He leaned toward her, so close she could smell his spicy aftershave.

"I don't know. I mean, I was the one responsible for causing a scene in your place of business."

"I'd hardly say you were to blame. That guy is a total schmuck. Always has been, always will be. Anyway, I don't need a reason to send you flowers. I saw them and I thought of you."

"Well, thank you again. Orchids are my favorite." Allison could feel herself blushing.

"Mine too."

"About Buck."

"I'd rather not talk about him anymore. He's a waste of breathing air."

"I couldn't agree more, but I'd really like to clear something up."

"Okay." Dempsey nodded and a shock of wavy brown hair dusted the lid of one brilliant blue eye.

"I didn't do any of the things he said. I never even slept with him. In fact, we didn't go any further than second base." Allison's expression was serious.

"Not second base!" Dempsey's face broke into a smile and he pulled Allison's hand toward him, covering it with his own. "If you think for a minute that I believed anything that asshole said, you couldn't be more wrong. In case you haven't noticed, Ali, I like you. I want to get to know you better. But I know you well enough already to realize you're not the kind of person, nor were you ever, who would go past *second base* with Buck Baird. I mean, then he'd really deserve to be called Lucky Bucky."

"Very funny." She smirked, feeling a little flutter in her heart. He liked her. "Moving on."

"Yes, moving on for sure." He sat back in his chair. "So your mom told me you're an artist?"

"I am."

"What kind of stuff?"

"Oil, acrylic, watercolor, pastel. I've even been known to do some sculpting when I'm feeling particularly creative. I try not to limit myself."

"Amazing." His gaze was fixed on her, so intently that even the vociferous din and distracting bustle of the surrounding patrons presented futile competition.

"Speaking of sculpting, I was going to ask you where you got that beautiful vase for the orchids."

"I thought you'd like that." He smiled, motioning subtly to someone over her shoulder, who approached the table with two cappuccinos and a plate of fresh-from-the-oven shortbread cookies. "A good friend of mine, Priscilla Alexander, owns a gallery in town. On Egg Hill Road. She hosts unbelievable exhibitions, some traditional, others on the cutting-edge side. All different mediums and materials. I'd love to introduce the two of you."

"I've driven past there, but I've never had a spare minute to stop in. I'd love to meet Priscilla."

"Cool. I'll set it up. Do you display your work?"

"Not really. I did when I was first starting out, but then I had so much interest from private collectors and, you know, after my husband passed away, it was easier to remain behind the scenes."

"Sure." He nodded and Allison chastised herself for mentioning Jack. No better way to kill the mood. "So what's with the five brimming bags I've got with your name on them? Are you having a party you didn't invite me to?" He tilted his head and she had to stop herself from reaching out and brushing his cheek with her fingers. Anyone else would have stumbled at the mention of her dead husband. Or at the very least said something excruciatingly awkward. But it hadn't even fazed Dempsey.

"I almost forgot about those! I'm making dinner for a friend."

"She's in for a treat."

"Actually, it's a he."

"Ah." His smile drooped into a frown.

"Oh no. It's nothing like that. He's an old friend from childhood. And he's married. His wife is also a friend. She had to go visit her parents in Florida and he's helped me so much with getting things in order around my house that I promised I'd cook dinner for him. And his daughter, Gia, who's in Logan's class."

"Then I can still ask you to have a drink with me next Saturday? Nothing fancy. I know a great wine bar on the outskirts of town."

"Um . . ." Allison froze, searching her brain for a reasonable out. But there wasn't one. She couldn't go on a date. She wanted to. Maybe. Or not. No, no. Definitely not. "The thing is, I'm not sure—it's just that . . ."

"You don't like wine?"

"No, that's not it."

"You don't like irresistible men?"

"No . . . that's not it."

"I understand. Say no more."

"I'm sorry." Allison looked down. What was wrong with her? Why was she incapable of accepting a perfectly desirable invitation from a perfectly gorgeous guy?

"Don't apologize." He stood up, resting his hand on her arm. "You don't ever have to apologize to me."

"Thank you."

"I'll go get your stuff." He walked toward the kitchen and Allison was left to marinate in humiliation. She could still change her mind. But it wouldn't be fair. To herself or to him.

"Hi, Allison." Sabrina appeared, standing over her, almost as if her timing had been choreographed.

"Hi, Sabrina." Allison forced a half smile.

"So what brings you to this fine establishment? The blueberry muffins are to die for!"

"Just picking up some things for dinner." Dempsey returned with his arms full. "Thank you." Their eyes met.

"I'll go grab the rest." He set the bags down at her feet.

"Must be some dinner." Sabrina winked at Dempsey while trying to sneak a peek at Allison's groceries. "Who's the lucky guest?"

"Charlie."

"Is that so?" Sabrina's lips curled into a malevolent grin. "I guess while the cat's away . . ."

"What?"

"Well, you know what they say—the mice will play!" She smirked. "Obviously, I'm joking."

"I'm sorry, I didn't hear you. . . ." Allison wasn't paying any attention to Sabrina. All she could think about was how she'd wrecked everything with Dempsey. Not that there was anything to wreck. Nor would there be now. Thanks to her.

"Oh, nothing." Sabrina sniffed. "Don't mind me. Enjoy your dinner. Tell Charlie I say hello."

"Right, thanks." Allison nodded absently.

And just like that, Sabrina turned on her stiletto heels and stalked off toward the bakery section, where she could be heard complaining that there were no more blueberry muffins and interrogating the counter attendant about when a fresh batch would be ready. Allison couldn't help but wonder what had made Sabrina the way she was. In part, she felt sorry for her. As her mother had always told her, people who take pleasure in making others miserable are usually miserable themselves. But what did Sabrina have to be miserable about? She had an attentive husband—or so she said—a smart and beautiful daughter, and enough financial security to never have to work a day in her life. Allison shook her head as Sabrina's fever pitch escalated. Charlotte was better than that, better than her. She just hadn't fully realized it yet.

"That was unbelievable. *You* are unbelievable. Those potatoes were out of this world." Charlie sat back on the couch in Allison's family room, rubbing his stomach. "I may never eat again, but if that was my last meal, I'll be a happy man." He motioned to the place next to him.

"I'm so glad you enjoyed it, but there'll be no sitting for me. Too much of a mess in the kitchen."

"Don't worry about it."

"Easy for you to say."

"No, I mean, don't worry about it, because it's done."

"Yeah, right." Allison looked at him quizzically.

"I'm serious. While you were up tucking the kids in, I cleaned everything up. Go check if you don't believe me."

"That's amazing. Thank you."

"Are you kidding? It was the least I could do." He rolled his damp sleeves down, buttoning them at the wrist. "See, proof of my labor. Plus, anyone who can get Gia to sleep within twenty minutes deserves a gold medal."

"Well, I can't promise they're asleep." Allison sat down next to him, folding her legs underneath her. "Logan's in his bed and she's in the trundle. There are flashlights and books involved."

"They're quiet. That's a feat in and of itself. You have no idea what bedtime is like at our house."

"She's welcome to stay and I'll drop her off in the morning."

"That's very nice of you, but you also have no idea what mornings with Gia are like."

"I guess I hit the jackpot with my baby."

"You could say that." Charlie motioned to the dendrobium orchids from Dempsey. "Those are nice. Secret admirer?"

"Not so secret."

"Oh." Charlie's expression changed. "I was kidding, actually. Are you . . . seeing someone?"

"No, nothing like that."

"Good," he answered quickly. "I mean, you know, I feel I should vet anyone who wants to date you."

"Is that so?"

"Absolutely. If Jack can't do it himself, I figure I'm the next best thing in the way of looking out for you."

"Well, you're too sweet. But I'm a big girl. Anyway, I'm not ready." Allison coiled a section of hair around her index finger.

"If you're not ready, then you shouldn't push yourself." He nodded confidently, as he always did. Allison wondered what it would be like to always feel so sure of yourself.

"*Thank you.* I think you're the first person who's said that to me. I swear, everyone's a matchmaker these days, including my own mother. It's remarkable how people always think they know what's best for you. Better than you know for yourself."

"I know the feeling." Charlie's brow knit.

"Let me guess. Charlotte?"

"Ding-ding-ding!" He smiled halfheartedly, and then his face turned thoughtful again. "Listen, speaking of Charlotte, there's something I've been meaning to talk to you about, but I didn't want to discuss it in front of the kids at dinner."

"Okay . . ." Allison wasn't sure what to expect. She'd made a promise to herself and to her mother not to get swept up in their marital problems, especially after the previous conversation she'd had with Charlie. And, anyway, she wasn't exactly the authority on maintaining long-term relationships.

"When I was here last time, I think I came off too brusquely."

"You were certainly passionate."

"Right." He fidgeted with his watch, a hulking gold Rolex with a face practically the size of a wall clock and hands almost as large as her fingers. It was a miracle his arm wasn't weighed down to the floor like a brick. What was it with men and watches? They could never be too big and a guy could never have too many, kind of like diamonds for women. "So I kind of want to explain myself, if that's okay with you." He looked up at her for permission to continue.

"Charlie, you don't owe me anything. And you definitely don't have to explain yourself to me."

"I know, but I want to."

"Okay. I'm all ears." *Please don't start bashing Charlotte.*

"What Charlotte and I have is complicated. There was a time when I was madly in love with her." He cleared his throat. "I still love her very much. She's a good person, Ali."

"You don't have to tell me that. I adore Charlotte."

"And I love that. I love that you see the good in her. The thing is, sometimes I feel like we've gotten so far from that and there's no way to turn back."

"What are you saying?" *Please don't tell me you're going to divorce her. I do not want to be the keeper of that secret.*

"I don't know. Nothing. Everything. I feel like I've lost control of us."

"Maybe you shouldn't be trying to control it."

"That came out wrong. What I mean is that there are days where I want to go to her and say, 'Let's run away. Let's sell the house. Let's pack up everything. Take Gia. And leave Wincourt. Go someplace where life is simpler.' You know?"

"I do."

"And then other days I think, 'What if Charlotte and I are already lost? Too lost to find our way back to each other?'" He sighed. "I hate the way I treat her sometimes. That's not who I am. I used to be a laid-back, go-with-the-flow, let-life-lead-you kind of guy. Not rigid and stubborn."

"I remember." Allison put her hand on Charlie's arm to comfort him.

"And you've reminded me of that. I feel like my old self when I'm around you. I don't know who I am anymore, Ali. There's just been so much stuff for so long now. Elizabeth, Gia, our conflicting parenting styles, no personal or romantic time ever, the small grievances that seem to balloon into major arguments in less than sixty seconds flat."

"Can't you talk to Charlotte? I know she's a reasonable person. And she loves you too."

"Does she? I mean, really, Ali. Does she love me? Or does she love being married and having a family? I honestly don't know anymore. But I do know I can't go on like this. She can't either. I can see her stress levels are through the roof. I know this is a terrible thing to say, but some nights I stay at the office late, even when nothing is going on, because I don't want to go home. Do you know what that feels like?" Charlie bent over and covered his face with his hands.

"No, but I can't imagine it's pleasant." Allison couldn't help but feel sorry for him. She'd cast him as the villain. The truth was, there was no villain. Charlie and Charlotte were two people so beleaguered by their own bitterness and resentment that they couldn't get out of their own way. Was that how people ended up in divorce court battling it out over a set of sterling silver flatware that neither of them would ever use? But they'd be damned if they'd let the other one walk away with it. "Is there something I can do to help?"

"You're doing it." He looked up at her with tired, bloodshot eyes. "I'm not looking for any answers. At least not tonight. I just . . . I guess I wanted you to understand where I'm coming from. And that I'm not a monster. I do love Charlotte. I do want her to be happy. For us to be happy. Only, I haven't figured out how to make that happen. How to get back to the way it was or even a version of that. I don't even know if it's possible anymore."

"Daddy?" Gia appeared in the doorway, her hot pink cotton nightshirt rumpled and her curly brown hair disheveled. "Is it time to go home now?"

"Yes, sweetie." Charlie stood up and Allison followed. "Thank you, again. Gia, can you say thank you to Logan's mommy for dinner?"

"Thank you," she whispered before her mouth stretched into a yawn.

"My pleasure, sweetheart." Allison bent over and gave her a kiss on the cheek, inhaling the sweet scent of little girl.

She'd always wanted a little girl. "You and your daddy are welcome here anytime." She hugged Charlie. "Drive safely."

After Allison had watched them climb into Charlie's massive SUV, she practically skipped to her art studio, throwing back the cloth she'd draped over her latest piece. She'd thought about it all through dinner and couldn't wait to add some of the necessary touches she'd visualized.

"Allison?" She heard Charlie's voice approaching before he appeared in front of her. "Sorry, Gia left her blanket. I knocked but you didn't hear."

"Of course, no worries. It's probably in Logan's room. Let me grab it." She scooted out from behind the easel.

"Thank you. I know it's ridiculous, but she can't sleep without it." Allison smiled knowingly. Logan's toy monkey had filled a similar purpose until he was about six.

A few minutes later, Allison returned, blanket in hand, to find Charlie staring at her painting. She lunged toward it, throwing the cloth back over it. "I'm not ready for anyone to see it yet." She realized she sounded more petulant than she'd intended, but she felt protective of this particular piece and she wasn't prepared to expose herself in that way yet. At least not to Charlie.

"Oh sure. I understand." He appeared somewhat wounded. "It looks amazing so far, but I should've asked."

"It's fine." She handed him the blanket.

"Okay, well, have a good night. Thank you on Gia's behalf for 'Blankie' and, again, for dinner."

"Of course." Allison waved as he left her studio. Suddenly she didn't feel like painting anymore. Instead she curled up on the couch in the family room with her journal. *My Dearest*

Jack, she wrote, and instinctively started sketching something, but her creative juices had ceased flowing. Frustrated, she tore the page out and began writing to him; the words came quickly, and without formal introduction.

Sometimes the pain was so visceral, she wanted to crawl out of her own skin. Sometimes it was there right in front of her, swinging back and forth like a pendulum, taunting her to reach out and grab it. To wring it until she'd squeezed it to a pulp. But, instead, she closed her eyes. And when she awoke, it was morning.

Chapter 17

I f Charlotte hadn't expected the worst, she might have been traumatized, just as Elizabeth had been when they'd arrived at their parents' shambolic condominium on Atlantic Avenue in Daytona Beach Shores.

Charlie had purchased the three-bedroom, three-bath corner unit in the stately oceanfront high-rise for them five years earlier when the upkeep of their house had become too much responsibility for them to shoulder, both financially and physically. When they'd first been given a tour of the fully furnished apartment, Charlotte's parents had oohed and aahed at every turn, declaring that it was fit for royalty. There was an expansive master bedroom with floor-to-ceiling windows overlooking the water, a gourmet kitchen with granite countertops, walk-in closets, a semiprivate elevator, a swimming pool, a fitness center, and a concierge to attend to your every need—he'd even bid them farewell by name on their way out. This had sealed the deal for Charlotte's mother, who'd exclaimed, *It's like* Cheers! And then her father had bellowed, *Norm!* at the top of his lungs, which had caused their real estate agent to flinch, before jotting a price down on a piece of paper and handing it to Charlotte.

To Elizabeth's shock and Charlotte's disappointment, their once pristine abode had gone from gorgeous to ghastly since the last time they'd visited. Upon walking through the front door, they'd been engulfed by the smell of rotten something or other. Eggs? Cheese? Whatever it was, the odor had been so overwhelmingly offensive that it had raised an immediate flag and impelled Elizabeth to make repeated gagging sounds. Further inspection, from room to room, had confirmed their suspicion. With their father confined to his bed, their mother barely able to walk ten feet without stopping to wheeze, and a biweekly housekeeper who was doing anything but keeping house, the place had gone to shit and beyond. The bathrooms reeked of stale urine, if there was such a thing.

Immediately, Charlotte had called a local cleaning service—one that cost a fortune but sent no less than six staff members to wash, polish, dust, and sweep every nook and cranny of any corporate or residential space, no matter how big or small. But even that hadn't been enough. The stench had seeped into the carpets, rugs, drapes, probably their clothing too. If possible, the walls had also absorbed it. With little help from Elizabeth, Charlotte had done twelve loads of laundry and reorganized every pill bottle in the medicine cabinet, tossing the ones that were expired. She'd stocked the refrigerator after three trips to the supermarket and had even rearranged all the kitchen supplies in every drawer and every cabinet, only after running them through the dishwasher multiple times. Finally, she'd done what she swore she'd never do. She'd given both her mother and father a bath. The circle of life at its finest.

There'd been no sitting by the pool or walking on the beach. She hadn't even dipped a toe in the water, unlike Elizabeth, who'd taken some time to work on her tan, insisting, "I can't very well come back from Florida looking all pasty." Under normal circumstances, her sister's behavior would have sent her into a tailspin, but she'd realized what her priorities were and that if the goal was to help her parents, she'd have to focus on that and deal with Elizabeth once they'd returned to Wincourt.

Unfortunately, to add insult to injury, their flight back to New York had been delayed six hours due to "weather" in the area, which meant Charlotte hadn't rested her head on her own pillow until three o'clock in the morning. And now it was nine a.m., following a taxing round of arguments with Gia about why she had to go to school, even though she preferred to spend the day with Mommy, shopping and having her nails done. Charlotte already needed a nap.

The phone rang and she lifted her tired body out of one of the chairs in her living room, where she'd been dozing off reading the latest copy of *People* magazine. Of course there were a ton of things to catch up on in light of the fact that she'd been gone for a few days, but her exhaustion was so oppressive that she'd decided to allow herself the morning to recharge.

"Hello?" Charlotte lifted the receiver to her ear, praying—for the first time—that it was a telemarketer so she could bark at them and be done with it.

"Thank *God*." Sabrina's voice came through the line.

"Oh, hey, Sabrina. What's going on?" Charlotte rolled her eyes in advance of a response.

"What's going on? That's exactly what I'd like to know." It sounded urgent, but everything sounded urgent when it came to Sabrina.

"Okay." She sat down again, this time sinking into the plush couch and stretching her legs down the length of it.

"You didn't tell me Charlie and Allison were having dinner while you were gone."

"What do you mean?" Charlotte sat up.

"I figured you didn't know." Sabrina's tone smacked of *I told you so*.

"Didn't know what? That they had dinner?" She hadn't known but was considering pretending she had if only to shut Sabrina down. Though she couldn't do that if she wanted more details, which Sabrina undoubtedly had and was practically panting at the chance to share.

"I *saw* her."

"Saw her what?"

"Allison was at DJ Gourmet with probably fifteen bags full of food. I think I saw caviar and strawberries."

"Really?" Charlotte swallowed a lump in her throat. That did seem a little much for dinner with a friend. And where had Gia been? Charlie had told her he'd stayed with their daughter, exclusively, when he wasn't at work. He'd actually bragged about it.

"Yes, really. But that's not the best part. Well, I don't mean *best*, but you know—"

"What? What is it?"

"When I saw her, I said, *and I quote,* 'I guess while the cat's away the mice will play,' and she didn't deny it! I told you that girl was not to be trusted!"

"That doesn't sound like Allison." Charlotte shook her head. Just yesterday, on the plane ride home, she'd been thinking about how nice it would be to talk to Allison. To confide in her about her awful trip. She knew that Allison, of anyone, would be empathetic. Sabrina hadn't even bothered to ask about her sick parents. Why would she, when instead she could call her first thing in the morning to drop a gossip bomb about her husband?

"Oh, really? The other day at school I saw her flirting with Craig. When I confronted him about it, he said I was being ridiculous and that she's a sweet, delightful woman. And, get this, then he suggested that maybe *I* should be more like Allison. Can you imagine?" Sabrina scoffed. "He said she was gorgeous too. I'm telling you, Charlotte. This Allison character is *not* to be trusted. I told Craig I don't want him associating with her anymore. I'm looking out for both of us here, Charlotte."

"I don't know what to say."

Could Sabrina be right? Could Charlie and Allison have had some sort of dalliance while she was caring for her ill parents more than a thousand miles away? Sabrina did tend to stretch the truth. But what if she'd been wrong about Allison? What if Allison was trying to steal her husband? And what about Charlie? Could he be trusted? There'd been a time when she'd have said yes, without a second thought. Though things between them had been exceptionally knotty lately. She couldn't even remember the last time they'd had sex. What if he felt the need to go elsewhere? Allison would certainly be an obvious choice.

"Well, if you want my opinion, I'd look into it."

"Right." Charlotte exhaled. She couldn't think straight. Her eyes were so heavy that it stung just to keep them open.

"Listen, I've gotta run. Flywheel class with Ginny in fifteen! Keep me posted. And, for Christ's sake, maybe you'll listen to me from now on."

"Okay, thank you, Sabrina. I'll talk to you later." Charlotte hung up. And then, paralyzed by both fatigue and insecurity, she sat staring at her living room wall for hours, cognizant of the fact that she'd never felt or been more alone.

Later that night, Charlotte sat on the same couch, in the same spot, staring at the same wall, waiting for Charlie to come home. She'd thought about calling him at work or sending him a well-articulated e-mail, but neither approach had seemed right. What would she have said? *Hey, so, by chance, are you having an affair with Allison?* Oh no, she needed to see the look on his face when she asked about their dinner. Surely, if anything was going on between them, she'd be able to read it in his eyes. She still knew him, no matter how far apart the two of them had grown. Somewhere, deeply embedded beneath the layers of bitterness and resentment that had piled one on top of the other over the last decade, he was still her Charlie.

The Charlie who had nursed her through having four impacted wisdom teeth removed and had held her hair back when the pain medication had made her sick to her stomach.

The Charlie who had squeezed her hand so tightly she'd thought it was going to crumble when she'd gone into labor with Gia. The Charlie who, just this morning, much to her astonishment, had left a note on her nightstand saying that he'd missed her, that he loved her, and that he was looking forward to seeing her when they were both awake. At the time it had seemed heartfelt. But now she was wondering if it was evidence of his guilt.

She heard him come through the front door and set his briefcase and keys on the table in the foyer. He'd probably assume she was sleeping until he saw the dim light on in the living room. She should be sleeping. After Sabrina's call, there'd been no relaxing morning or afternoon nap as she'd originally planned. How could she be expected to rest or even unwind after their conversation? Of course, the result was that she blamed Charlie for her delirious state. And delirious she was, having spent the entire day pacing and stewing. Stewing and pacing. The only benefit was that she hadn't been able to eat a thing, which might have helped offset the absolute crap she'd been forced to stomach while in Florida. It was no wonder her parents were a combined sixty pounds overweight.

"Charlotte?" Charlie called out in a stage whisper, so as not to wake the beast otherwise known as Gia. She didn't answer. "Hey, sweetie. Why are you sitting in here alone in the dark?"

"There's a light on."

"Barely. Is everything okay?" He approached her, sitting down next to her on the couch and leaning forward to hug her. She recoiled at his advance. "What is it? Your parents?"

"No." She shook her head, annoyed that he was being un-characteristically tender with her. "Did you have dinner with Allison while I was gone?"

"Yeah." He slid his shoes off.

"Why didn't you tell me?"

"I don't know. Because it wasn't a big deal."

"Wasn't it? I heard she went all out." Charlie was watch-ing her, she could tell, but she couldn't look directly at him as she'd hoped she could. She didn't want him to see the sadness or condemnation in her eyes.

"She cooked a nice dinner to thank me for all of the help I've given her around the house and for watching Logan while you guys were at Canyon Ranch."

"With caviar and strawberries?"

"Caviar and strawberries! Where'd you get that idea?" He laughed. "She made steak and creamed spinach. I think there was salad too, and some kind of cheesy potato thing. I assure you there was no caviar. There may have been straw-berries in the fruit salad she made for the kids, but that was about it." He rubbed Charlotte's arm, and this time she let him touch her.

"So Gia was with you?" She turned toward him now.

"Yes, Gia was with me."

"One big happy family."

"Charlotte, come on. It wasn't like that."

"Then why wasn't I invited? Huh? Why didn't she wait until I got back from Florida?"

"Honestly, I think she thought she was doing you a favor by feeding us on one of the nights you were away. I don't think it was anything against you." He brushed a wisp of hair out of her face. "What's going on, Charlotte? Where is this coming from?"

"Nowhere."

"Well, it has to be somewhere; otherwise, you wouldn't have known we had dinner in the first place."

"And why is that?"

"I already told you. I didn't think it was something so important that I needed to e-mail or call you while you were with your parents."

"Sabrina seemed to think it was important enough to mention to me after she saw Allison in town. She said something about while the cat's away the mice will play and Allison didn't argue."

"Are you serious? This is based on something Sabrina told you? Ridiculous. I'm not going to entertain it."

"She's my friend. And she was looking out for me."

"That's rich." Charlie sniffed. "Sabrina doesn't look out for anyone but herself."

"That's not true."

"Yes, it is, Charlotte. And I've heard you say the very same thing about her." He took her hand. "Come on, I think this is the exhaustion talking. Let's get you to bed." She pulled her hand from his grip. "Fine, have it your way. But I'm telling you, whatever ideas Sabrina has put in your head are ludicrous. I didn't do anything wrong. And Allison certainly didn't do anything wrong."

"Whatever." Charlotte folded her arms across her chest. Of course he'd defend Allison.

"I'm going upstairs. Feel free to join me once you've come to your senses." She didn't budge.

But a few hours later, when she'd finally decided it was time to go to bed, Charlotte walked toward the staircase, via the foyer, where Charlie had left his briefcase and keys on the table. In the garbage can next to it was a bouquet of white calla lilies.

Chapter 18

"Wow, this place is beautiful!" Elizabeth walked through Allison's foyer into the kitchen, where she could see the family room, dining room, and backyard all at the same time. "I love an open floor plan. It's so airy. Is that the right word?"

"Sounds good to me." Allison smiled warmly.

It was nice to finally be living in a house again after so many years. Apartments in Manhattan came at such a premium that anything bigger than a modest two-bedroom was more than she'd ever been able to afford. Now her home was someplace she could take pride in. Someplace she could really put her stamp on. After all, Allison had always had a keen eye for interior design. She could sit for hours flipping through *Elle Decor*, *Architectural Digest*, and *House Beautiful*, earmarking pages with fabulous finds, some within her budget, most well beyond. But wasn't that the fun of it? Scouring shelter magazines and then hitting flea markets and estate sales to re-create a space that would cost ten times as much if you paid retail. For as long as she could remember, she'd fantasized about working alongside an architect and builder to create her dream home and to then decorate it with unlimited funds. She wouldn't aggrandize—neither glitz nor overembellishment was her thing. Still, the home would be spectacular, with every detail just as she'd envisioned it. Fireplaces and window seats wherever possible. A true chef's kitchen, complete with professional appliances. And a bedroom with billowy white curtains opening to a breathtaking view. Because said home would most certainly be on the water.

"No sign of Buck." Elizabeth peered around the corner. "I'd say that's a good start."

"Seriously. What a jerk. I can't believe I let him get to me that way." Allison motioned to the couch in the family room. "Make yourself comfortable. Can I get you something to drink or eat?"

"Do you have Coke?" She sat down.

"Nope. How about Sprite?"

"Perfect." Elizabeth was still admiring her surroundings. "By the way, I'd have freaked out about Buck too. It was kind of intense."

"I felt like I was back in high school." Allison joined Elizabeth with two Sprites and a plate of freshly baked chocolate chip cookies. They'd intended to meet for lunch, but Elizabeth had gotten caught up at a job interview. "Okay, so these were supposed to be for Logan, but I think we need to eat them."

"Wow, you're like supermom. I *so* can't eat the cookies you baked for your son."

"You *so* can, especially because I can make another batch before he gets home."

"Any chance you want to adopt me?" Elizabeth laughed. "I could move in, say, tomorrow?"

"Well, thank you. But it's certainly nothing compared to Charlotte's house. That's a mansion if I've ever seen one." Allison grabbed two cookies and handed one to Elizabeth.

"Yeah, but it's so impersonal, don't you think? Plus, she doesn't bake."

"I see what you mean, but it's still gorgeous."

"I guess. It's just hard to feel at ease when you're afraid to sit on a chair for fear of creasing the fabric or, God forbid, smushing a pillow."

"You're too funny. Not that I don't love Charlotte, but it's definitely hard to believe you two came from the same parents. You did, right?" Allison raised an eyebrow.

"Yeah, we did. I'll admit it if I must."

"Speaking of Charlotte, I feel like she's been avoiding me a little. Is everything okay?"

"I think so. Though I'm always the last to know. We were out of town with my parents a couple of weeks ago and I'm pretty sure she's crazed when she comes back from a trip. Of course, she's permanently crazed, so I'm not really sure that would make a difference. What makes you think she's avoiding you?"

"She hasn't returned my three calls. And I kind of need to talk to her about the painting I'm doing for the Wincourt school gala."

"Weird. She's usually really anal about that stuff."

"I know." Allison had thought the same thing.

She'd been with Charlotte on more than one occasion when someone had phoned about something as trivial as a dress they wanted her opinion on or something as important as a doctor's appointment for Gia. She'd either dealt with it that very moment or sent herself an e-mail reminder to call back as soon as she was free. Allison had even gone so far as to comment on her impressive organizational skills. Could Charlotte be pissed off at her about something? Maybe Charlie had made a comment that had given her the wrong impression? Though, quite intentionally, she'd been careful not to speak badly about Charlotte to Charlie, namely, because she liked Charlotte and didn't think anything negative about her in the first place. But now she was questioning herself, replaying their conversations in her head to see where she might have gone wrong. The last thing she'd want to do was hurt or alienate Charlotte. Aside from Charlie, and now Elizabeth, Charlotte was the only friend she had in Wincourt. And Charlotte had been the first one to reach out to her in any kind of genuine way.

"Then again, she can be really moody and when she gets down sometimes she flies under the radar for a few days."

"Oh, okay. I'm sure it's nothing." Allison reached for another cookie. "So how are you? How was your interview?"

"It sucked. The guy was staring at my boobs throughout the whole thing. And my shirt wasn't even low-cut! I almost told him to take a picture—it lasts longer—but I need the money."

"I hear you."

"And of course I made the mistake of telling Charlotte about my job hunt while we were in Florida, so now she's harassing me every five minutes."

"You guys have such a funny relationship."

"You mean, because she thinks she's my mother?" Elizabeth

bit into her first cookie. "Wow, these are amazing. Is there anything you're not good at?"

"Plenty."

"Like what?"

"Well, let's see. I have a hideous singing voice, though it doesn't stop me from belting out eighties hits at the top of my lungs in the car. I'm not particularly good at sports. Any sports. And I'm awful at anything technology related. Microsoft Word is about the extent of my computer knowledge, which is why I save everything on my desktop; otherwise, I'll never be able to find it again."

"You don't e-mail?"

"A little. But only for work purposes. And I'd still rather call someone on the telephone."

"Nick's like that too. He says social media has ruined all personal communications in the world."

"I like Nick already." Allison slipped off her shoes and folded her legs underneath her, simultaneously propping a pillow behind her back and tossing one to Elizabeth to do the same. "When do I get to meet him?"

"Oh, um, whenever. I kind of assumed Charlotte and Charlie had filled your head with bad things about him already."

"No," Allison lied. Both Charlotte and Charlie had offered targeted jabs at Elizabeth's boyfriend more than once. "And anyway, I never pass judgment without meeting someone first. Why don't they like him?"

"Because he's not fancy like they are." Elizabeth rolled her eyes. "They assume that just because he doesn't make a ton of money or dress in expensive clothing that he's a loser."

"That's not fair."

"No kidding. You know what's remarkable? Never once has either of them asked me if Nick makes me happy."

"Does he?"

"More than anyone will ever know." Elizabeth looked down. "I don't talk about it much, but after I lost Cossette and then Rob left, I thought my life was over."

"I can understand that."

"Right, of course. I blamed myself, ya know? Obviously, now I get that it wasn't my fault. When I'm being rational. But I still think, what if I'd gone into her room to check on her? What if Rob had been home? What if she hadn't rolled onto her stomach? Or what if I'd been awake to watch her on the baby monitor? Would she still be alive? Would I still be married to Rob?" Elizabeth closed her eyes and shook her head.

"You can what-if yourself to death. No pun intended. Believe me. I've been there."

"Yeah, but you couldn't have felt responsible for Jack's death. That was a tragic accident."

"Oh really? Try this on for size. *What if* I'd gone on the ski trip with Jack and we'd driven instead of taking the bus? *What if* I'd tried to convince him it would be more responsible to stay home and continue looking for a new job? *What if* I'd watched the weather the night before and told him I didn't think the conditions were safe enough to be driving in? I've tortured myself with what-ifs too. But I can't imagine losing a child."

"Yeah, I don't recommend it. The amazing thing is that Nick, who has no children, is the only one who really understands.

Aside from you, I mean. Sometimes I feel like Charlotte wants me to move past it already, like, it's been ten years, get on with it already! Nick realizes that it's a part of the fabric of who I am now and that that will never change."

"I can appreciate that too. It's like the way people wonder why I've never remarried or even dated."

"Exactly." Elizabeth pulled her thick auburn hair off her face and twisted it into a loose bun. "I guess I just feel like Nick gets me. And he treats me really nicely, unlike Rob used to. And unlike Charlotte and Charlie treat him. Poor Nick doesn't get what he ever did to them."

"That's tough." Allison handed Elizabeth a napkin to dab the corners of her damp blue eyes.

"Yeah. Thank you." She accepted the napkin gratefully, using it to blow her nose too. "Maybe we should move on to a happier subject! Like . . . hmmmm . . . the hottie at DJ Gourmet. No pressure, of course. Just marry him already!"

"Of course!" They both laughed as Allison's phone rang. She grabbed it off the side table. "Hello?"

"Hi, Allison." Charlotte's clipped voice came across the line.

"Hey, Charlotte!" She and Elizabeth were still giggling, intoxicated by the buoyant shift in conversation.

"What's so funny?" Charlotte sounded subdued.

"Oh, nothing. I'm just sitting here with your sis."

"Elizabeth is there?"

"Do you have another sister I don't know about?" For some reason this made them laugh even harder.

"I'll call back another time. Sorry to bother you."

"It's no bother! I—" Allison started to say something else,

but before she could speak another word, Charlotte was gone. "That was strange. I think she just hung up on me."

"Welcome to my world."

"Great, thanks." Allison sighed. Now more than ever, she was convinced there was something wrong. She'd just have to figure out what that something was.

"Hello? Anyone here?" Allison called out, her voice echoing throughout the cavernous space.

She'd driven past the Alexander Gallery—situated on Egg Hill Road, prime real estate in downtown Wincourt—countless times, eager for a free moment to wander around the interior. But between shuttling Logan back and forth, to and from school and his various extracurricular activities, along with her usual errands, things around the house, and work commitments, she'd yet to have an opportunity. So when she'd received an introductory e-mail from Dempsey and the owner, Priscilla Alexander, had promptly invited her for a visit, Allison had jumped at the chance.

"Just a minute. I'll be right with you." Allison looked around, trying to place the origin of the melodious voice. Moments later, an elegantly turned-out woman, most likely in her early sixties, Allison estimated, appeared from behind a white wall. "So sorry to keep you waiting. The phone hasn't stopped ringing all morning." She held up a cordless receiver in her left hand and extended her right to shake Allison's. "I'm Priscilla Alexander. Pleasure to meet you."

"Allison Parker. And the pleasure is all mine." She was hardly able to keep her eyes from darting in every direction. "This place is spectacular."

"Why, thank you." Priscilla set the phone down on a nearby Lucite desk, sweeping her arm dramatically from one wall to the next. "Blood, sweat, and tears. And I didn't even create any of it!"

"One might say you created all of it. The watercolors are unique. I've never seen anything quite like them." Allison approached a section of the gallery to her right where four sizable paintings were hung at alternating heights. "Is that support made of leather?" She pointed to one of them.

"You know your stuff." Priscilla nodded.

She was a striking woman with prominent cheekbones, insightful brown eyes, and a head of thick, wavy silver hair extending well past her shoulders. Dressed elegantly in form-fitting tweed slacks and an eggplant-colored silk button-down cinched at her tiny waist, Priscilla belied the typical "artist type" Allison had been expecting. If anything, she looked more like an old-fashioned movie star.

"Thank you. There's always more to learn, though."

"I like the way you think." Priscilla nodded, revealing a warm smile. "So Dempsey tells me you're an artist too. Any friend of Dempsey's is a friend of mine. What a darling."

"I am. Though I'm not sure my work compares to what you've got here." They meandered from room to room together, winding in and out of small nooks, as if they were walking through a maze, while Priscilla narrated with background information on the various artists and their exhibits.

"As you can see, we don't confine ourselves to one genre. I like to offer a taste of everything. A creative smorgasbord, if you will. What's your preferred medium?"

"I'm like you. I prefer to dabble in different things. Oil,

acrylic, watercolor, pastel. Lately, I've been getting into more sculpting. I find it to be distinctively cathartic."

"I couldn't agree more." Priscilla indicated the chiseled bust of a woman sitting on top of a shelf at the far end of the gallery. "That one's mine. It's not for sale, though. I'm just learning."

"Wow." Allison approached. "Unbelievable. Is that you?"

"My mother."

"Striking resemblance."

"Thank you. I take that as a wonderful compliment. My mother was extraordinary both inside and out. I wish I was half the woman she was."

"I know the feeling." Allison had been missing her parents, specifically her mother, lately, especially with Charlotte's recent chilliness. Sure, they talked on the phone at great length at least once a day, but it wasn't the same. Another month and her parents would be home where they belonged. Where Allison and Logan needed them.

Together, Priscilla and Allison stood staring at the sculpture, lost in their own thoughts, until the telephone rang, cutting through the silence. "What did I tell you? We have an event this weekend with three new artists, and it's been nonstop. I'll just be another minute." She glided across the room, muttering under her breath, "Now, where did I put that phone?"

Allison drifted around some more, for a solid ten minutes, until Priscilla reappeared, looking visibly frazzled. "Is everything okay?"

"No, actually. One of those new artists I mentioned had to back out. Something about the flu."

"Oh, that's awful. I'm so sorry."

"This just leaves me in such a bind. I'll have to reorganize everything or else there will be two vacant spots on that wall." Priscilla pointed animatedly.

"I wish I could help."

"Me too. It's just a terrible predicament." Priscilla twisted her elegant features into a grimace and then all at once inspiration spread across her face. "Unless . . ." She turned to Allison, grinning expectantly.

"Unless what?"

"What if we show two of your pieces?"

"Mine? Oh, no, I couldn't."

"Why not?"

"I don't usually do big exhibits. My work is for private clients. Plus, you've never even seen any of it! For all you know, I can barely draw a stick figure."

"Well, I highly doubt that." Allison could practically hear the wheels in Priscilla's mind turning at warp speed. "Do you have a portfolio?"

"At home."

"Can you bring it by tomorrow morning?"

"I guess."

"Then it's settled. Problem solved."

"Wait, no, I'm not sure—"

"You wouldn't want to let an old lady down, would you?"

"Old lady!" Allison laughed. "Hardly. But if you're *desperate* . . ."

"Oh, I am."

"Okay, then. I can come back around nine tomorrow, after I drop my son off at school, if that works."

"Perfect." Priscilla hugged her spontaneously. "And do invite all your friends!"

They said their good-byes and Allison walked out onto the street, wondering if she'd made a dreadful mistake. She hadn't exhibited her work in years. Which pieces would she even show? Not the new one, which was as yet unfinished and still slated for the Wincourt gala, if she gathered enough nerve. She'd have to go through all her archived paintings and find the two that best represented her talent. Maybe they'd even bring in some good money.

As she approached her car, Allison noticed Missy sitting on a bench with her face buried in her hands. "Hey."

Missy jumped. "Oh God, you startled me."

"Is everything okay?"

"Not exactly."

"What's up?" Allison sat down next to her.

"My mother fell in her bathroom yesterday. Broken hip. She has surgery in two hours."

"Oh no." Allison rubbed Missy's back softly. "That's not good news. But at least a broken hip is fixable."

"I know. But I really want to go be there with her before the surgery and sit with my dad during it."

"Do you need a ride?" Allison still wasn't sure what the predicament was.

"No, thank you. The problem is that Sabrina promised to pick Miley up at school with Gabriella and she just backed out. She got a last-minute appointment with Serge."

"Who's Serge?" Allison never trusted people who went by one name only.

"Serge?" Missy's face registered shock. "He's only the

premier hair colorist in Wincourt. It's impossible to get in with him. Still, it's kind of bad timing."

"Sure." Allison didn't bother to suggest that perhaps Sabrina should get her priorities straight and that no hair appointment, with Serge or otherwise, could possibly be as important as helping out your best friend in her time of need. She knew it would fall on deaf ears or, even worse, that Missy would run back to Sabrina with a word-for-word recap of their conversation. "I can get Miley if you'd like."

"Really?" Missy perked up immediately. "I couldn't ask that of you. . . ." They both knew she could and would.

"It's no trouble at all. She can come back to my house and stay as long as she'd like. I've got plenty of food for dinner. Miley has a peanut allergy, if I remember correctly? And she hates mushrooms."

"Yeah, exactly. How did you know that?"

"You told me at one of Charlotte's Wine and Whines." Allison smiled. "Just call me and let me know when you want to come get her. No rush."

"Thank you *so* much, Allison. You have no idea how grateful I am."

"It's my pleasure, really."

Missy exhaled a sigh of relief. "Sabrina was definitely wrong about you."

Chapter 19

She'd gone back and forth a million times. Or at least that was how it felt. One minute she was wholly convinced that Charlie and Allison had engaged in raucous sex on the dining room table while Logan and Gia had been safely ensconced in his bedroom to ensure they didn't witness the spectacle. Charlotte had choreographed and then played out the entire scenario over and over in her head. She'd imagined Charlie clearing the table of dishes, food, and silverware with a passionate swoop of his arm, the way it happened in the movies, when there was no consideration for who would be cleaning up the inevitable mess. Then she'd pictured him drawing Allison toward him in one fluid movement, while undressing her with his penetrating stare. After that, they'd stripped down to nothing, desperate to ravage each other and unleash the raging torrent of lust they'd been denying themselves since the moment they'd laid eyes on each other that first day at school.

The next minute, she'd tell herself she was crazy. They'd

had dinner. That was all. So Charlie hadn't mentioned it. Why would he? As he'd said, he knew she was in Florida preoccupied with helping her parents. And he and Allison were friends. *She* and Allison were friends. They'd had an instant rapport. Not to mention that neither of them had ever given her reason to suspect anything before. Before Sabrina, that is. But why would she lie? Or even stretch the truth? She didn't stand to benefit from it in any way. Was it because she'd seen Allison flirting with her own husband? Charlotte couldn't imagine that. She'd never once seen Allison flirt. Period. Plus, Craig was hardly an Adonis. He wasn't even particularly attractive, save for his substantial bank account.

Charlotte had resorted to snooping through Charlie's things, justifying it to herself every which way possible, though all the while knowing full well she was doing something very wrong. How would she feel if Charlie went through her stuff? Not that she had anything to hide. She'd started with his office, meticulously turning over or unfolding every piece of paper—receipts, bills, solicitation letters . . . whatever she could get her hands on. She wasn't sure what she expected to find, but she was sure she'd know when she found it. His desk drawers had revealed nothing more interesting than his latest credit card bill, which wasn't really that interesting at all. She'd been disappointed, but why? Would uncovering something make her feel better? Highly unlikely. Still, it would be the ultimate fuck-you to Charlie, something she'd never been able to achieve during the course of their regular fights. He'd said it. More than once. But if she'd ever so much as muttered those words under her breath, he'd have left. Who knows for how long.

Feeling thwarted, Charlotte charged toward his closet, rationalizing that of course he wouldn't keep something scandalous somewhere as obvious as in his desk drawer. How could she have been so naive? She'd watched enough crime-solving shows to know better. Charlotte had then pulled down shoe box after shoe box, searching for that something. That something that would give her a jolt of satisfaction before she crumpled under the weight of disappointment and despair, crying her eyes out before confronting both of them with her triumphant discovery. That would show them. But the shoe boxes hadn't turned up anything. Nor had the pockets in every single one of his suit jackets and pants. He was either innocent or smarter than she was, and either way, she refused to believe the latter. She would not become one of those clueless wives blubbering to anyone who would listen about how she'd had no idea that her husband was screwing one of her closest friends, right under her nose. She'd listened to those women. And there had been many of them—the mothers of Gia's friends—who no longer drove luxury SUVs or carried the latest Gucci handbag. They didn't even show their faces at the nail salon anymore, having been downgraded to a life where giving yourself a manicure was not only acceptable, but the only financially responsible course of action. Maybe they'd gotten full custody of the kids, but that came with an unwelcome litany of new burdens for them to struggle with on their own. Charlotte would not become one of those women.

Allison had called half a dozen times. The last attempt had been to invite them to an art exhibit at the Alexander Gallery in town. When Charlotte had failed to reply to her message, Allison had e-mailed her again, copying Charlie. It had annoyed Charlotte, but she'd admitted to herself she'd have done the same thing in Allison's position. The position of being oblivious as to why—seemingly out of nowhere—Charlotte was ignoring her. Naturally, Charlie had answered immediately saying that they'd love to come! He never responded to her e-mails that quickly, and when he did, he never used exclamation points. Further proof? The devil on her shoulder said yes. The angel said this was classic self-sabotage. Charlotte was caught in a paradoxical purgatory, and with each passing day she was slowly driving herself mad.

Tonight would be a good litmus test, if nothing else. She'd be able to observe them. To watch the way they interacted. Would Charlie's gaze follow Allison around the room? Would he find ways to brush up against her? To whisper in her ear when he thought no one was looking? She'd have to stick to him like glue but still leave room for him to wander off from time to time, let up on the leash so the dog could dig its own hole. Charlotte would have to pay careful attention to Allison too. If Sabrina's notions were accurate, Allison was a sly one. Playing the wounded widow. How dare she? Had it been her plan all along to lure him with a protracted to-do list of household chores? To fill his belly with gourmet fare, crafted with love by none other than the tragic widow herself? Charlie had come home raving about Allison's culinary prowess. But had he also enjoyed her aptitude in the bedroom? Or did they seek out off-the-beaten-path hotels? The real seedy kind. That had actually made her laugh. If she knew anything about Charlie, it was that he did not do seedy.

He'd sooner be caught red-handed in a suite at the Four Seasons.

These were the thoughts that plagued her in the darkest hours of the night, while she lay awake in her marital bed, tossing and turning, unable to silence the boundless turmoil turning her mind faster than the wheels of a Mercedes convertible whizzing down The Autobahn.

Charlotte examined herself in the mirror. She'd told Charlie she'd meet him at the gallery, not that he'd offered to pick her up. She wanted to arrive on her own terms and with her own car, in the event that she needed a quick and dramatic escape.

"Just another dab and you'll be gorgeous," she said to her reflection, pursing her lips and dotting them skillfully with Chanel's Insolence gloss.

Insolence. *How appropriate,* she thought, before snatching her Prada clutch, smoothing her hair into place, and walking out the door.

Charlotte scanned the room for a familiar face. She'd never been to the Alexander Gallery, though she must have passed it a zillion times when shuttling Gia to and from school, not to mention all her errands and appointments around downtown Wincourt. She wasn't particularly interested in art, other than for its value. She knew that she and Charlie had some significant and expensive pieces gracing the walls of their home, thanks to Charlie's sound investing skills, but she couldn't tell anyone the first thing about them, not even the name attached to the hand that had painted them.

"Hey there." Elizabeth tapped her on the shoulder and she spun around, startled. She hadn't expected to see her sister. But why? Elizabeth and Allison were probably the best of friends by now, oblivious to the fact that they'd completely sidelined Charlotte. "Wow, you look really nice."

"Thank you. So do you." Charlotte had taken extra care when getting ready for tonight's event. If she was going to be in the same company as both Charlie and Allison—who already had the spotlight shining on her—she wanted to make sure she looked and felt beautiful. She'd achieved the former, if not the latter—how she would *feel* this evening remained to be seen.

"Where's Charlie?" Elizabeth browsed the throng of guests, most of whom were pointing and nodding at the various sketches, paintings, photographs, and sculptures scattered around the open space.

"He's meeting me here. I didn't want to be late." She was curious to see what time he'd show. He'd never once made it to a party, no matter how big or small, before eight o'clock, which would be close to the end of this one. But for Allison . . . "I'm sure he's caught up at work. What else is new, right?"

"Ooh, I see mini egg rolls. Want one?" Elizabeth took off into the crowd before Charlotte could answer. And then she spotted Allison across the room, with Logan at her side, talking to an attractive older woman. Allison turned around at that moment and caught her eye, smiling and waving and then excusing herself from the conversation to make her way in Charlotte's direction.

Allison looked stunning, as always. But tonight, her long

blond hair was flatironed into thick, glossy sheets and curled ever so slightly at the ends to give it just the right amount of bounce. And her face was made up, drawing out her most striking features—her light gray eyes and defined cheekbones. She was dressed in a floor-length, navy blue chiffon dress with a racer back that showed off her toned and tanned arms. She was, in a word, perfection. How silly, Charlotte thought, appraising her own simple black shift dress, that she'd dared to compete with that.

"Hey!" Allison beamed, pulling Charlotte into a warm embrace. "You look amazing!"

"Thank you." Charlotte's smile was flimsy. "And you look spectacular. No surprise there."

"Where have you been? I've practically been stalking you!"

"Busy, busy. You know how it is."

"Yeah, sure." Allison didn't seem sure, which afforded Charlotte a shock of satisfaction. "Well, congratulations on tonight. You must be very proud."

"Honestly, it was a last-minute thing, but thanks." Allison smiled feebly. Charlotte could see that she knew something was up. Something beyond Charlotte's busy, busy life, which definitely wasn't so busy that she couldn't have found time to return one of Allison's many calls. "Listen, I really want to show you my progress on the piece for the school gala. It's been a bit of an emotional roller coaster for me, and I trust your opinion. Do you have time this week? You could come over for lunch, if you'd like. I feel like it's been forever since we've had time for girl talk. I miss you."

She was trying. Too hard? Charlotte swallowed a pang of

guilt. If Sabrina was wrong about Charlie and Allison, Charlotte hoped she wasn't past the point of no return in the way of their friendship. Standing here with Allison now, part of her wanted to say, *Yes! A girls' lunch sounds fantastic! What can I bring?*

But what she actually said was, "Let me check my calendar and get back to you."

"Okay. Yeah, that sounds good." Allison appeared instantly deflated, and Charlotte felt like the mean girl. It was her inner Sabrina. And it came out only from time to time. Mainly when she was with Sabrina and Missy. Although every now and then, even when she was on her own, she might ridicule a salesclerk at Neiman Marcus or snap at the well-intentioned bagger at Whole Foods. Her mother called it entitlement. It wasn't a trait Charlotte was proud of. But everyone had their faults. At least she wasn't swigging white wine from her Klean Kanteen like so many of the other moms at Gia's school. *Sure it's water. Then why are you teetering on your Jimmy Choos at eleven a.m. on any old Tuesday?*

"Have you seen my husband?" Charlotte took a sip of the champagne she'd been handed on the way in.

"Oh yeah, he's here somewhere." Allison turned around, standing on her tippy-toes and craning her neck in search of him.

"Charlie's here already?" Charlotte couldn't mask her surprise.

"He was one of the first, actually. I think he was talking to Priscilla, the owner, about purchasing one of the pieces. And then I saw him talking to Missy after that."

"Missy's here?"

"Yup." Allison nodded. Since when had she and Missy become friends?

"So Sabrina is coming too?"

"Uh, no." She shook her head.

"You invited Missy and not Sabrina?" Charlotte was incredulous.

"Well, I mean, Sabrina and I aren't really friends. In fact, I'm fairly certain she doesn't like me, so I didn't see the point. Is that a problem?"

"Not for me." Charlotte laughed nervously.

Obviously Allison hadn't gotten the memo that no one put Missy on a guest list without Sabrina's name ahead of it. And the fact that Charlie, Charlotte, and Elizabeth were all there too . . . well, it was almost too good to be true. She couldn't help but be endeared to Allison all over again, even if just a little. If nothing else, she had guts. Not that Sabrina would have come. Allison was correct in her assumption that Sabrina wouldn't be heading up her fan club in the near or distant future. Still, it was definitely a bold move. Charlotte couldn't help but wonder what the repercussions would be when Sabrina got wind of the snub.

"I'm not scared of Sabrina," Allison said. *That makes one of us,* Charlotte thought. "Oh, here comes Charlie." He was walking toward them with Logan in tow, his hand placed firmly on Logan's back to help guide him through the mob. Charlotte felt an immediate twinge of affection for him. Would he have been a more present father if only she'd been able to give him the son he'd always wanted?

"Hey, babe!" Charlie leaned over to kiss Charlotte on the

lips. She let him linger for longer than usual in the presence of Allison, who wasn't even watching them. "You look great." A shiver ran up her spine as Charlie's eyes feasted on her from top to bottom.

"Thanks." She looped her arm through his. "So do you." Charlie had always looked his most dapper in a dark suit. She'd often thought how lucky men were to be able to wear them to both work and social functions, since they hid every imperfection—from a pot belly to a plump rear end. Not that Charlie had either. He'd been gifted, much like Allison and Elizabeth, with the enviable metabolism Charlotte had not. "Hi, Logan! Don't you look handsome!"

He grinned, showcasing his mouthful of metal.

"Say thank you, sweetheart. Gia's mommy just gave you a compliment," Allison advised, hugging him against her body.

"Uh, thanks." He shrugged, and at the same time, Allison's face lit up like a Fourth of July fireworks display. Charlotte followed her gaze to a strikingly handsome man who was moving in their direction.

"You made it!" Her grin stretched from ear to ear.

"Are you kidding? I wouldn't have missed it for the world." All at once it was as if the Red Sea had parted and Charlie and Charlotte had been swallowed up by a wave, rendering them nonexistent. Charlotte noticed that Charlie's smile had faded.

"You must be the famous Logan." He put his hand up for a high five and Logan slapped it, albeit reluctantly. Charlie cleared his throat.

"Oh gosh, how rude of me. Dempsey, these are my friends

Charlie and Charlotte. I've known Charlie for years and, as it turns out, their daughter, Gia, is in Logan's class." She faced Charlotte. "Dempsey owns DJ Gourmet, among other shops and cafés around the area. We went to high school together, if you can believe it."

"So you're old *friends*." Charlie emphasized the word *friends*.

"Not really. We barely knew each other back then."

"Hey, I knew exactly who you were! Though I can't say the same in return," Dempsey teased, and it suddenly became obvious to Charlotte that Allison was enamored with this man. Not Charlie. Silently she scolded herself for having been so stupid, not to mention gullible. What had possessed her to listen to Sabrina? A torrent of relief washed over her. Maybe she would take Allison up on that lunch invitation after all.

"Allison, darling." The elegant older woman Allison had been talking to earlier, whom Charlotte could only assume was the owner, Priscilla Alexander, approached. "I have someone interested in one of your paintings. Oh, hello, Dempsey." She kissed him on the cheek. "Mind if I steal her for a moment?"

"Only if you promise to bring her back." He winked and then turned to Logan. "Hey, buddy, I think I know where there's a secret stash of candy in the back. Wanna go see?"

"Can I, Mom?" Logan's eyes glistened at the prospect.

"I think that sounds like an excellent idea. Just no caramel with the braces, please."

Dempsey reached for Logan's hand and he took it willingly. "Really nice to meet you guys. Ali, I'll catch you in a few."

"So nice to meet you too!" Charlotte called after them.

"Yeah, nice to meet you," Charlie grumbled under his breath, as a dark cloud was cast over his face.

Charlotte pulled her husband closer to her side and he smiled at her, wrapping his arm around her waist. "Let's go grab a bite to eat. Chez Louis?"

She smiled back. "That sounds perfect."

Chapter 20

Allison sashayed into DJ Gourmet, frothing with antici-pation. She'd been waiting weeks to see the cake Dempsey had created for her birthday, having begged for a sneak peak at his secreted sketches again and again. But again and again, he'd denied her, visibly amused by her pleading and the playful banter that had ensued. When she'd first mentioned that she was planning an intimate get-together at her home to mark her thirty-fifth and had pointed to the chocolate and red velvet cakes in the case, asking Dempsey which one he thought would be a better choice, instantly he'd raised an eyebrow and shook his head. "No, no, no," he'd said, smiling furtively. "I'll make you some-thing special." She'd insisted it wasn't necessary, indicating that only a few friends would be in attendance and that all she needed was something small and simple. "I won't take no for an answer," he'd declared. And that had been that.

Even Allison's mother and father couldn't make it, not that it bothered her. There'd been a time when her birthday had been a source of untainted joy. On March first, inevitably she would wake up at the crack of dawn to announce, "My month has arrived!" Reliably her mother, and later Jack, taking the reins of her family ritual, would have some small token handy to commemorate the occasion, even though the actual date wasn't until the fourteenth. For whatever reason, birthdays had always been a big deal in her family, observed with an excess of food, cake, balloons, gifts, relatives, and good friends. If you called the honoree any later than ten a.m. to convey your happy wishes, best of luck talking your way out of it!

Allison would never forget the time she'd had an art history exam at Brown first thing in the morning on her father's birthday. She'd tried to reach him prior to entering the testing hall, but he hadn't answered. And a voice mail, she knew, simply wouldn't have cut it. Three hours later, she'd finally gotten ahold of him at the office. "Out of sight, out of mind, huh?" he'd teased. "I figured you'd forgotten about your old man." She'd apologized, knowing that he wasn't really upset. Then he'd added, "Even your brother remembered before you." They'd laughed together, well aware of the fact that her brother, Ethan, four years her junior and startlingly immature—as teenage boys often were—would probably forget his own birthday if their mother didn't remind him.

After Jack died, it had seemed impossible that she'd experience the same untainted joy at her birthday, or anything else, ever again. For years, March first had come and gone without recognition and the fourteenth had come and gone without fanfare. Her parents would give her cards and gifts from both them and Logan. Jack's parents would send a check with a note saying, *We didn't know what you'd like, so buy yourself something nice.* They'd meant well, but it had always irked her. How could they know what she liked? They never called. They never visited. They barely acknowledged her existence. But, as with the money they sent regularly, Allison's mother had always urged her to be the bigger person, to accept it graciously, aware of the fact that it might be all they could manage.

This year, for the first time in more than a decade, she felt like a little kid again. Or at least her pre-Jack's-death self. Maybe it was their fresh start in Wincourt. Maybe it was the cake. Maybe it was Dempsey. Whatever it was, she was desperate to bottle up the feeling and never let it go.

She'd been thinking about him a lot lately. Dempsey, that is. It could be at any given moment—while she was driving to school to pick up Logan, while she was studying a recipe to make for dinner, or even when she was painting—his face, his voice, his touch, would infiltrate her daydreams and afford her a flip of the stomach or a flutter of the heart followed by a quiet squeal that no one but she could hear. Sometimes she'd allow herself to play out entire scenarios in her head. Them going out for a romantic meal. Them walking on the beach barefoot, hands clasped tightly. Them kissing. Them . . . that was usually where it stopped. The ultimate hurdle to leap. While she'd yet to let another man's lips part hers, that she could at least imagine. But inviting him into her bed? What if she'd forgotten how to make love to someone? What if she panicked amid the throes of passion and ruined everything? Dempsey was as understanding and compassionate as any man she'd known; still, everyone had their limits.

They'd been talking on the phone every day lately. It had started the night of the art exhibit at the Alexander Gallery, when she'd let him take her home. She hadn't gotten a word in edgewise during the car ride, what with Dempsey and Logan prattling on and on about professional sports and video games. Who knew Dempsey was fluent in ten-year-old boy? He'd called her before bed. Just to say good night. And then he'd called her every evening after that. Their conversations never had a specific point or even a purpose. He just wanted to get to know her better. To understand who Allison Parker was—the woman, the mother, the artist. When Jack's name wheedled its way into their discourse, Dempsey never balked. Sometimes he even asked about him on his own. Allison had once commented, as lightheartedly as possible, that he shouldn't feel obliged to talk at length about her dead husband or even to seem interested. Dempsey had replied that Jack was a part of Allison and an even bigger part of Logan. And that was all that mattered to him. There was no sense in trying to either hide from or compete with a ghost. Jack was there to stay, in whatever way Allison needed him to, and Dempsey, for his part, was entirely comfortable with that. Whether it was true or not—and she believed it was—it was the right thing to say. It was something no one had ever said to her before. Everyone always seemed so caught up in the idea of moving on. Of compartmentalizing things. Her life before Jack. Her life with Jack. And her life after Jack. It was neat. Black and white. But Allison had never been a fan of black and white. She'd always preferred to live and work in a world full of blended shades and colors. Was there any other way to truly experience life? To take the good with the bad. The great with the grit. The utmost with the unthinkable.

He got that. He didn't have to say it. She just knew.

"Well, look who's here bright and early." Dempsey sauntered into the main area of DJ Gourmet wearing a plaid shirt, smeared with cake frosting and batter, over a snug white T-shirt and faded blue jeans.

"It's cake day, baby!" She beamed and let him lean in to kiss her on the cheek, close enough to her lips that it sent a shiver up her spine. That was as far as they'd gotten, even though every inch of her wanted to push him into the pantry and rip his clothing off.

"Oh really? It must have slipped my mind." He tried to keep a straight face, but his mouth was curling at the corners.

"Let's see it. Come on!" Allison walked past him, starting toward the kitchen.

"It's not in there." She turned back around to find him standing with his arms folded across his chest and a wily grin spread from ear to ear.

"Fine, I don't want it anyway." Two could play at this game.

"Great. So listen, I'll see you tomorrow night? I'll bring the cake with me."

"Come on!" she implored, putting on a pouty face. "Please?" She'd never been particularly adept at reverse psychology. She'd tried it on Logan more than a couple of times to no avail.

"Well, since you asked so nicely." He took her hand in his. "You can leave your purse here. It's safe."

"No worries. It's just my journal and a snack for Logan.

Can you believe I forgot my wallet at home for the third time this week? I've been such a space cadet lately."

"Well, everything here is free to you anyway, including your charming escort." He placed her bag behind the counter and led her through an open door in the back left corner of the café, where there was a large refrigerated room she'd never seen before. Dempsey removed his plaid shirt, revealing chiseled biceps, and wrapped it around Allison's shoulders. "Wear this. It's freezing in here."

"Thanks." She nodded, relishing his strong hands cradling her, as she peered around the space. There were shelves filled with all manner of herbs, fruits, vegetables, cold cuts, breads, and desserts. Then she spotted it. A large white cardboard box with her name printed in Dempsey's surprisingly neat handwriting on the side. "Aha!" She motioned to it, giggling giddily and rubbing her hands together.

"You're a sly one." He laughed, pulling the box down from the shelf and placing it on an expansive stainless-steel island in the center of the room.

"Let's see it." Allison reached her hand out to open the lid and Dempsey swatted it.

"Just what do you think you're doing?"

"You better not be messing with me!"

"Who, me?" He feigned offense. "All right, here goes. I hope you like it." He opened the box and Allison's eyes widened. It was, undeniably, the most magnificent cake she'd ever seen.

"Oh my God." She took a moment to catch her breath. "How did you do this? It looks identical to the real thing."

Dempsey had, quite realistically, re-created her favorite painting of all time—Vincent van Gogh's *Starry Night*—but she didn't know how he'd known it was her favorite; she was fairly certain she'd never mentioned it. The piece, which was among van Gogh's most well-known, was an interpretation of the view outside his sanitarium room window, though he was said to have painted it during the day from memory. As a small child, Allison had been drawn to the blue-and-yellow swirling sky over the serene village of Saint-Rémy, where she'd sworn she would live someday, even if only for one quixotic summer. And then there was the cypress tree on the left, which—as an adult and a widow—Allison had likened to the dark abyss she imagined had swept her sweet Jack away to a more peaceful existence.

"Well, I'm no van Gogh. So spare my ear." He put his arm around her waist, pulling her close to him. "But a little birdie told me you had an affinity for this particular piece of art. So I did my best."

"You did amazing. Thank you. Thank you so much." Allison wiped a tear from the corner of her eye and wrapped her arms around him, squeezing him tightly. When she finally let go, she didn't take a step back as she normally would have. She stayed there, her face less than an inch from his.

"I wanted you to have a perfect birthday," he whispered, brushing her cheek with the tips of his fingers and then tucking her hair behind her ear. He leaned in and placed the softest kiss on her lips, lingering there until she kissed him back.

"Thank you," she repeated, gazing into his eyes and kissing him once more before their bodies parted naturally. "I'm guessing that little birdie was my mother." She smirked, letting him take her hand again and lead her back into the café.

"A chef never reveals his source."

"I'm pretty sure that's a journalist, not a chef." Allison laughed, her heart still beating excitedly and her face still flushed. She wanted to process it all. The cake, the kiss, the way he'd looked at her. And she knew she would. On her way home and then a million times after that. But right now, all she could do was savor the moment. She'd brave the swell of emotions that were brewing inside her later. Much later.

"Details, details."

"Oh great." Allison sighed, spotting Sabrina walk through the front door.

"What's the matter?"

"Nothing. Just someone I know and would rather not have to talk to right now."

"Not Buck?" Dempsey looked around anxiously.

"No, nothing like that. Do you mind if I sneak out the back? I have a bunch of errands to run before I pick Logan up, and then I'm heading over to Charlotte's house to go over some stuff for the school gala."

"Of course, sure. Whatever you want." He pecked her on the lips affectionately. "I'll see you tomorrow, birthday girl."

"I'll have my party hat on!" She smiled. "Oh, I almost forgot. Let me know what I owe you for the cake."

"Get out of here, will you? I told you everything here is free to you."

"But it must have cost a fortune."

"Consider it my gift. I wouldn't have it any other way."

"Well, if you insist."

"I do."

"Thank you." Allison offered a quick wave and turned to weave her way through the crowd and toward the back door.

Chapter 21

"Hey! How are you? Come in, come in." Allison held the door open and hugged Charlotte as if they were long-lost sisters reuniting after a lifetime of being estranged.

"Honestly, stressed beyond belief." Charlotte exhaled for the first time in what felt like ages. "Every year, I tell myself I'm going to let someone else deal with all the busywork. And every year, I end up running around like a madwoman doing it all myself. I've been stuffing goody bags for days."

Organizing the annual Wincourt school gala, like any affair catering to the rich and privileged, was practically a full-time job, at least during the months leading up to the big event. Everything had to be just so. Anything short of perfection and you were destined to be ousted and replaced by someone hungrier, someone who'd been counting on you to fail, waiting for one little slipup so they could usurp your position faster than the Aston Martin in their ten-car garage. Perhaps a new mother who was desperate to prove her capabilities and roll out her Rolodex, dropping the names of her

"nearest and dearest" friends with fat wallets and even fat-
ter bank accounts, friends who were so near and dear they
barely recognized her walking down the street in the bright
light of day.

Charlotte had been that mother once upon a time. Of
course, Sabrina had told anyone who'd listen that she'd
decided—on her own—to pass the torch along after five
strenuous and thankless years helming the committee. But
everyone involved had known better. If she hadn't resigned,
she'd have been exiled. No one liked a tyrant, which—in Sabrina's case—was as euphemistic a characterization of her
governing style as could be warranted. When Charlotte had
stepped in to take over, she'd been in the fortunate position
of following a reviled predecessor. As long as she'd smiled
and treated the other volunteers respectfully, she was destined to be the Abraham Lincoln of the Wincourt school
gala. And that was how it had been for the first year. Until
the pressure had gotten to her too. By year two she'd found
herself snapping at people for no reason and even biting the
head off one of the new dads—the only man navigating the
rough-and-tough waters of know-it-all mommies who toted
a different Birkin bag to every meeting. After all, in this
group, where would philanthropy be without fashion?

John Billings—that had been his name; Charlotte would
never forget it. He'd been a seemingly pleasant guy who'd
mostly minded his own business. From day one, he'd been
emasculated by his peers for no other reason than being
there in the first place. You'd think at least one of the mothers
would have pointed out how refreshing it was to see a dad
so involved in his child's life. So what if his wife was the

breadwinner? What was wrong with that? Apparently, every-thing. Whenever John had opened his mouth to speak, offer-ing a typically intelligent and productive suggestion, the surrounding ladies would whisper and giggle; some had even made childish faces. Initially Charlotte had felt uncom-fortable for John and for herself, having to stand in front of them, pretending that she was oblivious to the inappropriate chatter. But eventually she'd started to resent John. Even though it wasn't his fault, his mere presence had become disruptive, and when his reaction to said disruption had been to become louder and more involved, Charlotte had been forced to shut him down in front of everyone. It hadn't been a proud moment, nor one she cared to recall. That evening she'd received a scathing e-mail from John's wife in defense of her husband, who—unbeknownst to anyone in the group—was in fact a very successful author who worked from home but still carved out time to devote to his son. Charlotte had very nearly written back suggesting that John might consider fighting his own battles, but instead she'd ig-nored it. And them. The following year, she'd learned that John's family had moved to a neighboring town, one with a less exemplary school system, but—with any luck—a more accepting parental body. She'd felt somewhat responsible.

"What's going on? I feel like we haven't spoken in for-ever." Allison motioned for Charlotte to sit down on the couch, where she'd laid out a spread of cut-up vegetables and baked chips with salsa. "I'm so sorry I couldn't make it to the meeting yesterday. I had to pick up Logan early from school because his stomach was bothering him."

"Speaking of which . . ." Charlotte nibbled on a carrot

stick. "I hate to do this at the last minute, but Charlie and I can't make it to your birthday dinner tonight. Gia's home sick with the flu and Charlie called me a few minutes ago to say he has to catch a flight to Boston tonight for an early morning business meeting that just came up. He said to tell you he's really sorry and that he'll make it up to you. I'd come myself, but for once I have no coverage."

"Oh, don't worry about it. I hope Gia feels better." Allison laughed. "Although I think that's going to make the guest list me, Dempsey, Missy, and Larry. I guess it'll kind of be like a strange double date!"

"Ooh, if you haven't heard from Missy yet, you probably will soon. Miley's home with strep throat, and last I spoke to her she thought she was coming down with it too." Charlotte felt legitimately sorry for Allison. She didn't have many close friends in Wincourt to begin with, and now two-thirds of them were dropping like flies at the eleventh hour. "Why don't we plan another celebration when everyone's feeling better?"

"Perfect." Allison smiled contentedly and Charlotte could tell it wasn't the kind of thing she'd let bother her. Unlike Charlotte, who took it to heart and immediately questioned intentions when anyone canceled plans with her. "Dempsey made a huge cake, though, so if Gia's feeling better, feel free to stop by for a care package."

"About this Dempsey character . . ." Charlotte grinned. "I think I'm going to need a few more details, my friend."

It felt good that things were back to normal between them, or as close to normal as they could be in the wake of Charlotte's cold front. After she'd seen the way Allison had

looked at Dempsey at the art exhibit, she'd been more convinced than ever that there was nothing going on between
Allison and Charlie. And while she'd certainly noticed how
it had irked her husband to see Allison and Dempsey so
clearly enamored of each other, she'd since rationalized that
Charlie probably felt like his position as Allison's protector
had been commandeered by a virtual stranger. It wasn't that
he had romantic intentions toward her, but rather that he
wanted to be there for her since his childhood best friend
could not be. Charlie liked playing the knight in shining ar-
mor. It was one of the reasons Charlotte had fallen in love
with him in the first place. She'd wanted to be saved. She'd
needed to be. And he'd offered her the fairy tale. What girl
wouldn't have fallen for that?

Charlie had shared very little with her about Jack. But every time his name came up, she could see that it troubled
him. She'd never pushed or prodded, assuming he'd speak
his mind when he was ready, but it all made sense now.
Much more sense than the two of them having an affair. She
hadn't bothered to disclose this revelation to Sabrina. Mainly
because she didn't want to be talked out of it. Sabrina had
offered enough snide remarks about Allison and Charlie—
both separately and together—at the committee meeting
yesterday. The last thing Charlotte needed was to give her
reason to extrapolate.

"It's crazy, right? Everyone always says you'll meet someone when you least expect it, but I never actually believed
it was true, especially because I've been kind of closed off to it."

"Kind of?" Charlotte raised an eyebrow.

"Fine. Completely."

"So what's different this time?"

"I don't know." Allison sat cross-legged and leaned against the armrest of the couch, facing Charlotte. "He's just so laid-back. And smart. And he doesn't push me. But at the same time, he's direct. It's like I know he's interested, but he's waiting for me to move things along."

"So the fact that he's the most stunning man I've ever seen has nothing to do with it, right?"

"Well, that doesn't hurt." Allison blushed and Charlotte could tell she was more than smitten.

"So nothing's happened yet?" This was the kind of girl talk Charlotte had always imagined herself engaging in when she and Charlie had first moved to town. She'd pictured an intimate group of women congregating at her house every week to share stories, divulge secrets, and be there for one another through the good, the bad, and the ugly. Instead she'd fallen in with the likes of Sabrina and Missy.

"Just one kiss." Allison covered her face with her hands. "It was sooooooo good, though, Charlotte. I felt like I was twelve all over again."

"You were kissing boys when you were twelve?" Charlotte had waited until she was sixteen. Well, she hadn't so much waited as the boys hadn't exactly been lining up. She knew sixteen was late, but *twelve*? "Like, with tongue?"

"Oh yeah, and way too much of it, actually. First kiss. Mike Katz. Coolest boy in the sixth grade. Turned out to be a total tool. Wish I'd known that before I let him slobber all over my face."

"Gross." Charlotte thought for a moment. "Do you think you'll sleep with him?"

"Mike? Definitely not. He's married with five kids."

"Very funny." Charlotte reached for a celery stick and dunked it in salsa. "You know what I meant."

"God, I don't know. I mean, part of me wants to. Badly. But it's too soon. And I'm just a wee bit terrified."

"So, you haven't since . . ." Charlotte trailed off.

"Since Jack."

"Eleven years. Wow." Charlotte processed the information, even though, if she'd thought about it, she already knew it to be the case. Allison had confided in her that she hadn't so much as gone on a date since Jack had died. "You may be the only person I know who has less sex than I do."

"I mean, I have to assume it's like riding a bike, but—you know—it's different with everyone."

"I'm probably not the best person to ask. I've only had sex with three people. And the first guy was a one-hit wonder. Minus the hit part."

"Including Charlie?" Allison was unconvinced.

"Including Charlie. Why? What's your number?" Her eyes widened in anticipation. "Wait, weren't you and Jack married when you were practically kids? And didn't you meet at summer camp? Please don't tell me you were sleeping around by thirteen." All Charlotte could think about was Gia. Gia with her baby fat around the belly. And her chubby little cheeks and hands. Fine, so she was only turning ten, but the mere concept that a boy's tongue could be in her mouth within two years and God knows what after that made Charlotte want to enroll her in a convent. Stat.

"I definitely was not having sex when I was thirteen. More like sixteen. And, even though Jack and I met at camp, we broke up, or whatever you want to call it, at the end of every summer. We didn't start dating seriously until after college." Allison smiled wistfully and then laughed guiltily. "Let's just say I had some fun when I was at Brown."

"You dirty girl!"

"Who, me?"

"Well, I think you're going to be just fine with Dempsey. He seems like a great guy. I'm happy for you."

"We're not walking down the aisle yet." Allison's phone buzzed. "Speak of the devil." She read the text message that had just come in. "Another one bites the dust."

"He can't come tonight either?" Charlotte watched Allison's face for even a hint of disappointment.

"Apparently the whole basement of DJ Gourmet flooded last night from a broken pipe. He's up to his waist in water. He feels terrible." Allison typed a message back to him. "Oh well, I guess it'll be me, my baby boy, and cake for ten!"

"That sucks. I'm so sorry."

"Are you kidding? Logan's all I ever need. And as you said, we'll celebrate when everyone is healthy and dry!" Allison popped a chip in her mouth. "Plus, Dempsey's my date for the gala, so I'll get to see him then."

"Speaking of which, how's the painting coming? Can I get that sneak peek?" Charlotte had given Allison carte blanche for the piece they planned to auction off. She'd told her that this year's theme was "hope for the future" and that anything even remotely related to that would be fine. After seeing her work at the gallery exhibit, Charlotte had been even more buoyant about Allison's talent and her contribution to the event.

"Not now." Allison smiled. "I just need to add the finishing touches, and then it'll be done."

"Well, I can't wait." Charlotte smiled effortlessly.

Finally, after weeks of one manic day followed by the next, she felt relaxed, even if only for a brief space in time. Allison's house was so much warmer than her own, so much more lived in, despite the fact that she'd only moved in six months ago. It was the kind of place where if you spilled something on the carpet by accident, no one would have an aneurism. Or if there were errant crumbs dusting the countertop, World War II was unlikely to break out. Why couldn't she be more like Allison? Charlie probably wondered the same thing. Hadn't he indicated as much without saying it directly? Still, she couldn't help but like this woman, even though she secretly wanted to be her.

"I meant to e-mail you the details, but things have been crazy. Remind me what you need?"

"The name of the piece, approximately what it would go for if you were selling it, dimensions. And any specific information about it, like if there's a story or what medium you used. All that good stuff."

"Easy enough. Though with my forgetfulness lately, I should probably write it down." Allison surveyed the room for a pen and paper.

"That reminds me, I have your purse. You left it at DJ Gourmet."

"Oh my God. I didn't even realize that. What's wrong with me? Wait, but how do you have it?" Allison was visibly confused.

"I guess Dempsey gave it to Sabrina since she came in

after you and thought you were going to be at the meeting yesterday."

"Oh right."

"Then she left it with me when you canceled because I told her I was coming here today. But I didn't get a chance to stop home like I thought I would. If you need it I can bring it by later. Maria is doing school pickup and drop-off for the foreseeable future, so I won't see you there."

"Nah, it's no big deal. I'm just glad I know where it is. I guess I should be happy I also forgot my wallet at home yesterday, so at least I have that! Can you bring it to the gala?"

"Absolutely. As long as you bring the painting!"

"Sounds like a foolproof plan."

Chapter 22

Her birthday had been blissfully uneventful. In a way, she'd felt strangely grateful that everyone had canceled at the last minute. Sure, she would have delighted in playing hostess. After all, it was one of Allison's favorite pastimes. Still, sitting on the couch with Logan, with their feet up on the coffee table, eating cold sesame noodles and moo shu pork out of the containers while they watched *The Voice*, was truly the best gift she could have asked for.

After gorging themselves on Chinese takeout, they'd shamelessly wielded two forks, no plates in sight, and dug into Dempsey's birthday masterpiece, alternating between feeding themselves and feeding each other. Ultimately, they'd barely polished off one-tenth of the cake, which they'd both found surprising given their marathon eating spree. An hour later, plummeting from his sugar high, Logan had fallen into a deep egg-roll-and-icing-induced food coma on her lap, where she'd let him rest for longer than necessary, while stroking his warm forehead and raking her fingers through his thick, shiny brown hair. Jack's hair. Even though Logan's still smelled like little boy.

Allison often wondered how long she had until she turned into a pumpkin—until she became persona non grata in Logan's life. It felt impossible to digest, must less endure, that one day she'd be an embarrassment. That there would come a time when he'd be annoyed to arrive home from school and find her there, in *his* space. When she'd no longer be able to "hang" with him and his friends, chatting about their days, or cheer loudly on the sidelines at his soccer games. Even worse, what if he gave up crawling into her bed when he'd had a bad dream or on weekend mornings, so they could snuggle and watch cartoons until their stomachs were grumbling so loud Allison was forced to finally get up in search of sustenance? He couldn't. She couldn't.

Depending on her mood, this train of thought could lead Allison down a long path of what-ifs or what-would-happen-whens. *What if* Jack was still alive and they had three kids by now? Would she still love Logan as much? Would he still be her entire world if there was a mini Allison or two running around? *What would happen when* Logan went to college? *What if* he wanted to go somewhere like UCLA or Oxford? *What if* he moved to England? *What if* he married a Brit and had little British babies, and she saw him only twice a year for tea, scones, and stiff upper lips? *What if* he forgot about her and she ended up old and alone with fourteen cats and only three litter boxes?

This was where her musings typically ceased. Rationally, she knew that most of these scenarios were exaggerated fabrications, but she couldn't escape the unknown, and that

scared her. Even eleven years later, she missed having someone to depend on, someone's hand to grab when there was
turbulence on an airplane, someone to hold the dustpan
when she shattered a wineglass on the dining room floor,
and someone to tell her it was all going to be okay, whether
they were sure of it or not. For now, she had her parents. But
no one was more aware than Allison that life was fleeting.
Here today, gone tomorrow. More like here this minute, gone
the next. That was one place she wouldn't let her mind go.

On the contrary, today was a happy one. Dempsey had
sent an extravagant bouquet of thirty-five pink, purple, and
yellow roses to commemorate each of her thirty-five years,
displayed in another stunning hand-painted vase from the
Alexander Gallery. Logan had after-school activities followed
by a playdate with a friend, so Allison would have most of
the day to paint. And the best part of all, her mother and father had returned from California the previous evening,
and her mother was sure to arrive at any moment.

Allison danced around the kitchen, singing into a wooden
spoon while the eighties station blared in the background.
"We built this *city*! We built this city on *rock and rooooolll!*
Built this city . . ."

"I knew I should have given you voice lessons." Allison
whipped her head around to find her mother standing in
front of her. "I also should have told you the importance of
locking your front door."

"Mom!" Allison ran around the island and practically
pummeled her mother. She was a sight for sore eyes, a well-
rested, slightly tanned version of herself, but not looking a
day older. "You scared the crap out of me."

"Hello to you too, sweetheart." Her mother squeezed her back, steadying herself on a chair to maintain her balance. "I guess you're happy to see me?" She sat down at the breakfast bar and Allison sat next to her, turning her stool so they were facing each other.

"You have no idea."

"I suppose Logan's at school?"

"Yeah, sorry. Apparently, at this age, pulling them out because their grandparents just came home is not an acceptable excuse. But he's beyond excited that you and Dad are coming for dinner tonight."

"I can't wait to get my hands on him. I've been in hug and kiss withdrawal for months. It's been treacherous."

"I can only imagine." Allison grinned. Suddenly, her world felt complete again, and so many of the things she'd been worrying about over the course of the last few weeks seemed insignificant.

"So listen, don't kill me, but I have an eleven o'clock hair appointment with George. I can't stay for long."

"Mom." Allison moaned.

"I know, I know. But there's no one in California who gives a cut like George. I'm desperate."

Her mother had been getting her hair cut, colored, and styled by George Fortier for as long as Allison could remember. When she was younger, she loved going to the salon with her mom, if you could call the spruced-up basement of George's shack of a house that. He'd always have loads of candy and he'd let Allison dress up his miniature poodle in ridiculous outfits. In the last three decades, George had come a long way. Now he worked out of his very own space called the Fortier Spa, located on the main drag in Wincourt central—prime real estate. In addition to his services, he employed a full staff devoted to massages, facials, manicures, pedicures, and so on. George had done Allison's hair and makeup on her wedding day.

"Fine, I'll let you off the hook." Allison smiled. "This time."

"How very generous of you." Her mother smiled back. "Now, tell me how everything went with Charlotte before I have to run." Allison had been keeping her mother abreast of all the goings-on in Wincourt while she was away, including what little drama she had in her own life. She'd even let on that things might be getting romantic with Dempsey, though she'd been careful to keep her feelings close to the vest on that one, mainly so as not to disappoint anyone.

"It went fine. Well, actually, it was like nothing had ever been off." Allison hopped off her stool and rounded the breakfast bar to fetch them each a glass of water.

"Maybe nothing ever was off." Her mother accepted the drink gratefully and Allison sat back down.

"I thought about that, but there's no way. People don't just fall off the face of the earth for weeks on end."

"Remind me again."

"We went on that trip to Canyon Ranch. Everything was great."

"I remember that."

"Charlotte and I really connected, you know? I thought I'd finally met someone who could be a real friend."

"Right."

"And then bam! She stopped returning my calls and, honestly, it seemed very intentional. When I finally saw her at the gallery that night, she was colder than usual, though she seemed to warm up throughout the evening. After that it was like everything turned back to the way it was. And then yesterday it was like nothing had ever happened at all."

"That is a little weird. You're sure you weren't reading something into it? Maybe she was just busy."

"I'm sure. It all started when she went to see her parents in Florida. I even had Charlie here for dinner while she was gone, so he and Gia didn't have to fend for themselves."

"Do you think that bothered her?"

"Why?"

"Maybe she felt left out. Didn't you say she's very sensitive? And I know their relationship is on the rocks."

"I never thought about that." This, Allison realized, was the precise reason she needed her mother around. Like Charlotte, her mother understood people. She knew what made them tick, what made them glad, what made them sad, and what plain old pissed the shit out of them.

"I may be wrong, but knowing that she's generally insecure, she may have felt put aside, or . . ."

"Or what?"

"Jealous."

"Jealous of what?"

"That you were filling in for her while she was out of town. Women can be very territorial. And you have been spending an awful lot of time with her husband."

"What's that supposed to mean?"

"It's not supposed to mean anything coming from me, sweetheart. But think about it from Charlotte's perspective."

"I don't know." Allison shook her head.

"I don't know either. But I'm glad things are back to normal."

"I guess." Allison thought for a moment. "Maybe I didn't know Charlotte as well as I thought I did."

"I wouldn't overanalyze it." Her mother stood up and kissed her on the cheek. "Sometimes, my dear, you are blessedly unaware of how beautiful you are and that some people may view your very presence as a threat."

"You get paid to say that!" Allison laughed and walked her mother to the front door, disappointed that she had to leave so soon, despite the fact that she'd be seeing her again within hours.

"I wish." Her mother blew another kiss. "Love you, sweetheart. See you tonight."

Allison closed the door behind her and sat down on the sofa before the phone rang. She reached over to the side table to grab the cordless receiver.

"Hello?"

"Allison? It's Elizabeth." She sounded serious.

"Oh, hey, Elizabeth. How are you?" They'd been talking only sporadically over the last month, ever since Elizabeth had gotten a job in sales for a major pharmaceutical company. The pay was on commission, but to both Elizabeth's and everyone else's surprise, the customers had really taken to her. Apparently, her direct, no-nonsense approach was exactly what the doctor—or pharmacist—had ordered.

"I'm good. Really good." She cleared her throat.

"Well, that's great to hear."

"There's something I have to tell you."

"Okay. Is everything all right?"

"Better than all right." Elizabeth paused. "I'm pregnant."

"What did you say?" Allison was sure she'd heard wrong.

"I said I'm pregnant." Elizabeth's voice cracked.

"Oh my God!" Allison shrieked. "Are you serious?!"

"Dead serious." Elizabeth sniffed, and Allison could tell she was crying.

"Those better be happy tears."

"The happiest of all time."

"Oh, Elizabeth. I could not be more thrilled for you." Allison knew all too well what this meant to her. How losing her first child had altered her life forever. How she never thought she'd see the light of day again, even if she was standing directly under the sun. How nothing could make it go away. Nothing could make it better. Except maybe this. "I didn't know you guys were trying!"

"Neither did I!" Elizabeth laughed manically. "When I had Cossette, there were some complications. After that my gynecologist told me that my chances of getting pregnant the natural way were only a little higher than one percent. Nick and I have never had enough money to think about fertility treatments, and even if we had, I don't know. I guess I never thought he really wanted kids."

"Oh."

"Don't worry, he does!" Elizabeth blew her nose loudly into the phone. "I think he might be happier than I am. He's already gone to the toy store to get him a football."

"*Him?*"

"Yeah, did I mention it's a boy?" Allison could practically hear Elizabeth beaming through the phone line.

"Wait a minute. How far along are you?"

"Sixteen weeks today. I had one of those CVS tests, which tells you the sex! Who knew?" Allison did. She'd had every test in the book with Logan. Not because of her age. She'd been way too young for any concerns there. But because her mother and her doctor had decided it was the best course of action given her circumstances. The very last thing Allison had needed was to give birth to a child with developmental or health issues when she could barely take care of herself.

"Unbelievable. What did Charlotte say?"

"Nothing. I haven't told her yet."

"Are you kidding?"

"I wanted to wait until I was really sure, you know? And then you were my first call."

"Wow, I'm so flattered, but you have to call Charlotte immediately. She's going to be over the moon."

"I hope." Elizabeth sounded skeptical.

"I *know*."

"You're probably right. She's just been so crazy with all this gala stuff that we've been on each other's nerves more than usual lately. I'll wait until Sunday when she has time to breathe."

"You're going to make me keep my mouth shut for *two days*?"

"If I can wait sixteen weeks, you can wait two days."

"Fair enough." Allison smiled. "Congratulations again. And if you need anything at all, you know where to find me."

"Thanks. That means a lot." Elizabeth hung up after promising that she'd keep Allison well informed and that they'd go maternity-clothes shopping soon.

Allison lay back on the sofa, stretching her body from one end to the other and resting her head against a throw pillow.

For whatever reason, she couldn't shake the feeling that everything was finally falling into place.

Chapter 23

Charlotte stood in the middle of the empty ballroom at the Wincourt Country Club marveling at the results of her handiwork. So she hadn't polished the floors or set the tables. But she had picked out every plate, fork, knife, spoon, napkin, tablecloth, and chair. She'd even given the busboy a quick tutorial on how to spray the floral centerpieces to keep them hydrated and glistening. It was this attention to detail that had landed her the coveted position of cochair of the gala in the first place.

Of course the *co* part was something of a joke. Charlie hadn't lifted a finger in the way of plans and preparations, nor had she expected him to. His job—and it was an important one—was to open his wallet and keep it open leading up to and throughout the evening. He'd agreed to said role, and he hadn't even balked when she'd asked him to purchase a fifth table of ten bearing a hefty price tag of five hundred dollars a seat. That would bring their grand total to twenty-five thousand dollars in guests alone. Not to mention the items they'd bid on in the silent and live auctions or the impromptu "anonymous" donation she'd ask Charlie to give as a match for whatever was raised. Of course, everyone would know who'd given the money, but it was so much classier to at least affect obscurity.

Somewhere over the course of the week, between pounding the pavement to gather last-minute contributions and sating herself with a bottle of wine while reading over the final program, Charlotte had decided this would be her last hurrah. It was actually possible to overstay your welcome as chair, even if you were doing a bang-up job year in and year out. She hadn't reached that point yet, but she wanted to go out on top. Kind of like *Seinfeld* or *Sex and the City*. Charlotte knew it was better to leave them wanting more, rather than be pushed out like Sabrina had been. Her ego was far too frail for that, and unlike Sabrina, she had neither the capability nor the inclination to live in denial.

She checked her watch. It was six thirty. Within the next thirty minutes, upward of four hundred men and women bedecked in the finest suits and the fanciest dresses would be crowding into the cavernous space where Charlotte was now standing alone, appraising her reflection in a mirror-covered wall. She knew she looked beautiful, which was a rare feeling for her. But when she had someone else to do her makeup and hair in the expert fashion she so desired and when she'd practically starved herself for the better part of three weeks so she could squeeze into a size four, emerald green, strapless taffeta Oscar de la Renta gown, even she had to admit she was breathtaking.

Eduardo at the Frederic Fekkai salon in Greenwich had

swept her glossy brown hair, which had been freshly high-lighted with blended streaks of deep red, into an effortless chignon with a few well-tamed, loose wisps to frame her face. And then his colleague Greta—who, Eduardo had told her, had worked with the likes of Gwyneth Paltrow, Kate Hudson, and Cameron Diaz—had painted her face in the way she imagined an artist would create a masterpiece. Ten small strokes here, five targeted dabs there, a series of brushes, and a dot, dot, dot on her lips until she'd glanced at her like-ness out of the corner of her eye and nodded her head in approval.

She'd choreographed the day as a cruise director would devise a schedule of activities for her passengers. Running a tight ship was paramount to the success of any sizable fête, and Charlotte would be damned if even one little thing went wrong, though inevitably it would. That was what damage control was for. And she was ready, armed with everything from first aid kits to needles and thread, not to mention the number for the closest hospital programmed into her cell phone in the event that 911 simply wasn't good enough. It was all part of the master plan, down to the half hour of solitude she'd left herself to contemplate the evening ahead.

What she hadn't premeditated was her discovery of the night before. Now, standing alone in the dimly lit silence, she laughed bitterly at the irony. How long and far had she searched to uncover this very piece of information? How many hours had she spent agonizing, torturing herself, vac-illating between certainty and questioning whether she'd gone absolutely mad?

She'd thought about acting on it immediately. But confrontation wasn't her strong suit. It never had been. Still, fueled with the two glasses of champagne she'd had on the limo ride over, and the cocktail hour in her immediate future, there was no telling what she might do or say.

She inhaled deeply and then exhaled, desperate to release the ugliness that was stirring inside her like a tornado gaining speed with every twirl and swirl. It felt both infuriating and exhilarating at the same time. Charlotte refused to be made the fool. She thought back to a period in her life before she'd met Charlie, when things had been so simple. When the idea of charting your course and figuring out what mark you wanted to leave in the world was as easy as saying it out loud. Or writing it down on some bucket list you'd scribbled while drinking a glass of cheap white wine over Indian takeout in your teeny-tiny apartment barely big enough to maneuver around in. Naturally she hadn't appreciated any of that at the time. The ability to come and go as she pleased without having to answer to anyone. The opportunity to watch what she wanted on television and to eat what she wanted for dinner without the nuisance of other opinions. The sheer bliss of spreading out across the whole bed, even if it was only full-sized, because why not? There was no one else there to snore or kick or wake up to in the morning with a perma-scowl on their unshaven face. Sometimes she wondered if that was what life was all about. Never feeling content in the present until the present was the past. And always assuming, hoping, even praying that there was something better, something more fulfilling on the horizon.

Charlotte sat down and kicked off her shoes—four-inch-high black silk Manolo Blahniks with a silver buckle encrusted with sparkling green gemstones to match her dress. Charlie would arrive any minute, she guessed. She'd asked him to meet her there so she could finalize some last-minute details on her own. Soon after, the other guests would arrive. She'd plaster a smile on her face to belie the surge of fury that was rousing in the pit of her stomach. She'd give her speech, stressing all of the important points she'd rehearsed. People would laugh. A few might even dab at a crocodile tear in the corner of a dry eye. The others would be plugged into their smartphones, following a sporting event or answering e-mails that couldn't wait the length of her ten-minute monologue, which everyone there knew was really a ten-minute pitch for the exceptional Wincourt school district, which—what do you know?—happened to need their money. She leaned against the back of her chair and took everything in. For tonight, this was her reality. Tomorrow, things would be different. Very, very different.

By the time the clock struck nine, the gala was in full swing. Charlotte had air-kissed and schmoozed. She'd chugged three more glasses of champagne in quick succession, but only after delivering an articulate and persuasive speech with eight hundred eyes focused solely on her. She'd also managed to avoid Allison, who'd been trying to grab her attention ever since realizing her artwork was not on display. "Just a minute," Charlotte had said, holding up a dismissive index finger on each occasion that Allison had approached her in her body-hugging nude gown embellished with the most subtle but intricate beading. Of course she looked gorgeous. That was to be expected. She even had Dempsey on her arm, the most flattering accessory of all. Charlotte wondered, for a passing moment, how all this would affect him. And then she dismissed the thought. Dempsey and Allison weren't married. They didn't have a child together. He would be fine. If anyone was the victim, it was her. There was no mistake to be made about that.

"Charlotte, is everything okay?" Charlie tugged on her arm, pulling her away from the bar. "You might want to slow down on those."

"I'm fine." She looked past him. Eye contact wasn't an option at this point. It was all she'd been able to manage to remain civil for the last two hours. "And I'm perfectly capable of monitoring my own alcohol intake."

"I'm not saying—"

"There you are!" Sabrina squealed, running toward her as fast as her Jimmy Choos would carry her. Charlie cleared his throat to indicate that she'd interrupted him, but predictably Sabrina didn't notice. And if she did, she certainly didn't care. For once, Charlotte was thankful for Sabrina's insolence. "I've been trying to track you down all night!"

"Sorry, I've been crazed with attending to every last detail." Charlotte rolled her eyes as she watched Charlie's follow Allison and Dempsey around the dance floor.

"You don't have to tell me how it is." Sabrina put her hand on Charlotte's arm. "I've been in your shoes. Five times."

"I know." Charlotte nodded. "I can't believe you kept coming back for more!" It was always easier to nourish Sabrina's ego rather than to placate her or, God forbid, point out that this night wasn't about her anymore.

"I must have been a glutton for punishment, because it

wasn't easy. That's for sure." She exhaled, as if her past efforts were still burdensome. "But you're doing a good job too." She smiled, and Charlotte did a quick translation. *I could have done it better.*

"Well, thank you. That means a lot coming from you." Charlotte glanced over Sabrina's shoulder to see that Allison was making her way toward them. "Sorry to be rude, but I just have to run over and check on the items for the live auction. I'll only be a minute."

"Charlotte, wait . . . ," Charlie called after her, but she scurried away as quickly as possible, swallowing her entire glass of champagne on the way. It wasn't until she'd reached the auction area that she realized Allison was right behind her.

"Hey." Allison touched her on the shoulder and she jumped. "Are you okay?"

"I wish everyone would stop asking me that," Charlotte snapped. She couldn't help herself.

"Okay." Allison smiled, but Charlotte could see the concern on her face. "Is there anything I can help you with?"

"You've done plenty already."

"Speaking of which"—Allison spoke slowly and carefully, as if she was handling a volatile child—"I noticed that my painting isn't on display."

"Yeah, sorry. It just didn't work out." Charlotte turned her back to Allison and started tidying up the silent-auction area.

"What do you mean it didn't work out?"

"Exactly what I said."

"Charlotte, I'm going to need a little more of an explanation.

I worked very hard on that piece. It was an enormous emotional investment, as I'm sure you can imagine."

"Well, I'm glad it was cathartic for you, but—for our purposes—it wasn't right. It was an executive decision." Charlotte moved down the line of items, returning pens to their clipboards and pretending to check the lists of bids, while Allison trailed her.

"Who's the executive?" She was clearly confused and annoyed, justifiably so. There'd been nothing wrong with her painting. It had been perfect. And, more important, it would have raised a lot of money for the Wincourt school system. But for once, Charlotte didn't care about that. Even if it had garnered a million dollars, she wouldn't have used it.

"I am. I am the executive. And it was my decision not to include it. Now, if you'll let me get back to what I'm doing here, I'd really appreciate it, okay?" She started to walk away again, but this time Allison grabbed her by the arm.

"No, it's not okay. I want to know what's going on here, Charlotte. There's obviously something wrong."

"Not now, Allison. This is neither the time nor the place."

"Yes, now."

"Excuse me?" Charlotte spun her head around, and suddenly, staring Allison directly in the face, she couldn't hold back any longer. Not for another week. Not for another day. Not for another minute or even another second. "Did you think I wouldn't find out about you and Charlie?" Charlotte's tone was fierce and increasing in volume as she pursued Allison with pointed finger, forcing Allison to retreat, one step at a time. "Huh? *Did you?*"

"Charlotte, I don't know what you're talking about." Allison shook her head fearfully.

"Bullshit." She practically spit the word at Allison. "You're a slut. And a husband stealer!" Charlotte was now yelling so loud that the guests on their half of the room had quieted down and the band had stopped playing, noticing that a crowd was gathering. "You thought you could just prance into this town and into our lives with your pathetic little 'poor me, poor widow' act. But it was all a ruse. You're a master manipulator—I'll give you that. Pretending to be my friend. Pretending you needed help fixing things around the house. I should have seen through you from the start."

"Charlotte, *please*. Can we walk outside and talk about this?" Allison's tone was hushed as she eyed the door.

"No, we cannot!" Charlotte stomped her foot.

"I don't know where this is coming from, but if we could just talk rationally—"

"Rationally?" Charlotte cut her off. The entire room had fallen silent and all eyes and ears were on them. It was now or never. She cleared her throat and pulled herself together as best she could. "I read your letter, Allison."

"My letter?"

"Yes, your letter. You know—the one in your journal? The *love* letter to my husband!" A collective gasp rippled throughout the throng of guests.

"What the hell is going on here?" Charlotte looked up to find Charlie standing by Allison's side with a hardened expression shrouding his face.

"What's going on . . ." She stopped for a moment, searching the mob until she found Dempsey, and their eyes locked. "What's going on is that your little girlfriend here wrote all about your love affair in her diary. Or whatever you want to call it. I guess the cat's out of the bag now."

"Charlotte," Allison pleaded.

"Get out." Charlotte pointed to the exit.

"Please, Charlotte, don't do this."

"I said, *get the fuck out!"*

Allison looked at Dempsey, who bowed his head in disappointment, and then raced out the door. What Charlotte hadn't expected was that Charlie would run after her.

Chapter 24

Allison sat on her family room couch sobbing, her knees hugged to her chest, while trails of wet black mascara streamed down her cheeks. After fleeing the ballroom of the Wincourt Country Club, she'd sprinted to her car and sped home as quickly as possible, nearly spinning out of control on three different turns. She knew she shouldn't be behind the wheel, but she didn't care. She had to get away.

She'd thought about calling her parents. About unleashing her despair on them. But she wasn't a child anymore. They'd seen her through too much already. And she didn't want to alarm them, especially since they had Logan sleeping at their house for the night. She needed to be alone, she decided. To replay the events of the evening in her head, specifically her conversation with Charlotte.

What letter could she be referring to? Allison had never written anything more salacious about Charlie than that he was helping her. That he was being the friend Jack would have wanted him to be. At first, Allison had been dumbfounded, not knowing how Charlotte had gotten hold of whatever evidence she thought she had. And then it had hit her. Charlotte had been in possession of her journal for days now. It was unthinkable that this woman whom she'd called her friend would have engaged in such a blatant invasion of privacy. That not only had she given herself permission to look inside, but once she'd seen what the journal contained, she'd allowed herself to indulge in Allison's innermost thoughts, feelings, and confessions, mostly to her late husband.

Still, now, Allison couldn't focus on that. What was done was done. She'd been humiliated in front of everyone from Logan's school, a number of her parents' friends and acquaintances, and—most important—Dempsey. She'd seen the look on his face. Disappointment. Regret. Perhaps a bit of disgust. All because of nothing. Not that anyone would believe her over Charlotte. She didn't have a leg to stand on in Wincourt. Whereas Charlotte, by comparison, was the captain of the ship, and she'd thrown Allison overboard without a second thought.

What would she do now? Where would she go? She couldn't very well stay in Wincourt with a scarlet letter emblazoned on her chest. Logan would be teased at school, no doubt. And she'd have to face Charlotte every day. Just when Allison had thought she was finally settling into her new life. Just when she'd decided that taking a leap of faith had been the right decision after all. Just when she'd finally found a man she wanted to be with and who wanted to be with her, even if they hadn't defined their relationship yet. It was too much for any one person to handle, and suddenly she was yearning for Jack. He'd know what to say, she told herself. He'd know what to do. He'd protect her. Allison's heart ached, and looking around her vacant house, she felt hollow inside.

Just as she was about to go up to bed, to sleep until she couldn't sleep anymore, the doorbell rang, and for a moment, she hoped it was Dempsey. All she needed, all she desired, was for him to take her in his arms and tell her it was all going to be okay, even if it wasn't strictly the truth. But when she opened the door, it wasn't him, and the lump that had been residing in her throat swelled nearly to the point of suffocation.

"Thank God you're here." Charlie was standing on her front porch, still in his tuxedo, which was now drenched from the unexpected downpour that had erupted only minutes after she'd arrived home.

"This isn't a good time." Allison shook her head sluggishly. Everything was moving in slow motion, it seemed, including her.

"Please, Allison. I need to talk to you."

"Not now. Maybe tomorrow. I don't know."

"It's about Jack." Charlie's green eyes were passionate but empathetic. If he was using Jack's name in vain, he should be ashamed of himself.

"Fine." She stood staring at him, waiting for him to say whatever it was he'd come to say. She was too numb to think beyond that.

"Can I come in? It's a little damp out here."

"I suppose. But not for long. I'm exhausted." She turned to walk back inside, allowing Charlie to close the door behind him.

"Of course, I understand." He followed her to the sofa and she motioned for him to sit down. "I'm really wet, actually."

She looked at the clean, dry cushions and shrugged. "Whatever."

"Oh, okay." He nodded and sat across from her. Then he took a long, deep breath and exhaled. "I can't tell you how sorry I am for what happened tonight." He reached for her hand, but she recoiled. Allison saw him wince, but she didn't have the energy to care.

"You're not the only one." Her voice was monotone. Charlie wasn't to blame. That she knew. But it wasn't as if they could remain friends after this, so what was the point?

"I'm appalled by Charlotte. I have no idea where she got this idea or what she thinks she read. . . ." He paused, as if waiting for Allison to say something. What did he expect? An admission that she actually had written him a love letter? A denial? He knew the truth. In fact, now they were the only two who did.

"Neither do I." Allison cleared her throat, which was parched and raw. "But I do know that you shouldn't be here."

"We haven't done anything wrong."

"It doesn't matter, Charlie. Charlotte seems to think otherwise, and frankly, I've heard enough from her to last me a lifetime. I don't owe her an explanation. But you do. You need to go home to your wife and stop helping me."

"I can't." Charlie hung his head.

"You have to."

"No, I really can't." He was adamant.

"What does that mean?" She certainly hoped he didn't expect to stay the night. That was out of the question.

"I mean I can't stop helping you. I owe it to you and Logan. I owe it to Jack."

"You keep saying that, but you don't owe us anything."

"You don't know. . . ." He trailed off, pressing his fingertips to his temples.

"I don't know what?"

"Allison, I don't know how to tell you this."

"Just say it." He was making her anxious now. What more could go wrong?

Charlie looked up and Allison could see that his eyes were swimming in a pool of tears. "I'm the reason Jack died that day."

"Excuse me?"

"I'm the reason Jack was on that bus." He repeated himself, this time looking her directly in the eyes.

"That's ridiculous." She stood up. "I don't have time for this. You can go now."

"Allison, please. Sit down. Let me explain." She listened to him, against her better judgment. "Okay. Here goes." He took a deep breath. "I'm not sure if Jack ever told you this, but we ran into each other on the street a few months before—" His voice cracked. "Before the accident."

"I think I vaguely remember him mentioning something."

"He told me about the job. The one he really wanted at Brower Fisk. He said it was his dream job."

"Right."

"The thing is, I was looking too. The boutique firm I was with had just gone belly-up, and I was desperate to find something. I'd been interviewing for months and nothing was turning into an offer. So I called my uncle, who knew someone high up there."

"And?"

"And I got the job. A favor for the old man. I stole the job from Jack. What's worse is that Jack had invited me on the ski trip so he could introduce me to some of his colleagues. He was helping me while I was screwing him. If he'd gotten the job at Brower Fisk instead of me, I'd have been the one . . ."

"Dead."

"Dead."

"Wow. Okay." Allison tried to absorb the weight of Charlie's words, to react to them in the appropriate way, but she'd been rendered incapable of emotion. She was officially crippled inside.

"If you hate me, I'll understand. When I found out what had happened, I was sick. And then Brower was bought out by Cooper Paine and we moved up here. I still work there, for fuck's sake."

"Right." Charlie was watching her, no doubt waiting for a big reaction. Any reaction. She just didn't have it in her to say more.

"I wanted to call you so many times, Ali. To tell you what I'd done, but I was too much of a goddamn chicken. And I didn't want to add to your pain. I know that sounds pretty pathetic now, but it's the truth. If that's worth anything."

"Uh-huh." Allison nodded deliberately.

"I've carried it with me for years. Believe me when I say that. I never even told Charlotte. She still doesn't know." He sniffed and she noticed a tear escape from the corner of his eye. "When we saw each other that day at school and you said you'd moved back to Wincourt, I felt like I'd been given a second chance. It was as if serendipity was standing right in front of me. I knew that I could never make up for what I'd done. But I also knew that I needed—and *wanted*—to help you and Logan to the greatest extent of my capabilities. I should have said something sooner."

"It's not your fault." Allison spoke the words, though she wasn't sure whether she meant them. Still, what else was there to say? Was she supposed to hold him accountable now? Or was he looking for an out? If the latter was the case, he could have it. At the time she probably would have cursed and thrown things at him, told him that he was in fact to blame. But more than a decade later, she'd developed perspective. And anyway, her mind was currently crowded with bigger problems.

"You don't have to say that."

"I know."

"I'm not telling you this to assuage my own guilt, Ali. I'm telling you this because I want to be able to move forward. I want you in my life. I want Logan in my life." His voice was urgent.

"I don't really see how that's going to be possible after what happened tonight."

"It won't be easy, but we can get through this. I know we can."

"Charlie, you need to go home and work things out with

Charlotte, first and foremost." Allison mustered an awkward half smile.

"Work things out? I think it's time I admitted to myself that Charlotte and I are past the point of repair. I mean, really, what's left of *us*?"

"Okay." Allison exhaled, wearied by the prospect of having to play therapist to Charlie yet again.

"Maybe all this time I've found some solace in the idea of starting over. It's been so refreshing to feel like someone needed me. To feel like you and Logan could lean on me, since that certainly doesn't happen with Charlotte and Gia anymore."

"What are you trying to say, Charlie?"

"I don't know."

"Listen, Charlie, I appreciate your confession tonight, and I'm letting you off the hook. But unless there's something else, I need to ask you to leave now."

"I'm sorry, Ali. I didn't—"

"Please, Charlie. You need to go home to your wife."

Chapter 25

Charlotte paced back and forth from one side of her bedroom to the other, vacillating between primitive rage and consuming grief. How could they have done this to her? How could *he* have done this to her? Not only was Charlie screwing Allison behind her back, but he'd made a choice. And that choice had not been in Charlotte's favor. He'd decided, without so much as a cursory glance in her direction, to run after Allison when she'd fled the scene, leaving Charlotte standing there alone with four hundred people staring at her, mouths agape. She'd been humiliated by both of them in the worst possible way, and now, more than an hour later, Charlie had yet to return home.

What had she expected Charlie to do? She'd asked herself this same question over and over. But over and over, she'd failed to find an answer. If he'd tried to apologize, admitted his shortcomings, would she have forgiven him? Would that have quieted her public outburst? Probably not. Still, it would have been preferable to the alternative—

abandoning her in front of everyone who was anyone in their small rumor mill of a town. She'd never be able to show her face again at school or at the country club or at the hair salon. And even if she dared, the stage whispers and bowed heads would be enough to send her on her way, never to return again.

Charlie would probably try to blame it on her. She was prepared for that eventuality. He'd say they could have worked it out in the privacy of their own home. That she'd embarrassed him. How many times had she heard that? How many times had he kicked her under the table during one of his business dinners to not so subtly indicate that she should shut her mouth, because whatever it was she was saying wasn't to his liking? She was sick of it. All of it. The bickering, the jabs muttered under his breath but loud enough for her to hear, the knock-down, drag-out fights. Those were the worst. They took everything out of her and then some. And the aftermath was almost as bad as the fights themselves. Two, three, four days—sometimes even a week or more—where they'd go through the motions of life, walk through the hallways of the same house, and sit at the same dinner table like two strangers, both of them fuming inside, certain of how right they were and how undeniably wrong the other one was. Eventually the tension would either dissipate or Charlotte would be forced to apologize if she ever wanted to regain a semblance of normalcy. Oftentimes she found herself saying she was sorry when she didn't even know what she was supposed to be sorry for. But at some point, she'd come to the realization that it didn't matter. The source of the battle was moot to Charlie, as long as he won the war.

Charlotte slipped out of her gown, letting it fall to the floor in a heap. Normally she'd have gingerly returned it to its hanger, scouring it for any stains or snags, and covered it with a garment bag so Janna could bring it to the dry cleaner first thing Monday morning. She kicked off her six-hundred-dollar shoes and let them bounce off the wall and onto the carpet, where they'd sit, straps tangled, until she had either the energy or the wherewithal to care about picking them up. She opened the top drawer of her dresser and reached for the first nightgown she could find and then wriggled her tired body into the silky fabric. Charlie had bought it for her on their third trip to Paris. She'd seen it in the window of La Perla and fallen in love. Later that evening, before going to sleep, she'd found the box on her pillow tied with a big white bow. She'd tried it on, modeling it for Charlie, as if she was on the catwalk. He'd said she looked beautiful in it but that he quite preferred her wearing nothing at all. They'd made love twice that night. It may have been the last time that had happened.

She pulled back the covers on her bed, ready to climb in, when she heard the front door slam and the sound of Charlie's pounding footsteps ascending the stairs. She turned around and there he was, looking impossibly handsome in his damp, shriveled tuxedo with his lips pressed into a thin line. Part of her wanted to run to him. To tell him she was sorry for everything. That she wanted to start over. That they could leave Wincourt once and for all, find their way back to each other again. But another part of her, the part of her that knew better, folded her arms across her chest and glared at him.

"I'm just here to pack some things." He walked toward his closet, not bothering to look at her.

"Where are you going?" She followed him.

"I don't know, Charlotte. Anywhere but here."

"Well, isn't that fabulous. I'm sure your girlfriend would be thrilled to have you shack up with her. Or did she throw you out?" Charlotte could only assume that he'd been with Allison all this time, consoling her, possibly even making passionate love to her.

"Leave me alone, Charlotte." He grabbed his black leather carry-on and started throwing shirts, pants, socks, shoes, and underwear in haphazardly. It took every bit of her willpower not to take the bag out of his hands and pack it for him in an orderly fashion. The truth was that she knew what he needed better than he did.

"I'm sorry, but I'm a little confused as to why *you're* angry with *me*. Aren't you the one who's been fucking my friend for the past . . ." She paused, realizing she had no idea how long their affair had been going on. The only point of reference she had was the letter Allison had written to him that fateful night after she'd had Charlie and Gia for dinner, while Charlotte had been tending to her sick parents in Florida. ". . . for God knows how long."

"You have no idea what you're talking about." He turned toward her now, almost running her over on the way out of his expansive walk-in closet.

"I read it with my own eyes!" Charlotte flailed her arms in the air. "You must think I'm really stupid."

All at once he stopped. Dropped his bag on the floor. And looked at her. He finally really looked at her. "I don't think you're stupid, Charlotte. But I do think you're wrong. No, I'm sorry. I *know* you're wrong. And whatever proof you may think you have is bullshit. Okay? It's fucking bullshit. And, frankly, I don't give a shit anymore."

"What's that supposed to mean?"

"What do you think it means, Charlotte?"

"That you don't love me anymore." She sat down on the bed and started to cry, softly at first.

"Honestly, Charlotte, I don't know how I feel. But I do know one thing. I don't know you anymore. The woman I fell in love with was fun. She was happy. And optimistic. She smiled more than once in a blue moon. At me. You used to smile at me, Charlotte, and that was all I needed to turn the worst day into the best day. You were funny and light-hearted. You worked hard, but you played harder. I don't know that woman anymore. I've spent so much time pray-ing she'd come back to me. And, believe me, I know I've made mistakes. We both have. But now, I don't know. I just don't know."

"So you think I'm pathetic and insufferable." Charlotte was sobbing now, and her whole torso was quivering.

"I don't think you're pathetic. I think you're bored. I think you've been bored for the last decade. I know you're busy. I know you find things to fill your day. But it's not enough. If it was, you wouldn't be on my back every goddamn minute of every goddamn day." His voice was growing louder and Charlotte could see the veins in his forehead stretching his skin.

"Don't yell at me! I'm not the one who had the affair. I didn't do anything wrong!"

"Keep telling yourself that, Charlotte. Go ahead. And let me know how that works out for you." He bent his head and shook it back and forth. "I'm leaving. Tell Gia I'll call her to-morrow."

"So that's it? You're just walking out?" She didn't want to fight, but she didn't want him to go either. If he left, there was no telling what would happen. Why hadn't she thought this through? Why hadn't she considered the ramifications?

"That's it, Charlotte. I'm just walking out."

And with that, he picked up his bag, turned his back on her, and left.

The next morning, Charlotte was awakened from a deep sleep by the piercing ring of her telephone. "Hello?" She grunted into the receiver in a raspy voice.

"Char? It's me."

"This isn't a good time, Lizzy."

"I have something to tell you. It's important."

Charlotte rubbed her eyes and sat up in her bed. The very last thing she needed was to deal with her sister's problems. She had quite enough of her own at the moment. "What is it?"

"Jeez, you sound grumpy."

"I don't have time for this, Lizzy. Just tell me what it is so I can go back to sleep."

"Well, fine, if you're going to be that way about it." Elizabeth paused, presumably waiting for Charlotte to beg her to come out with it. "I'm pregnant!"

"Lizzy, I just told you I don't have time for this. When you decide you want to tell me what's really going on, let me know."

"I'm not messing with you, Char; it's true! Can you believe it? After all this time?"

Charlotte was wide-awake now. "Are you serious?"

"Dead."

"Oh my God."

"I know! Isn't it the best news ever? We're so beyond excited. You're going to be an aunt!"

"Slow down." Charlotte took a sip of the lukewarm water on her nightstand to dampen her parched throat. "Just how do you and Nick plan to support a child? I certainly hope you don't expect me to bankroll this new hobby of yours."

"It's not a hobby, Charlotte. It's a child."

"Whatever. Have you thought about how much this child is going to cost?"

"Nick just got a new job. That was the other thing I was going to tell you."

"Well, let's be honest. Nick has had at least a dozen new jobs in the last, what, two years? And when he gambles away your diaper money, what are you going to do then? Come running to me, that's what."

"Are you kidding me?"

"No, I'm not kidding you. This is so like you to do something completely irresponsible, like get knocked up, without even thinking about how you're going to manage it or how it might affect other people."

"I'm so sorry, Charlotte, that I didn't consider how my having a child would ruin your life! I was hoping you would be happy for me like Allison was, but I guess I should have expected this."

"You told Allison before you told me!?" Charlotte was fuming now. How dare she?

"I did, because I wanted to wait until your mind was free of all your important gala crap. And I felt badly about it. Allison made me feel badly about it. She said I should tell you straightaway. That you'd be over the moon. But apparently, you can't get out of your own way long enough to see that this is something I've been waiting years for. You know how important this is to me, Charlotte."

"You know what, Lizzy? I've got a great idea. Why don't I just disappear and Allison can be Charlie's new wife, Gia's new mom, and your new sister. I think everyone would be a lot happier that way. And it would save me a whole lot of fucking hassle. How does that sound?"

"Truthfully, it sounds pretty good to me."

"Fuck you."

"No, fuck you, Charlotte. Fuck you and your perfect life. Or should I say the perfect life you pretend to have, because we all know it's a facade. Fuck you and your fancy house and your fancy cars and your fancy fucking clothing and all that stuff that doesn't mean anything. Fuck you. You don't even want me to be happy. Because if I'm happy then you won't be the one who has everything anymore. And that's all that matters to you. Isn't that right? Well, guess what,

Charlotte? Look who has everything now. Me. Good luck finding yourself another sister."

"You don't mean that."

"Yeah, I do." Elizabeth was quiet for a moment. "In case you were wondering, it's a boy."

Chapter 26

"It's just me!" Allison's mother announced, letting herself in the front door. "Not a thief or a serial killer, in case you were concerned." She walked into the kitchen carrying two stuffed bags of groceries.

"Good to know. The last thing I need right now is to be robbed or murdered," Allison deadpanned, taking the bags from her mother and kissing her on the cheek.

"You really need to start locking your door. I mean, for God's sake, you're all alone here."

"Not *all* alone." Allison looked at Logan, who was lounging on the couch with his feet on the coffee table, entranced by some tween-type show on Nickelodeon.

"You know what I mean." She started unpacking green apples and purple grapes the size of silver dollars.

"One more episode before lunch!" Allison called out.

"Okay, Mom." He wagged his arm in the air. "Hi, Grandma."

"Hello, my darling." She smiled in his direction and then turned her attention back to Allison. "So?"

"So, what?"

"So how are you doing? You must feel relieved."

"I'm not sure that's the word I'd use."

Two days after the gala, Missy had appeared on Allison's doorstep in an effort to mend things, to finally be the friend she'd said she always wanted to be, and to repay Allison for her goodwill the day of her mother's hip surgery. She'd said that she went to Charlotte and asked to see Allison's "love letter" to Charlie. Missy had insisted that something didn't add up. She'd also confessed that Sabrina had come clean the day before, admitting that she'd read the letter first, the whole journal, in fact, and had intentionally earmarked that page in order to pique Charlotte's curiosity.

Missy had then taken the journal back to Allison, who'd explained—in no uncertain terms—that said letter had been intended for Jack. That she'd ripped out the sketch on the page before it, which had read *My Dearest Jack* at the top, in a fit of frustration, and that if she hadn't, the separation between her journal entry from that night—the night Charlie and Gia had been over for dinner—and her profession of love to her dead husband would have been abundantly clear.

Missy had maintained that she was finally fed up with Sabrina and divulged that right about the time Allison had moved to Wincourt, Sabrina had discovered that her husband, Craig, was having an affair, apparently not his first. Sabrina had sworn Missy to secrecy, threatening to "ruin her life" if anyone found out. It wasn't that Sabrina had thought Allison was the culprit, but still, she'd represented everything Sabrina despised in other women—not to mention that she'd felt Allison was usurping her place as Charlotte's best friend.

In other words, the whole thing had been a dreadful misunderstanding. A misunderstanding that had impacted too many lives and relationships.

"Have you spoken to Charlotte?"

"Only briefly yesterday afternoon."

"What did she say?"

"What could she say? She's sorry. Humiliated. She understands if I can never forgive her, but she hopes that I will. At some point."

"What did you say?"

"I said I need time. That I get where she was coming from now but that it's not that easy." Allison handed her mother some tea. "Mom, I went into town to go to the bank yesterday and it felt like everyone was staring at me. It doesn't go away just because it was a mistake or because someone apologizes."

"I agree." She accepted the steaming mug gratefully and rubbed Allison's back with her free hand. "I think it was awfully generous of you to even accept her call."

"Yeah, well, I'm sure she's suffering right about now. I can't imagine this helped things with Charlie. There's still a lot of damage that's been done."

"I know, sweetheart. But it will get better, I promise."

"I hope you're right."

"I know I'm right." She cupped Allison's cheeks in her palms and kissed her on the forehead. "And now I'm going to take my grandson to the diner for grilled cheese and French fries, if you don't mind."

"I thought I was going with you."

"I think it's better if you stay here."

"Excellent. Even my own mother is embarrassed to be seen with me."

"Don't be ridiculous. I just think you might have a visitor—that's all." She motioned to Logan to let him know it was time to go. "It wouldn't kill you to put a little makeup on."

"*Mom.*" Allison arched an eyebrow. "What have you done?"

"Nothing you won't thank me for." She wrapped her arm around Logan's back. "You ready?"

"Yup!" He nodded eagerly.

"Bye, sweetie. Have fun with Grandma."

"I will."

"Bye, Mom."

"Good-bye, darling." Allison's mother waved over her shoulder. "Remember a little blush and mascara! And running a brush through your hair couldn't hurt!"

Reliably, twenty minutes later there was a knock at her door. As Allison went to answer it, she couldn't quell the jittery sensation that had settled in the pit of her stomach.

"Hey, you." A smiling Dempsey appeared on her front porch looking more handsome than ever. He paused for a moment before taking her into his arms and squeezing her against his warm body. Unwittingly, she started to cry

"I'm so sorry," she said.

"You have nothing to be sorry about." He stroked the top of her head. "I know the truth. All of it."

"Who told you?" she asked, even though she was pretty sure she knew the answer.

"A little birdie."

"Oh yeah?" She laughed through her tears and took his

hand in hers to lead him inside. "The little birdie struck again, huh?"

"Something like that."

"I'm so sorry, Dempsey," she repeated as they sat next to each other on the couch in her family room.

"It's not your fault. None of it's your fault. I'm the one who should be apologizing."

"For what?"

"For doubting you for even a minute. I know you better than that. You'd never get involved with your friend's husband, or any married man, for that matter."

"And I'd never betray you. What we have is so important to me."

"Me too." He leaned in to kiss her softly on the lips. "Me too." The phone rang, infringing on their moment.

"I don't have to get that." She gazed into his gentle blue eyes.

"Go ahead. I'm not going anywhere." Allison got up reluctantly and walked into the kitchen. When she returned a few minutes later, there was a confused expression blanketing her face.

"Who was it?"

"Jack's parents. Nancy and Bill."

"Oh?"

"They said they want to come visit for Christmas. That it's been way too long. And that they're finally ready to be the grandparents that Logan deserves."

"Wow." Dempsey pulled her onto his lap and swathed his strong arms around her waist. "That's great, isn't it?"

"I think so." She leaned back and rested her head on his chest. "I mean, yes, definitely. I'm just surprised is all."

"You know what this means, right?" He nuzzled his face into the curve of her neck.

"What?"

"Only good things to come. Very good things."

I have to admit tonight was really nice. It felt like being part of a family, even though it wasn't entirely my family. Does that make sense? I think most people take it for granted, you know? Husband, wife, kids—all gathered around the table for dinner. As I said, it felt nice.

But now I miss you. I miss you so much. These last few months have been a roller-coaster ride and, through it all, being able to express my feelings and thoughts to you has been the greatest gift. Still, I want you here with me all the time. I know that's not possible given the circumstances, but it's true. And I'd never lie to you.

I want to touch you again. To hold your face in my hands and kiss you. To make love to you. I want you sleeping next to me every night. I need that.

I love you and I always will.

Good night, my precious. Until we meet again . . .

xoxo, A

Five Months Later

Chapter 27

"You're going to have to give him back eventually." Elizabeth smiled contentedly, marveling at how natural Charlotte looked cradling her sweet little nephew in her arms.

"Says who?" Charlotte kissed the newborn on his teeny-tiny button nose and brushed his hair off his forehead. "I can't believe this wild mane he was born with. You were completely bald until you were two."

"I was not!" Elizabeth protested.

"You were so. I have the photos to prove it. And you had all these dimples too, so you kind of resembled a golf ball." Charlotte sat down next to Elizabeth on the couch in her cluttered apartment. "I'm sending Janna here on Monday to clean this place up." She looked around at all the boxes—some partially unpacked, some not. "You've got a ton of stuff."

"I know." Elizabeth sighed. "Don't get me wrong, I'm thankful for all of it, but it feels a little overwhelming right about now. I'm feeding him every few hours. And when I'm not, I'm just so exhausted."

"Can Nick help?"

"He has been. It's tough, though. He's at work all day, sometimes until nine at night. And then he comes home and wants to see the baby. After that he tries to make headway in the opening-presents department, but it's a lot. He's even written thank-you notes."

"Impressive."

"I feel like I haven't slept in a week. And do you see this?" Elizabeth pointed at her ratty, smelly, oversized white T-shirt with milk stains at the nipples and an unidentifiable orange smear down the center. Orange juice? "Let's just say I haven't showered in over forty-eight hours."

"Well, that's about to end."

"Yeah, right. I don't think this one will be sleeping through the night anytime soon."

"No, but you will be." Charlotte nodded definitively and then went back to cooing. "Isn't that right, you delicious doll? Your mommy needs some rest too."

"And how do you suppose that's going to happen?" Elizabeth arched an eyebrow. "Please don't tell me you're planning to move in."

"Very funny." Charlotte made a face at her sister. "Remember when I told you my gift was slightly delayed?"

"Yeah."

"Well, she arrives tomorrow."

"She?"

"Beatrice."

"*Your* Beatrice?"

"*My* Beatrice."

Beatrice had been Charlotte's saint of a baby nurse when she'd had Gia, and although she'd since gone into retirement, Charlotte had called her and begged her to come help Elizabeth. She'd offered to pay her double her already exorbitant salary and Beatrice had readily agreed, with the caveat that she couldn't start until late August, after she'd returned from her daughter's wedding in Jamaica. Since the baby hadn't been due until September first, Charlotte had expected Beatrice to be waiting at Elizabeth and Nick's apartment—as a surprise—when they'd come home from the hospital, but, alas, the best-laid plans . . .

"That's amazing! But you've done so much already." Charlotte had accompanied Elizabeth to every one of her prenatal checkups that Nick couldn't be at. She'd also helped her prepare the nursery, rolling up her sleeves and wielding various tools that—to both her surprise and Elizabeth's—she was fairly adept with.

"Don't be ridiculous. That's what sisters are for." Charlotte sniffed. "Now can you please leave me with my nephew and go hose off? I can smell you from here."

"You don't have to ask me twice." Elizabeth jumped up, kissed her baby on the cheek, and shoved her armpit in Charlotte's face. "Take a whiff of that!"

"You are disgusting! Get away!" Charlotte shrieked as Elizabeth giggled and skipped toward the bathroom. As soon as Charlotte heard the water running, she lay back on the couch and closed her eyes. It was remarkable to think how far they'd come in the past five months.

Within forty-eight hours of the Wincourt school gala and

Charlotte's falling out with Elizabeth, once the massive mis-understanding had been revealed, Charlotte had been left shocked, relieved, and furious all at once. More than that, she'd been mortified. She'd caused a scene in front of hundreds of people. She'd humiliated herself and those she loved. She'd jeopardized her marriage, her friendship with Allison, and her relationship with her sister. And for what?

She'd e-mailed Charlie immediately to explain. He hadn't been answering her calls in the wake of their hideous fight, and she'd hoped—prayed—that this would be the first step toward bringing him around. And then she'd phoned Allison. Their conversation had been awkward at best. In fact, Charlotte had been taken aback by how kind Allison had been, given the circumstances. She'd said she needed time. That now she had a better understanding of where Charlotte had been coming from, but that this enlightening information still didn't erase what had happened. Charlotte had said she understood. That if Allison never wanted to speak to her again, she couldn't blame her. They'd hung up after only a few minutes, just as her cell phone had trilled with a return message from Charlie, letting her know that he would be home the next day. He needed a little more time to clear his head, he'd said, but they would talk then.

And talk they had. For four hours. Charlie had told her about his shame over stealing the job from Jack all those years ago and the inherent guilt that had been weighing on him for over a decade. He'd said that he wanted to make things work between them. That even though he'd been livid after Charlotte's outburst at the gala, it might very well have been the wake-up call they desperately needed. He'd confessed that he felt lost, that he hated the way he treated her. That he wanted their marriage to be solid and full of love and that he was willing to work on himself and with Charlotte to put the pieces of their life back together. Then he'd handed her an envelope with three tickets to Hawaii and said, "We leave next week. No work calls. No stress. Just you, me, Gia, and the beach." He'd told Charlotte that he'd even scheduled sailing lessons for him and Gia, professing, "I want to be the father she deserves and the husband you deserve. It's about time."

After that, they'd made the most passionate love they had in years, in broad daylight, with their bedroom door wide open. So what if no one had been home? It had still felt deliciously rebellious.

"I'm a new woman!" Elizabeth materialized twenty minutes later, interrupting Charlotte's reverie. She looked astonishingly slender for someone who'd recently given birth, affording new meaning to the phrase *the pounds just fell off.* There'd been a time when this would have irritated Charlotte to no end, but her rapport with her sister was different now.

"You look it." Charlotte smiled. She'd never seen Elizabeth so happy. "I forgot to tell you Mom called earlier. She'll be here on Saturday."

"Great!" Elizabeth took the baby from Charlotte, nuzzling her face against his. "I can't believe Dad will never get to meet him."

"I know." Charlotte shook her head, willing herself not to cry. "He would have adored him."

Five months earlier, they'd received a call from their

mother in the early morning hours saying that their father had died in his sleep. *His heart couldn't take it anymore,* was what the doctor had said. *Take what?* Charlotte had asked. But she'd never gotten an answer. And what did it matter anyway? He was gone. The one and only good thing that had come of his passing was that it had reunited her with Elizabeth. They'd agreed to put aside their differences on the heels of a heartfelt apology from Charlotte. She'd begged for Elizabeth's forgiveness and said that, above all, she hoped that they could move forward together as sisters who supported each other and wanted the best for each other. After all, with one parent gone and another whose health was questionable, they were each other's only real familial support system.

"It's impossible not to." Elizabeth lifted up her clean shirt and let the baby latch onto her breast.

"Can't argue there. Though it would be nice if he had a name. Have you decided on one yet?"

"We have."

"And?"

"Leo. Leo Graham."

"Oh my God." Charlotte's eyes watered. "After Dad. Mom will love that. I love that. And I love him."

"Good thing. Because he's expecting his auntie Charlotte to shower him with lots of expensive loot."

"I can do better than that."

"Oh yeah?"

"What would Leo think about a playmate?"

"I'm sure he'll be thrilled to play with you too, Char."

"Oh no, not me. I was thinking more along the lines of a first cousin."

"What?" Elizabeth zeroed in on Charlotte's belly. "I thought you'd put on a couple of pounds!"

"Gee, thanks." Charlotte laughed. "But I'm not pregnant."

"You guys are trying? That's so exciting!"

"Not in the way you're thinking."

"Okay . . ." Elizabeth looked confused.

"Charlie and I are pursuing adoption."

"Wow."

"I know." Charlotte smiled. "There are so many kids out there that need loving homes. And Charlie and I can give them everything they need and more."

"Them?"

"One to start! Let's not get ahead of ourselves." She wrinkled her forehead. "You don't think it's crazy, do you? Starting over."

"No, Char. I don't think it's crazy at all. I think it's perfect."

Chapter 28

"Hey, stranger." Charlie walked toward her looking more casual than she'd ever seen him, in black Nike running shorts, a plain gray V-neck T-shirt, and sneakers. Even his typically obedient short hair was longer and tousled.

"Hey, you." Allison hugged him but didn't linger for long, as she once would have. "I'm really glad you could make it."

She hadn't seen too much of Charlotte or Charlie over the past few months. After the scene at the gala, Allison had thought it appropriate to take some time and space, even once she'd learned of the mix-up. It certainly shed light on Charlotte's caustic performance, but still. She could have come to Allison. She could have given her the benefit of the doubt. Would Allison have acted that way if she'd been in Charlotte's shoes? She thought not, although it was impossible to say for sure. What if it had been Jack whom she'd suspected of having an affair with her friend? What if she'd had proof, as Charlotte had thought she had? She'd asked herself a million and a half questions along the same lines. And all she could come up with was time and space. Wasn't absence supposed to make the heart grow fonder?

Allison had bumped into Charlotte a few times around town. She'd seen the two of them out to dinner on three separate occasions. They'd all been exaggeratedly polite, wearing awkward smiles and exchanging pleasantries. Charlie had mentioned the weather more than once. And Charlotte had extended a lunch invitation, which Allison had yet to take her up on. She would eventually, sooner rather than later, she suspected. She still liked Charlotte and knew that there was a future for their friendship. She just wanted it to feel organic, not rushed. Most recently, Allison had mingled with her at the hospital when Elizabeth had delivered Leo and they'd laughed and bonded in the way they used to. Charlotte had apologized again and again, insisting that— more than anything else—she wanted to rebuild their friendship, if Allison would be so generous as to give her a second chance. It was a first step, and Allison could tell that Charlotte was being genuine.

Ironically, since the night of the gala, Allison had grown much closer to Elizabeth than she'd ever been with Charlotte or Charlie. They were alike in so many ways, even though to the naked eye it didn't seem that way. Allison had come to know the real Elizabeth, who was fun and down-to-earth, if a touch sarcastic and snarky every so often. They'd taken long walks together in Wincourt Park. Allison had been by Elizabeth's side to register for all her baby gear, when Nick had been called into work. And, in turn, Elizabeth had been a steadfast sounding board and listening ear for Allison, who'd been more than a little deflated after Charlotte's attack and Charlie's admission about Jack.

The only person Allison had not seen at all was Sabrina. She'd heard through the grapevine that Sabrina had checked herself into a rehab facility in Southern California. She'd also noticed that Sabrina and Craig's house was for sale, and Elizabeth had told Allison that Charlotte had said they were looking to move to Rye, New York—only twenty minutes south of Wincourt, but still the chance for a fresh start. That was the funny thing about the suburbs of Manhattan. You could live fifteen, even ten minutes, in any direction and your world would be entirely different, everything from the schools your kids attended to the people you associated with, right down to the supermarket you shopped at and the dry cleaner that laundered your clothing.

"I took the day off. It's part of the new leaf I turned over."

"Oh yeah?" Allison had remembered Elizabeth mentioning something about Charlie leaving his job at Cooper Paine and how he and Charlotte were working on their renewed relationship. She'd said she hoped it would last for more than a few weeks for Charlotte and Gia's sake. Apparently, her wish had come true.

"Yup. My life was a mess. I don't have to tell you that." He looked down at the ground. "I told Charlotte about Jack. You know, how I stole the job from him. . . . I can't tell you how sorry I am, Ali."

"It's okay." Allison touched his arm gently. "There's no way you could have known."

"I left Cooper Paine."

"I heard."

"It didn't feel right. It never did. Before or after Jack died. Charlotte's been very supportive." He smiled for the first time. "I'm at a great new firm in Greenwich. It's still a big job."

"I'd expect nothing less." Allison smiled back.

"Right." He laughed. "But the hours are more flexible. I can be home for dinner now most nights. Spend more time with my family. And since Gia has been gone for the whole summer at camp, Charlotte and I have really had time to focus on us. Things are good."

"I'm happy for you guys."

"Thanks. Obviously it would have been easier to figure all this out a little more privately, but such is life. I guess."

"If there's one thing I've learned it's that life always throws you curveballs when you least expect them." Allison craned her neck to peer down the street. "I see the bus!"

Allison hadn't been able to sleep at all the night before. She'd missed Logan so terribly for the last eight weeks, while he'd been at Camp Tawana having a grand old time, or so he'd said in his very short letters, all of which Allison had saved so she could read them over and over, hanging on his every word. She'd written to him every single day, as her parents had her first summer at sleepaway camp. She'd also worried every single day, peppering both her mother and Elizabeth with her tried-and-true litany of what-ifs. *What if he doesn't like the food? What if his bed is uncomfortable? What if he cracks his braces? What if he doesn't make friends?* She knew Gia was there with him, and that helped ease her mind, but Gia was loud and outgoing, whereas Logan was more re-served, even a bit shy sometimes.

"I can't wait to see my girl." Charlie rubbed his palms

together anxiously until the big yellow bus pulled up in front of them and came to a complete stop.

"Mom!" Logan ran down the stairs as soon as the driver had opened the door, flinging himself into Allison's waiting embrace. Behind him, Allison noticed a striking tall and slender young girl with shiny brown hair cascading down her back. She walked straight over to them, and Allison wondered if she was a friend of Logan's—or more. The thought of her baby having a girlfriend was almost too much to bear.

Logan gave Charlie a high five.

"Hi, Daddy." Gia looked confused. Allison and Charlie exchanged startled glances and Charlie took his gorgeous daughter in his arms.

"Oh my God! I almost didn't even recognize you! I'm so sorry."

"I lost some weight since visiting day."

"I can see that." Charlie couldn't keep his eyes off of her.

"Are you proud of me?"

"Gia, sweetheart." He knelt down in front of her, held her close to him, and then at arm's length. "I'm proud of you in every way, but it has nothing to do with how you look." Gia beamed at him. "Now let's go get some ice cream and head home to see Mom and Aunt Elizabeth. I think they have a surprise for you."

"My new cousin?"

"You got it!" He turned to Allison. "Ice cream?"

"Nah, I've got my parents waiting at home with this kid-do's favorite lunch." She ruffled Logan's hair, which was way too long from not having been cut for two months. "I'll see you guys tonight?"

"We'll be there."

Later that evening, at the Alexander Gallery, Allison stood in front of her painting, hugging Logan close to her and silently musing about how far she'd come.

"It's breathtaking." Charlotte appeared beside her, holding Charlie's hand.

"I second that," Charlie agreed.

"I wish we'd featured it at the gala. I'm such an idiot."

"Don't be so hard on yourself." Allison rubbed Charlotte's back instinctively. "If it sells, I'm giving the money to the Wincourt school system anyway."

"That's too generous." Charlotte shook her head. "Especially after—"

"Hey, now," Charlie interrupted. "Fresh start, remember?"

"You're right." She caressed his cheek affectionately.

"Is that Dad?" Logan asked, unaware of the inherent meaning in Allison's painting.

"In a matter of speaking."

"It doesn't look exactly like him."

"I know," Allison smiled. "It's an interpretation."

"You've never painted Dad before."

"I guess I wasn't ready."

"He looks happy." Logan nodded.

"He is. And so are we." Allison kissed the top of his head. "It represents hope for the future." She winked at Charlotte. They both knew that the theme of the gala had since taken on more meaning than either of them had ever anticipated.

"Oh." Logan nodded again, absorbing the weight of Allison's words as well as an eleven-year-old boy could.

"Hello, hello! Sorry we're late." Allison's mother rushed over to the group, with her father close behind. "There was some kind of fender bender on Lockwood and the whole street was backed up. We had to park five blocks away and walk."

"Well, you're here now and that's all that matters."

"Where's Dempsey?"

"I'm right here." He tapped Allison on the shoulder and wrapped his strong, tanned arms around her, lifting her off the ground before kissing her tenderly on the lips. "I wouldn't have missed it for anything."

"I love you." She gazed into his adoring blue eyes.

"I love you more."

Allison's mother winked at her father. And Charlie squeezed Charlotte's hand. They all knew that things could never go back to the way they once were. That their lives would never be the same. But, finally, there was hope.

Photo by Jen Goldberg Photography

Emily Liebert is the award-winning author of *You Knew Me When*, published in September 2013. She's been featured on *Today, The Rachael Ray Show*, and *Anderson Cooper 360°*, and in *InStyle*, the *New York Times*, the *Wall Street Journal*, and the *Chicago Tribune*, among other national media outlets.

Emily is currently hard at work on her fourth and fifth books. She lives in Westport, Connecticut, with her husband and their two sons.

WHEN WE FALL

···································

EMILY LIEBERT

A CONVERSATION WITH EMILY LIEBERT

Q. What is your average writing day like?

A. When I'm writing a first draft of a book, which is about six months out of the year, not including edits, I do my best to actually sit at the computer and write for about four hours a day. Some days I feel it; some days I don't. But I always try to push myself. Then I let what I've written marinate and go back to it later in the day, when I decide if it was inspired brilliance or total crap. I typically write between the hours of ten in the morning and three in the afternoon. I'm not someone who can write all day. I have two little boys, so my mind is fried by nine o'clock at night and then it's reality TV time!

Q. When you are writing, do you use people you know as inspiration? What about celebrities?

A. Oh yes! In fact I draw most all of my inspiration from my own past experiences and the experiences shared with me by my friends and family. I always tell people they should stay on my good side or watch out—they may be the villain in my next novel! As far as celebrities, I do tend to mention some either by real name or pseudonym—you may be able to guess who they are! My novels are about the world we live in now, and our culture is so inundated with all things celebrity that a reference here and there is a must.

Q. What is your writing process? Plan ahead or dive right in? How many drafts do you typically write of your novels?

A. I'm a planner in all areas of my life and my writing is no exception. I put together a detailed outline before I write even the first word. I typically write half the book (roughly fifteen chapters, give or take) before I go back and read from the beginning, though I always go back and edit each chapter after it's written—either later that day or the next morning. Sometimes reading through the previous chapter helps me get into the groove for attacking the next one. Then I write the second half of the book and do one final read through before sending it to my editor. After that, my editor and I will go through a few drafts, maybe two or three. My writing is very concise and, as a former editor, my writing is also very clean.

Q. What was your journey to becoming a published author?

A. I wrote one novel, which was very autobiographical—even though I claimed it was fiction. I was fortunate in that I had a platform since I was already a magazine editor-in-chief and had written hundreds of articles for various magazines. I pitched eighty agents and was very lucky to have three offers for representation. Unfortunately (and fortunately), that novel never sold. I'm now thankful for that, even though it was a serious bummer at the time. That novel will *never* see the light of day! Afterward I decided I wanted to write another novel, but first I was inspired by a great idea for a narrative nonfiction book. This was in 2009, just as Facebook was really exploding. I thought, with all of the hundreds of millions of connections on Facebook, there must be some amazing stories evolving. I told my agent at the time. She loved the idea. And *Facebook Fairytales* was born! After that book was published in April 2010, my career took a turn and I switched agents/agencies.

Q. What do you think is the biggest myth about being a novelist and what advice can you give to readers who want to write a novel of their own?

A. The biggest myth is that all you have to do is sit down and write a book—in your pajamas. There is so much more work involved in being a published author. In fact, about half of my time is spent on marketing, publicity, and networking. You can write the best book in the world, but if no one knows about it, you're kind of screwed. As far as advice, I always tell burgeoning authors to write what you know. Write about something you're passionate about. Force yourself to sit down at the computer every day, or as often as you can, and put words to paper. Ask family and friends to read it. Develop a thick skin. Everyone gets rejected. Believe me, I've saved every rejection note I've ever received. And pajamas are okay some days.

Q. How did you come up with the idea for When We Fall?

A. I've always been interested in the bonds of female friendship—what draws women to one another and what pulls them apart. Another common theme in my novels is to examine the age-old question of whether or not women can really "have it all."

In *When We Fall*, specifically, I also wanted to explore the theme of loss. For Allison, it was the loss of her husband and the father of her son. For Charlotte, it was the loss of love in her marriage. And for Elizabeth, it was the loss of her daughter.

I was so interested in the idea of showing how these different types of personal loss impacted the lives of my leading ladies. Further, since I grew up in Manhattan and then moved to the suburbs as an adult, I knew I wanted the main character to be struggling with what it means to say good-bye to a place that holds so many memories and then to move to a town that's essentially a completely fresh start.

Q. What are you working on at the moment?

A. I'm working on my next women's fiction novel, which will publish in June 2015. And then I'll start writing my fourth novel/fifth book, which will be released in spring 2016.

QUESTIONS
FOR DISCUSSION

1. Who do you relate to most: Allison, Charlotte, or Elizabeth? Why?

2. Why do you think Allison and Charlotte are drawn to each other at first—what characteristics make them similar/different?

3. What are your thoughts on Allison and Charlotte's different parenting styles?

4. Do you think Allison and Charlie's friendship is inappropriate? Can men and women really be friends without romance getting in the way?

5. Do you think Charlie had real romantic feelings for Allison?

6. What is your impression of the sibling relationship between Charlotte and Elizabeth? Whose side are you on?

7. Did you find yourself disliking any of the characters along the way?

8. Do you fault Charlie for holding on to the secret about Jack for so long?

9. Were you rooting for Allison and Dempsey? Charlotte and Charlie? Allison and Charlie?

10. Do you think friendships such as Allison and Charlotte's can really be patched up after such a major falling-out?

11. Is there a real-life Sabrina you know?

12. What do you predict will happen with Allison, Dempsey, Charlotte, Charlie, and Elizabeth? Sabrina? What would you like to see happen?